The Legacy

Susan X Meagher

THE LEGACY

© 2009 BY SUSAN X MEAGHER

ISBN (10) 09799254-4-4
ISBN (13) 978-0-9799254-4-3

THIS TRADE PAPERBACK ORIGINAL IS PUBLISHED BY BRISK PRESS, NEW YORK, NY 10023
FIRST PRINTING: OCTOBER 2009

Acknowledgments

A very big debt of thanks to Linda Lorenzo. Her skills, good humor and speed made what could have been a difficult edit into a pleasure.

As always, Carrie made the book pretty. She's a great cover designer and an even better girlfriend.

By Susan X Meagher

Novels

Arbor Vitae
All That Matters
Cherry Grove
Girl Meets Girl
The Lies That Bind
The Legacy

Serial Novels

I Found My Heart In San Francisco

Awakenings
Beginnings
Coalescence
Disclosures
Entwined
Fidelity
Getaway
Honesty
Intentions

Anthologies

Undercover Tales
Outsiders

To purchase these books go to
www.briskpress.com

Part One

Noel Carpenter opened her front door with one hand while trying to get a good look at the official-looking, heavy envelope wedged among her usual mail. She started to drop her things on the table by the door, but remembered halfway through the act that she didn't have room for a table in her new apartment.

Absently, she walked to the coffee table, dropped everything except the ivory-colored envelope, and spent a few moments scanning it. It was from a law firm in Delaware. Why would a firm in Delaware send her anything? She'd been there for a holiday, but she certainly didn't know anyone who lived there. She was tempted to open up her computer and research the firm before going further, but the envelope was too enticing and, on impulse, she decided to open it.

Noel almost laughed at herself when she realized she had been holding the letter as though it were a bomb. Boldly, she slid a fingernail under the flap and dumped the contents into her palm. She unfolded the cover letter and read, the words starting to swirl before her eyes. She'd never, ever wanted to know, but the woman had hunted her down. Why? Why now? What good would it do anyone? After re-reading the letter several times and beginning to feel sick to her stomach, she sat down and compelled herself to take a few deep breaths. When she was confident she wouldn't lose her lunch, she reached for the phone. Whom to call first? April was the obvious choice, but she was emotionally invested in the whole mess. Her mom and dad would worry about her and probably hop in their car and drive down. That left Andy. He'd be able to understand the documents and help determine if this was some nasty mistake. Hitting the third speed dial button, she anxiously waited for an answer. Relief swept over her when she heard her brother's voice.

"Andy? It's Noel. Can you swing by my apartment on your way home tonight?" She sucked her lip between her teeth and bit it lightly. "I just found out who my birth mother was." Her stomach was in full revolt when she added. "No, I meant 'was.' She just died."

⌐

"You're killing me. You're absolutely killing me!"

"Calm down, Toni. I'm only doing my job." Heidi Naylor got up from her desk and put her hand on her friend's shoulder. "You know I'll do whatever I can to help you out, but I can't lie to this woman." Fondly, she reached out and tucked Toni's dark, thick, straight hair behind her ears, knowing it would fall as soon as Toni leaned forward again. She kissed her tilted head. "I'm always a little disappointed when your hair doesn't taste like chocolate."

Toni gave her a quizzical look, then smiled, her eyes losing the hooded character they took on when she was troubled. "I chewed my hair when I was a kid, but not because I thought it'd taste good."

Heidi gave her a quick hug, then sat back down. She started to browse through the commercial real estate listings on her computer and pointed one out. "Look at this one. This place has been upgraded and it's selling for three hundred thousand dollars more than…say…this one." She clicked on another listing.

Toni leaned over to get a better look, and Heidi discretely sniffed to see if she could deduce what job Toni was working on. She detected new-sawn wood. "Are you working on that new deck for Jackson?"

"Yeah," Toni said as she read the listing information. "I'm half done. It'll be ready for the first warm day. You know how he likes to shove people out on that patio, even when it's freezing out."

"He's a good businessman. Using the patio gives him another ten tables."

"It's more important to make people comfortable," Toni groused. She used a finger stained with pitch to point out. "This one doesn't have as many bathrooms. Maybe that's why it's less."

Chuckling, Heidi said, "You stick to construction. I'll stick to real estate. An extra bath doesn't add three hundred thousand dollars to a bed and breakfast."

"Well, you didn't have to tell this woman…this Noel…to upgrade the whole place. If she does much work at all, I'll never be able to buy it."

Heidi reached under Toni's barn jacket and tickled her waist. The muted giggle that earned gave testament to just how miffed Toni was. "I'm sorry," Heidi said. "I know how much you want The Sandpiper. But I've got to do my job."

"Yeah, yeah." Toni snapped her dark leather baseball cap on her head and adjusted it to perfection without aid of a mirror. "Everybody knows the price of everything, and the value of nothing." She turned and sauntered out of the office. Once she was outside, Heidi watched her lean into the blowing gale that pelted her with snow and hail.

Toni Hooper paced in front of The Sandpiper, occasionally crossing her arms over her chest and jumping up and down to try and stay warm. She was early, as she often was, and underdressed for the winter weather, as she always was.

Her head was bare, her gloves unlined, her barn jacket more appropriate for fall than winter. Her worn cowboy boots provided no warmth, and they made walking on the icy sidewalk treacherous. But she loved her boots, and their practicality was secondary.

Even though it was frigid out, she was too occupied with her conflicting feelings to pay much attention to the weather. She aided in the search for Noel for months, cramming bits of research in whenever she had a spare moment. Her dedication to the quest was unstinting, and ordinarily she'd get a great deal of satisfaction from meeting the fruit of her labors, but it was all too late now. Months too late, and Toni couldn't help but mentally kick herself for not working harder, for not coming through when she was most needed.

She turned and looked at the house where she'd spent so much time and wished once again that Noel had appeared on the scene in time. Now, she was forced to admit, Noel was right on time for ruining her plans, and that made Toni want to slug her.

A small, white car crept down the street, and Toni's heartbeat quickened. She knew most of the cars that the locals owned, and this was not one of them. She peered into the car when it slowed down even further, and was surprised to see an attractive woman of about her own age, with slightly wavy golden hair. The window of the car rolled down and the driver called out, "Are you Toni or Heidi?"

"Toni. Heidi's not here yet."

"Want to get in while we wait? You look like you're freezing."

"Oh, I'm freezing, but I don't mind." Toni walked over to Noel's car. "You can park anywhere you want."

"I guess I'll just stay here. Let me get closer to the curb." Before Noel could move, another car approached.

Toni said, "That's Heidi," and went to meet her.

⌒

Once her car was properly parked, Noel took her first long look at the property she'd inherited. Heidi said it held ten guest rooms and seven baths, plus a good-sized apartment on the first floor, but from the front, it didn't look that big. In fact, it looked like it could easily be a single-family home.

It had been painted white—quite some time ago, given the flaking and peeling. It wasn't an eyesore by any means, but it didn't look distinctive or lovingly cared for. She glanced over and saw Toni help Heidi pull a big leather bag from the car and carry it for her to the walkway. There was something gallant about the way she did it; matter-of-factly, rather than the showy let-me-get-that-for-you-little-lady attitude that some butchy women adopted.

Toni was definitely on the butch side, but Noel thought that her standing next to Heidi accentuated that fact. Noel had been around enough businesswomen to peg Heidi as someone who spent a lot of time and a good bit of money to look good. Her medium brown hair was accented with blonde highlights and her coat was more stylish than warm. Leather gloves that fit like skin also couldn't have provided much warmth.

When Heidi waved to her, Noel had to brave the elements herself. She got out of her car and stood on the sidewalk where the three of them raced through brief introductions, then darted for the front door. While they waited for Heidi to get the door open, Toni inserted the toe of her boot under several severely cupped boards on the porch. "That's a lawsuit waiting to happen."

"Don't even say things like that," Noel said, her voice high.

"Owning a piece of property like this terrifies me."

Heidi finally got the key into the lock and jiggled it to make it turn. They all stood in the entryway for a minute relishing the relatively warm air. "Is this the first time you've owned anything?" Heidi asked.

"No, we, I had a house, but I…sold it." She showed a smile that was decidedly put on. "But this is a whole different league."

"Not really," Heidi said. "Real estate is real estate."

Noel took off her knit hat and flipped her honey-colored hair over her shoulder. Pale blue eyes narrowed and she said, "What is that smell?"

Toni grimaced. "Probably the refrigerator. After Max died none of us had the sense to come over and check things out. It was a couple of weeks until it dawned on me. I cleaned the darned thing out, but I think it's ruined."

"Maybe we should start in the kitchen," Noel said. She gave the woman an encouraging smile. For the life of her she couldn't understand why Toni seemed to feel responsible for cleaning out a woman's refrigerator, that oddity added to the weird vibe she was getting from the handywoman.

They walked down the wide hallway, with Noel following Toni. There was something about the way she ambled along that reminded Noel of a cowboy. Maybe it was the boots, or the worn jeans and barn jacket, but the effect was incongruous for the Delaware shore.

They bypassed the staircase that led to the second floor, and Toni led them through a big parlor then turned left into a surprisingly narrow, very outdated kitchen. At the far end of the galley-like space, there was an ill-fitting door that was letting in far too much ice cold air. "Good thing you're not open for the winter season," Toni joked.

"I'm not going to be open for any season," Noel said confidently.

"As soon as I can get this place into shape, someone else can worry about it."

Toni looked like she desperately wanted to say something, but she held back. Heidi took a quick glance at her and said to Noel, "If you'd like to get rid of it right now, Toni's very interested."

Puzzled, Noel glanced from one woman to the other. "But you told me I'd be able to get more for it if I fixed it up."

"I think you can. But there's always a risk…"

"I'm sure that's so, but you seemed pretty confident of your opinion before. Have conditions changed in the last couple of weeks?"

"Well, no, but if you sold it now, you'd save yourself a lot of trouble. It all comes down to how you value your time and how much risk you're willing to take."

Noel noticed that Toni was fidgeting. Because of what, she didn't know. "What are you prepared to pay?"

Toni's chin was pointed at her chest and her dark eyes were almost hidden by the angle she held her head at. "I'm not sure. What are you asking?"

Noel frowned slightly at Heidi. "I'm not sure. Did you print out the listings for comparable properties?"

"Yeah, I did, but there isn't much up for sale now. Prices have really taken a hit so people are only selling if they have to. The few I have are further down the Maryland shore."

"So they aren't really comparable?"

"Uhm, not technically. But take a peek anyway." She handed her listing sheets for three properties. Noel looked through them, trying to ignore Toni, who was shifting her weight, still acting like she was about to burst.

"These are pretty expensive." She looked Heidi in the eye. "Is this place worth as much as these?"

"More. Rehoboth is more expensive than these areas. More in

demand, too."

"Well, Toni, if you can make me an offer that seems competitive, I'm more than happy to consider it."

"Well, that's what I wanted to talk to you about," she said, seeming more at ease now that she was speaking. "I could pay what it's worth, but I'd need for you to carry a second mortgage."

"Oh." Noel was just about to refuse her out of hand when Toni jumped in again. When she spoke, her voice had an almost desperate quality, and Noel found herself feeling sympathy for the woman.

"I talked to someone at the bank. I only qualify for about five hundred thousand dollars, and that's a lot less than you'll want. But I'll do anything to make this work. Anything," she emphasized, her big brown eyes taking on a puppy-like sincerity.

Noel was saddened when she said, "I'll talk to my brother, who's also my tax advisor, but I'm not crazy about doing that if I can sell it outright." She watched Toni's eyes, vividly seeing the disappointment. "But, like I said, I'll think about it."

Toni sighed heavily. It was clear she'd been shot down, but she didn't seem angry. Just sad. Noel hated feeling like she'd kicked Toni's dream to the curb, so she changed the subject. "What would you do if you were to renovate, Heidi?"

Surveying the kitchen, Heidi said, "If this were a home, I'd suggest redoing the kitchen and even enlarging it. But most B&B owners like to keep their kitchens fairly minimal. If I were you, I'd replace the appliances, obviously add a dishwasher, and put a new heavy-duty floor in. Other than that, I wouldn't touch it."

Toni pushed her hair back over her ear and wrinkled her nose. She discretely pointed at the door. "You might want to fix that."

Heidi removed a notebook from her bag and started taking notes. Noel did the same, but she used a big black organizer. Toni shoved her hands into the back pockets of her jeans and rocked on the narrow heels of her boots while she waited for her companions.

Noel walked over to check the cabinets. The doors creaked and wouldn't stay closed; the ill-fitting drawers were sticky, needing two hands to get them closed. "I don't think I'd buy a place where the kitchen was this…" She glanced up and saw Toni nearly glaring at her. "Dated," she finished weakly.

Heatedly, Toni's sharp voice snapped, "Max made the best breakfasts in town for over twenty years in this kitchen."

Heidi put her hand on Toni's arm and pulled her close, then put an arm around her waist and gently patted her.

Noel's eyes widened at this display of familiarity. Toni read gay, but Heidi definitely didn't, and Noel couldn't quite figure out if they were lovers or close friends or just very affectionate townies. No matter what they were, this whole thing was weird. Toni was as prickly as a cactus, but the wistful expression on her face when she said she wanted to buy the house was so heartfelt that Noel nearly wanted to hug her. She knew she was coming to this game late, and that there were years of history between the others, but this was extra innings and she was just entering the stadium.

"It's no reflection on Max to say the obvious, honey," Heidi said, her voice soft and almost loving. "This kitchen must be seventy-five years old." The soothing tone she used changed when she turned her attention back to Noel. "You could do a lot in here, but I think you might be wasting your money. I'd hate to see you put fifty thousand dollars in and have the new owner want to tear it out. I'd suggest doing the minimum and seeing how the property is received. If having an older kitchen is a hindrance, you could replace it later."

Noel nodded, and made a few notes in her planner. Giving a businesslike smile, she said, "Let's move on."

They went through the house room by room. Toni was still a little irascible, insisting that almost nothing needed to be done to make the house attractive to a new buyer. The three of them were squeezed into the smallest of the bathrooms, with Toni saying, "Sure, you could strip this room down to the studs and make it beautiful. But nobody complained about it and Max was sold out through the summer every year. You can't sell more rooms than you have."

"Of course you can't," Heidi soothed, "but the new owner won't be Max. Prospective buyers are going to see this place like Noel is seeing it, only they won't be as forgiving."

"I'm sure that this worked great for Max," Noel said, continually perplexed by the way both women behaved, "but if I were staying here, I'd want an updated bathroom. But then, I don't like to stay in B&Bs, so my perspective is probably off."

Toni's face was blank as she gazed at Noel for a few seconds, then turned and left the room. Noel held back and said to Heidi, "Is...uhm...Toni your...girlfriend?"

Heidi took a quick peek down the hall, seeing Toni leaning against a window. "My girlfriend?" The way she stressed the word was another oddity.

"Yeah."

"No, she's not." It appeared that Heidi was intentionally trying to keep her expression neutral, confusing Noel all the more. "Toni doesn't do relationships."

Yet another strange thing to tell a client. "But you know her well, right?"

"Oh, yeah. Really well."

"I can't figure out the vibe here. Is the kind of work I want more than she can do? Or is she only interested in buying the place? I've never seen anyone less willing to take on a big job."

"Oh, no. Toni could take this place apart and rebuild it. And even though she'd like to buy it, she knows her chances are slim. The issue is that she and Max were very close, and I think it upsets her to have you say things that...are too honest."

"Then maybe I should find somebody else to do the work. I don't want this to be a struggle."

"I can help you find someone else, but Toni is really the best, and she knows this place like the back of her hand. She's done all of Max's repairs for the last twenty years."

Noel started to speak, then stopped. "Is there something…were Toni and Max more than—"

"No," Heidi laughed. "They were just friends. But Toni's very protective of her friends."

"I suppose that's a good thing, as long as you're one of her friends."

"Just about everyone in town is. Toni's a gem, and if you hire her, I guarantee you'll agree with me."

It took over two hours to go through the whole house, and they didn't even attempt to go to the basement. Heidi had another appointment, so she had to leave quickly. She handed Noel the keys, then dashed away leaving Toni and Noel standing uncomfortably in the parlor.

Noel patted her planner. "With everything we talked about today, I could spend anywhere from two thousand to two hundred thousand dollars."

"I might have been too subtle when I pointed this out," Toni said, looking a little sheepish, "but I think you could spend less than ten thousand and have the place shipshape."

Noel sat down on an overstuffed sofa and scanned the room which was jammed with knickknacks, objects d'art, and junk. She would have commented, but she'd learned to keep her opinions about Max's decorating skills to herself. "How would you spend my ten thousand dollars?" Her pen was poised over a fresh page in her planner.

Toni sat down opposite her, once again looking a little like a cowpoke sitting in the parlor. Her knees were splayed and her hands dangled between them. She seemed uncomfortable, as though she belonged out on the range rather than cooped up inside. In what was no doubt a nervous habit, she played with her hair for a few seconds, tucking it behind her ears, then she gazed at Noel and spoke decisively. "I'd true up the front and rear entry doors, I'd redo the front porch and the back stairs, then I'd build an arbor or a gazebo in the side yard." She paused, clearly thinking. "I'd probably put a swing or some nice Adirondack chairs by the arbor, then I'd rip up the front sidewalk and put in some big, irregular pavers." With her arms folded across her chest, she nodded once. "That's it."

"I wouldn't have guessed any of that."

Shrugging, Toni said, "You asked. I know the house, I know the guests, and I know the town."

"I can't argue with that, but it just seems to me that people would like a more modern, cleaner place."

Cheeks flushed, Toni said, "She was sick for six months. All of her friends did what we could to keep the place up to snuff, but we got behind on the housekeeping. It seemed more important for us to spend time with her in the hospital." She slumped back into the sofa, looking like she'd been unfairly chewed out.

"No! I wasn't referring to dirt or clutter," Noel said, although she easily could have been. "I just think people like a more modern feel. I meant clean as in spare."

"What do you think about her?" Toni asked in an accusatory tone. "Don't you even have any questions?"

"About Maxine?" Noel's open expression closed tight. There was no way in hell she was going to open up to this strange woman. No way.

Toni slapped her open hands onto her knees. "Yes, about Max. It meant so much to her to find you, and it kills me that she died before she could."

Noel didn't say the obvious, that waiting until your child was forty-five years old wasn't really rushing, but she nonetheless tried to be diplomatic. "I didn't know her, Toni. I never met her, and I never tried to find her." She stood up, adopting the polite, businesslike mien she'd shown through much of the day. "I'm going to go home and try to make some decisions. I promise to call you about your proposal."

"Fine." Now Toni was all business, too. "If you're going to fix it, you'd better start with the porch. It's a hazard. And a buyer will notice the wind whipping in through the back door."

"Okay. Can you send me an estimate?"

Rolling her eyes, Toni stood perfectly still for a few moments, then said, "Three thousand for labor, plus materials. That'll depend on what you want to use."

"Uhm, I'd like a written estimate if you don't mind. My brother is helping me make decisions, and he's very persnickety."

"Fine," Toni sighed, clearly aggrieved.

"I'd like to get started soon. Do you have time?"

"Yeah. As long as we don't get a lot of snow or ice, I can start right away."

"Great." Noel extended her hand and shook Toni's. "It was good to meet you."

"You too." As Noel started to leave, Toni asked, in a voice filled with frustrated interest, "Are you married or have kids or anything?"

"No," Noel said, turning briefly to face her. "I teach third grade. That's enough kids for me." She started to walk away, but stopped and added, "I just got out of a ten year relationship. With a woman."

"Wow," Toni said, looking surprised. "Max would have been blown away."

"Was she...?"

"Oh, no." She laughed and her face grew animated for the first time. Her eyes shown with affection and her smile was sweet and full. "She always said she was gay from the waist up. She loved women, but didn't understand the sexual attraction."

Laughing rather coldly, Noel said, "Sometimes it's just the opposite for me." With that, she departed, leaving Toni to stare at the empty doorway, a befuddled expression on her handsome face.

⌒

The next afternoon, Heidi pushed open the door of a dimly lit bar and smiled when the few inhabitants raised their arms in unison to shield their eyes from the glow of the setting sun.

"I was hoping you'd be here," Heidi said to Toni. She sat on a bar stool next to her friend and said to the bartender, "Our pal doesn't look like she had a good afternoon."

"So I've heard." The bartender, a silver-haired woman whose kind, sharp eyes belied her age, added, "I think I'm getting a pretty one-sided description of Max's daughter."

"I liked her," Heidi declared. "She didn't waste our time, she accepted all of our comments, and she seemed very professional."

"She called me this afternoon. She won't hold a second mortgage for me, so she's gonna fix it up and dump it like a piece of trash," Toni said, glumly. "She didn't even want to discuss price. It clearly means nothing to her. Nothing at all." She leaned over and rested her head on her crossed arms.

"A lot of people don't like to carry paper," Heidi said, rubbing her back gently, "even though it's a pretty good investment. Maybe she's just risk averse."

"She's gay," Toni said, her words accompanied by a smirk from Jackie, the bartender.

"Really? I wouldn't have guessed." Heidi looked at her friend for a few moments, then in a casual tone, asked, "Are you going to put her on your to-do list?"

"No way," Toni said, feeling slightly disgusted at the thought.

"Toni says she's not very attractive," Jackie commented.

"Get me a gin and tonic and I'll set you straight." Heidi turned and stuck her tongue out at Toni. "She has beautiful blonde hair, really pretty pale blue eyes, and is model thin. She dresses nicely too." After another quick tongue exposure, Heidi took a sip of her drink. "We didn't talk about her personal life, but I assume she's some kind of professional."

Toni took a sip of her beer. "Teaches third grade, her hair's probably dyed, she likely wears tinted contacts, and she's not thin, she's skinny. When she was sitting down her coat opened, and she was flat as a board. She's all bones and hard angles."

"You're just saying that because you liked her so much," Heidi teased.

"I don't think she's really Max's kid. How does Max's dark, coarse hair turn into that shiny blonde stuff? Max had brown eyes, not those pale blue ones. She didn't look a thing like her."

"Yes, she did," Heidi said. "They had the same build, but Noel doesn't have Max's adorable beer belly."

Fondly, Toni said, "I'll never understand how that woman was so skinny and managed to have a gut."

"Genetics, I guess," Heidi said. "But Noel obviously didn't get that from her mother."

Toni spent a moment reconsidering her newfound belief that it was just as well Max had never been able to meet her daughter, but quickly reminded herself that Noel was the kind of prissy, tight-ass woman Max had no patience with. She stood up and put a five dollar bill on the bar. "No, she didn't. She didn't get her mother's trusting nature, either. I've got to go home and type up an estimate for my new boss. Whoopee."

They watched her leave with Jackie commenting, "The only way she would've liked that girl is if she'd handed her the keys and the deed."

⌒

Two weeks later, Noel returned to Delaware to check on Toni's progress. The weather had been warmer than normal, and Toni had been able to use every day to her advantage.

Noel got out of her car and took out her planner, making notes on the progress. Then she snapped a few pictures with her phone. She was down on her hands and knees when Toni came up behind her. "Boo," she said quietly.

Laughing, Noel got to her feet and dusted off her knees. "You're going to have to do better than that. I have eighteen eight and nine-year-olds who do their best to drive me crazy every day." She pointed to the half-finished porch. "You've done a great job."

Toni hooked her thumbs into the side pockets of her jeans, and rocked back on her boots. "Do you have experience in building?"

"Some, but I've never had a porch built. My brother gave me a long checklist of things I should watch for. He's a CPA," she said as if this explained everything.

"Mind if I look? CPAs might know things about porches that I've missed."

Somewhat reluctantly, Noel turned the book around. Toni scanned the list, nodding with satisfaction. "This is a good list."

Noel reclaimed her book and snapped it closed.

That abrupt gesture almost made Toni reassess her thoroughly considered decision to try to be friends with Noel. She knew that's what Max would have wanted, and if she couldn't buy The Sandpiper maybe she could convince Noel to run it. But even Max wouldn't have wanted her to have to grovel to get even a chink out of this icy woman. Casually, Toni asked, "Is your brother adopted too?"

"Yes. All three of us are."

"Three?"

"We have a sister."

"Where do you fall in the lineup?"

"I'm the youngest. My brother is five years older and my sister's just a year older."

"That's pretty close in age."

"Yeah. The agency was reluctant to place me with my parents since my sister was so close in age, but they gave in. Luckily."

"That must be kinda nice…not to be…alone. Well, maybe you don't think of it as being alone…because…you know…" she trailed off weakly, wishing she'd started a conversation about the weather.

"Do you have any siblings?"

"Yeah." Toni scratched at her head, and wished once again that she hadn't opened her mouth. "I've got a younger brother and a sister."

"Then you know how nice it is," Noel said curtly. "I can pay you for the rest of the porch. Just give me a second to write a check."

Toni followed along behind her, watching impatiently as Noel used the hood of her car to write the check. She was desperate to make a few suggestions, but everything she said had come out wrong. Still, she couldn't let her ideas drop. Things needed to be done to make The Sandpiper shine again. "It's a little early to start, but I think your next project should be to paint the exterior."

Turning, Noel narrowed her eyes a little as she handed Toni the check. "Do you just not like to be indoors?"

Showing an embarrassed grin, Toni said, "No, I like to work

indoors, I just think curb appeal is important."

Noel smirked. "Now you're starting to sound like a real estate agent. Two weeks ago you said nothing needed to be done."

"Well, I've spent a lot of time outside the last two weeks, and I've been looking around at the neighbors. The Sandpiper is the homeliest inn on the block. You're not gonna get people to look at the inside if they don't look at the outside."

Noel sighed heavily. She leaned against her car and let her eyes wander along every part of the house. It did need to be painted. "I'm not sure this is the best time to do it. Maybe I should see if I can stir up any interest first."

"I talked to Heidi, and she thinks it would help attract buyers. She says it sets a bad first image or something like that. She said it's hard for a buyer to get over that."

Noel twirled her pen in her hand as she continued to look at all the peeling paint on the most exposed parts of the house. "I assume you know someone who paints houses?"

Showing her most attractive grin, Toni said, "It just so happens that I do. My friend Roxy is a painter, and she and I work together on big jobs if I don't have anything else going on."

"This is gonna cost me an arm and a leg, isn't it?"

"It'll be less than a new bathroom." She bit her lip, and started to add up the numbers. "I think."

"Great. But I need seven of those, too."

"If we get the facade fixed up, you'll probably change your mind about that."

"It's more likely that I'll be broke before I get there."

Smiling that charming smile again, Toni said, "I guess that's a possibility." Her voice took on a more enthusiastic tenor when she said, "The other thing I wanted to talk to you about is my idea for the side yard." She jogged over to a bare patch of lawn to the right of the porch. "If you had a pretty arbor here and a couple of nice chairs, you could serve wine and cheese out here at night. People love that."

"You keep forgetting that I'm not going to be serving anyone anything. If I come to Rehoboth Beach this summer, it's going to be to look at women and lie on the beach. In that order." She started to walk around to the driver's door of her car.

"I'll have Roxy send you the estimate on the paint job. And I'll toss in an estimate on building an arbor."

"I'll entertain Roxy's estimate," Noel said, smiling tightly. "But not yours. I hope the weather stays warm for you. Bye-bye."

Toni waved goodbye to the departing car, quietly saying, "Bitch."

⌒

A few days after her visit to Rehoboth Beach, Noel received a notice from her postal carrier that a package was waiting for her. She wasn't able to get to the post office until Saturday, and had to wait in a tediously long line. The return address read "Hooper, Rehoboth Beach, DE."

Grousing to herself, she got into her car and opened the heavy box which contained nearly every possible device for recording information—note cards; spiral notebooks; two Rolodex of different vintage; greeting cards, some with notes enclosed; two ancient floppy disks of a type that hadn't been used in years and one of a more recent time. Some of the material was organized, assumedly by Toni, but most was held together at best by rubber bands. A piece of paper from a spiral notebook lay atop the mess. Toni's bold hand had written, "Most of Max's regulars don't know about her death. Heidi thinks it would be a good idea if you notified them. I can help out if you have trouble sorting through this stuff. I know it looks like a mess, but the latest floppy disk is pretty current." The note was signed with a very large T.

Noel stared at the note for a long time, then calmly wadded it into a ball and threw it against the windshield, while uttering a sharp expletive. Toni might think she held the cards, but she'd never played against Noel. She'd do things in her own way, on her own time. Max's so-called regulars were of no interest to her, and if Toni wanted to communicate with them, she was more than welcome. Noel would make sure she had the addresses by dumping them on her head the next time they were compelled to be in contact.

⌒

The next Sunday afternoon Noel and her sister April entered an attractive diner in Rehoboth Beach. Toni was sitting in a booth, and she stood up and waved when they entered.

"Hi, there," Toni said, smiling at April, who returned her smile with matching enthusiasm. "I didn't know Noel was bringing anyone. I'm Toni Hooper."

"This is my sister, April," Noel said.

Toni extended her hand and she and April shook. "It's very good to meet you," April said.

They all sat down and Toni kept smiling, looking from Noel to April and back again. "You look a lot alike."

"I guess we do." April took a quick look at her sister. "Kinda."

Toni looked at April's hair, which didn't share the shine or texture of Noel's, even though it was roughly the same color. Her eyes were brown, and her face was a little rounder and more open than Noel's. Still, there was something about them that suggested they were related. "Do you live close to each other?"

"Not very," April said. "Do you know the DC area?"

"Not well. I've been to Baltimore a bunch of times, and to all of the monuments and memorials in DC, but that's about it."

"Well, my husband and I live not too far from where we all grew up. Suburban Maryland. Our brother is a little closer to Noel in Baltimore." She made a face. "None of us are crazy about Noel being where she is. I don't think it's safe for a single woman."

"It's fine," Noel said, clearly having had this discussion before. "I've been there for twelve years, April."

"But you were in a house before. Now you're all alone in that old place." She shivered noticeably. "The hallways are so dark."

The waitress approached and put her arm around Toni's shoulders. "You guys ready?" she asked, leaning against Toni as though she were a wall.

They all ordered and, as soon as the waitress left, Noel handed Toni the client list she had cobbled together. It had taken an hour of persuasion from April, her brother Andy, her mother, her father and her grandmother to get Noel to do the work. Andy finally won the point by convincing her that being able to present a new owner with an up-to-date client list would handsomely pay off. Toni spent a few minutes going over every name, nodding occasionally. By the time their drinks arrived, she was ready to launch into her pitch.

"I know you're not going to like this, but I've put a lot of thought into this and I think you have to open for the summer."

April pinched her sister's shoulder and said, "That's just what I've been telling her. I've never known anyone who owned a B&B. I'd love to come down here for a few weeks with my kids."

Looking very interested, Toni fixed her gaze onto April and said, "You have kids? Tell me about 'em."

Sulking, Noel sipped her soda while her sister told Toni all about her two sons. When she had the opportunity, Noel interrupted. "I guess I haven't made my position clear. I'm a teacher. I'm happy being a teacher. I only want to be a teacher. There is no part of me that wants to run any sort of hotel. That includes B&Bs, inns, hostels, campgrounds, and shelters." She looked at Toni to make sure she was listening. "Do you understand that?"

Giving her a sharp look, April said, "Noel, you don't have to be rude."

"I'm not." She looked at Toni again and the determination in her eyes softened along with her tone of voice. She'd been reminding herself on a daily basis that Toni was clearly well-intentioned. To be hanging in after having her offer shot down either indicated intense loyalty to Max's wishes or a wide masochistic streak. "I'm not trying to be rude. I'm just trying to be clear. You act like you think I want to be convinced. I don't."

Toni leaned back against the red leatherette seat which squeaked noisily as she settled into it. A half smile covered her handsome face and her dark eyes focused intently on Noel. "I know you don't want to do this. But I also know you're willing to do a lot of work to maximize your profit. Am I right?" She smiled with ill-disguised satisfaction when Noel reluctantly nodded.

"I'm only trying to tell you my opinion of the best way to do that. I know a lot of the people on your list." She rolled the list up into a tube and slapped it against the table a few times. "Most of them have been coming here for years, and they're not a flexible bunch. They like things the way they've always been."

"I think many people are like that," Noel said. "But things change. People die. Businesses change hands. People adapt."

Toni's smile had less gusto when she replied, "True. But if you want to hand the new buyer a list full of satisfied customers, you'll reconsider."

"No, thank you. I'll send the notice out when I get home. I'm going to make it clear that The Sandpiper is for sale, and if it's open this summer it will be under new management." Noel tried not to glare, she really did, but she wasn't very successful. Toni was so ridiculously persistent!

They were interrupted with the delivery of their food, and Toni effortlessly changed the subject, making the sisters laugh with her tale of a raccoon who'd decided to move under the new porch, and her ultimately successful quest in evicting him.

⌐

After lunch they drove over to The Sandpiper. The new porch made the dwelling look much sharper and more cared for, and Noel and April were effusive in their praise of Toni's workmanship. Noel pointed to the vertical boards Toni had nailed in to hide the empty space under the stairs. "Did you have to put those there to keep the raccoon out?"

"No, but I would have. I thought it looked nicer with a little skirting. I hate it when you can see underneath a porch."

"I've got your check for the rest of the work, and April helped me pick out a color for the clapboards."

Toni looked at the paint sample and nodded sagely. "This will look very good." She smiled that charming smile at April. "You have a very good eye. What do you think about using a contrasting trim?"

"I think it's a must. Noel thought you wouldn't have to paint the trim, but I told her it would look silly if you didn't." She scowled at her sister. "See? I told you."

"You could get away without painting it," Toni conceded, "but I think this pale yellow would look great with a dark green trim." She turned and drew her index finger across the landscape, dotted with inns and B&Bs. "None of the other places have that color scheme. The Sandpiper would look fresh and clean, and I know that's important to Noel."

"I'd love green," April said, excitedly. "I'll pick a color out and send it to you, okay?"

"Do I get a vote?" Noel asked.

"I'm lending you the money for the paint job, so I should get to pick the color," April said, giggling.

Rolling her eyes, Noel said, "I don't think Toni wants to know how I've had to grovel for loans to do this."

"Oh, I do. If April has the money, she's the one I have to impress."

"You already have," April said, nearly batting her eyes.

Possessively, Toni put her hand on April's shoulder and guided her to the side lawn. "Maybe you're the person I should talk to about my idea to put either an arbor or a gazebo in right here."

This time, Noel didn't try to hide her scowl. She tried to make it fiercer. This was seeming more and more like the times April would flirt with Noel's boyfriends just to see if she could make them notice her. It had been almost thirty years since that had last happened, but Noel wasn't quite over it. Almost, but not quiet.

⌒

They were thirty miles from Rehoboth before April had exhausted her list of superlatives for Toni—her skills, her charm, and her ideas. Peevishly, Noel said, "I hope you're planning on giving me the arbor, because I'm not paying for it. I'm tapped out."

April patted her leg in a motherly fashion. "Consider it a gift from me and Ed. And I think it's gonna be fantastic when we sit out there this summer. Toni was thinking just what I was when it comes to planting. She really knows her plants."

"There's one species she doesn't know, and that's Determined School Teacher. It can be dangerous."

"Oh, don't put that face on. Toni's remarkably charming and you know it. You just don't like sweet-talking women."

"I have nothing against sweet-talking women. She's just not my type."

"She's my type," April said, her laugh almost giddy. "Men don't show me that kind of attention any more. I loved how she looks you in the eye and acts like you're the most important person in the world." She looked at her sister's face, watching her reaction. "Come on. You can't say she isn't attractive."

"Not to me. She's too butch." ·

"Right." April's voice betrayed her suspicions. "You hate butch women. That's why you wanted to move to California to track down that woman from Terminator 2. The one with all the muscles."

"It was her acting that attracted me," Noel said, a guilty smile starting to show.

"Why do you stop and stare at every female cop or firefighter?"

"Respect for public servants."

"Military personnel?"

"Patriotism." Noel made a face. "I might be attracted to butch women, but not to Toni."

"I can see how you'd think that. Her broad shoulders and strong hands must be a real turnoff. And that thick, dark hair. Ugh! Who could stomach that? Not to mention those bedroom eyes and adorable smile. Yuck."

"I didn't say she was ugly, April. She's too pushy. And she acts like she knows it's only a matter of time until I do just what she wants. I don't find that attractive."

"Well, I do, and if Ed leaves me, I think I'm gonna turn to the dark side."

"I'll mention that the next time I talk to my personal handywoman, a position I'm itching to make redundant."

Part Two

*T*wo weeks after her last visit to Rehoboth Beach, Noel reached Toni on her cell phone. "I don't know what kind of people visit B&Bs, but someone should make sure that they're not licensed to carry handguns."

"Hello, Noel," Toni said, her voice nearly purring with pleasure. "When can we expect you?"

After a long exhale, Noel glumly said, "School's in session until Memorial Day, and it starts up again after Labor Day. I can't change the schedule, and I have to show up every day, even when some idiots I don't know are crying about their vacations."

"When's your first reservation?"

"At the end of April. The guy threatened me with a lawsuit!"

"That doesn't surprise me. People are very territorial about their vacations. When's your last one?"

"The second week in October. Why anyone would want to go to the beach in October is beyond me, but two women from Vermont are going to be there over my dead body if it comes to that."

Unable to stop herself from laughing, Toni said, "Don't worry about the shoulder season people. We'll figure something out. If you can be here for the big months, everything will be fine."

"Easy for you to say! You don't have people gunning for you."

Toni's voice took on a soothing, soft tone. "You won't either.

There's a woman here in town who house sits for the various B&Bs. I'll talk to her today and see if she's available. Don't worry about a thing."

"Can I ask you a question?"

"Sure."

There was a lengthy pause while Noel tried to figure out a way to ask her question in a polite manner. "Why do you care so much? Are you just a nice person?"

Toni's pause was just as lengthy as Noel's had been. "Yes. I'm just a nice person."

They hung up and Toni walked over to the window of the house she was working on. The first buds were starting to show on the flowing plum tree just outside, and she recalled how happy Max always was at the first sign of spring. She started to mist up while complimenting herself on at least getting Noel to The Sandpiper for one year. She owed Max an awful lot, but she figured her debt was just about paid. Now it was up to Noel. She either had some of Max's magic when it came to her guests, or she'd run back to Baltimore at the end of the season. It was on her.

⌢

That evening, Toni sat on a bar stool, sketching on a pad with a charcoal pencil. Her expression was composed, and slightly studious. But there was a lightness about her that evening that compelled Jackie to wander over and speak to her.

"You look happy tonight. Working on something special?"

Toni's eyes shifted from her pad. "Yeah. I'm trying to do something a little different with the arbor I'm making for The Sandpiper."

Jackie laughed, and slapped Toni on the arm. "I had a feeling you'd break her down."

Toni shook her head. "I didn't break anybody down. Noel just realized that she's got to make some smart decisions now to get what she wants in the end." A thoughtful look settled onto her face, and she said, "She's not a bad person. I was a little too quick to judge her."

"You?" Jackie asked, recoiling in horror. She jumped back when Toni tried to grab her.

"She didn't come across very well at first, but I'm starting to like her."

"Oh-oh. Next thing you know she's gonna be on your to-do list."

Smiling slyly, Toni said, "I could do worse."

"Did her boobs grow?"

"I haven't seen 'em lately," Toni said dryly. "But it's hard to find a girl who has everything that you like."

"Last time you talked about her, she didn't have anything you liked."

"She must've had a bad day the first time I saw her," Toni said seriously. "When I saw her a couple of weeks ago she looked a lot better." She made a gesture with her hand, hovering around her head. "Her hair looks a lot better now, and her eyes really are pretty. She's got a nice mouth too."

"Maybe she had plastic surgery." Jackie took another step backwards just in case Toni reached for her.

"She didn't have plastic surgery," Toni said, scowling. "She just looks better. She seems nicer, too. I didn't think she had a sense of humor, but she does."

"Well, maybe she'll luck out and get to take you for a spin."

The look on Toni's face was almost seductive. "I think we could both have fun on that ride." She sat there after Jackie left, thinking about Noel. She was actually damned good-looking, and since she neither looked nor acted like Max, it wasn't creepy being around her. She was feisty, for sure, and there were few things Toni liked better than a feisty lover. And since Noel had to return to Baltimore in the fall, she could prove to be the perfect summer catch. Time would tell.

⌐

On the Thursday before Memorial Day, Toni was replacing a lock set on a restaurant Heidi was listing. She was rushing, and nicked herself with a screwdriver, making her jump and shake her hand vigorously.

"You don't seem like you're in the zone today," Heidi said.

"Oh, I've got a couple of things to finish over at The Sandpiper before Noel gets here tomorrow night."

"Tomorrow night, huh? Is she excited?"

"I wouldn't go that far," Toni chuckled. "I talked to her earlier in the week and she sounded nervous. She and her sister and their mom have been working on recipes that Noel can whip up without a lot of trouble. Apparently she can cook, but she's not used to cooking breakfast for a big crowd."

"Have you been talking to her a lot?"

"Not really. Just when something comes up. Why?"

"Just wondering. No reason."

"That'll be the day. You're always plotting something."

"Maybe I'm turning over a new leaf."

"Yeah," Toni said suspiciously. "That's likely."

⌐

Toni went by The Sandpiper on Saturday morning. It was early, just after seven, and Barbara, the inn babysitter, was getting ready to leave. Toni spotted her coming out the back door and smiled to herself when it looked as though Noel was going to grab onto her skirt to stop her from leaving. "Run for it, Barbara!" Toni called out.

Noel looked up and met Toni's eyes. Pleadingly, she said, "Don't let her get away."

In her soft British accent, Barbara said, "You'll be fine, dear. It's just like making breakfast for your own family."

"I've never made breakfast for my own family, and I don't want to start now."

Imploringly, Barbara looked at Toni. "You've got to give this girl a pep talk. I made batter for pancakes last night, and we've already put two dozen scones in the oven this morning. She doesn't have a thing to worry about."

"I've got some time until I have to get to work," Toni said. "You'd better run while you can, Barbara."

"If you let her leave, you've got to stay," Noel insisted.

Toni laughed, completely content. She couldn't have picked her timing better. "I can give you a hand today and tomorrow; then you're on your own."

Noel reached out and tugged at Toni's denim shirt. "I'm gonna handcuff you to the stove. You're the one that got me into this."

Toni held up her hands, still smiling indulgently. "Guilty as charged." She followed along behind Noel, trying to catch a look at her ass through shorts that Toni considered far too baggy.

～

By 11 a.m. everyone had eaten and a few guests were sitting in the parlor lingering over coffee. The two young gay men that Toni had arranged for were upstairs cleaning the rooms, and Noel was busy drying and putting away the dishes as quickly as Toni handed them to her.

"Yes, I do know where everything goes, but if I put it all away you'll never learn," Toni said.

"Do you think I didn't think of that?" Noel leaned against the counter and laughed. "You probably think I'm the ditsiest woman you've ever met."

"Not at all. When I first met you, I thought you were rigid and overly serious. Seeing your panicked side has rounded you out."

"Great. Now I seem like I'm bipolar."

"No, you seem like a perfectly normal person who's doing something she's not used to. But I guarantee you'll get into the flow." Toni snuck a look at her watch and her eyes nearly bugged out. "I've gotta get going. I'm just starting a big job." She put her hand on Noel's shoulder and squeezed it. "Call me if you need anything."

She started for the door with Noel saying, "You've been a real lifesaver. I have to think of some way to thank you."

"Oh, you'll think of something," Toni said, showing her teeth. "I've got a few ideas if you can't think of any," she added quietly once she was sure Noel couldn't hear her.

⌒

Toni called Noel the following Friday. "Do you have any interest in getting away from your new digs for a few hours?"

"If you've found me a buyer, I'll give you half the proceeds. No, I'll give you three-quarters." She laughed, but the sound was weary. "Who am I kidding? You can have it all. I just want to go home."

"Someone needs an attitude adjustment. I'll be there at six o'clock. Do you drink alcohol?"

"All I can get my hands on," Noel said, feeling a little perkier.

⌒

Toni showed up a little early, but Noel was waiting for her. As soon as Toni opened the back door, Noel grabbed her purse from the counter and pointed in the direction from which Toni had just come. "Out. Out."

As they walked along the side yard, Toni asked, "Is it really that bad?"

"I should be a stoic, but I'm not in the mood. I despise it." Noel's smile showed she was teasing, at least a little bit.

They reached Toni's truck and Noel stood back and appraised it. "This is the coolest truck I've ever seen."

"Thanks," Toni said opening the passenger door. "It was my dad's."

As Noel tried to judge how best to get into the high-riding truck gracefully, she gave Toni a concerned look. "Is your dad…?"

"What? Dead? Oh, no. He just found another piece of junk to rehabilitate. May I?"

She'd placed her hands on Noel's waist and when Noel felt the hands compress against her and easily boost her into the cab, she nearly swooned. She was slowly changing her mind about Toni's persistence, now beginning to find it rather appealing. As for her looks, well, she was exactly the type of woman that she'd been attracted to her entire adult life.

Toni continued to talk and Noel had to mentally slap herself to focus. "I usually buy his projects from him. Drives my mother nuts because he could sell them for a lot more, but I think he hates to have them get too far away."

Toni walked around to her side and got in. Noel asked, "What year is this?"

"Things must be bad if you don't even know what year it is." She grinned unrepentantly at Noel's playful glower. "It's a '55 Chevy."

"Boy, I wish my dad was interested in cars. The only thing he ever wants to talk about is the stock market and planning for my retirement."

"I lucked out in the dad department. We watch baseball together and compete for who has the best tools."

Noel ran her hands over the slick dash and shifted her weight in the dove grey bucket seat. "Is any of this original?"

Toni sat for a moment, letting her dark eyes scan the interior. "Nothing much." She patted the seat next to her thigh. "These are from a Mazda 929. I guess you could say the dash is original, but it's been repainted."

"Did you help with the renovation?"

"Yeah, sure. My dad's much more of a mechanic than I am, but I'm not bad. My biggest contribution was the bed." She twitched her head towards the rear of the truck and waited for Noel to turn around. "I made the oak stringers and fitted the stainless steel too."

"That's fantastic! It looks like a brand new truck, but they don't make trucks this beautiful anymore. Now they're all sheet metal and plastic." Noel turned around and settled into her seat, putting on her seatbelt. "I love the color, too."

"Viper red," Toni said, her voice sounding a little sexy. "My dad's choice. I would have gone with sea mist green."

"This must attract a lot of attention."

With a sly smile, Toni nodded. Her voice had deepened into a purr. "Sure does."

She turned the engine over and they sat in silence for a moment, the big-block V-8 rumbling underneath them. It felt like a massive vibrator rumbling under her butt. Noel would have made a saucy remark to someone she knew better, but Toni was so overtly flirting with her that she found herself uncharacteristically shy. "Where are we headed?"

"Let's go to Jersey. Whenever Rehoboth drives me nuts, I go

out of state."

"Jersey it is."

⌒

To Noel's surprise, they didn't drive the whole way. Toni guided her truck to a parking lot by the ferry in Lewes, and they got out. Noel looked around at the assembled crowd. "I'd heard there was a ferry, but I've never taken it."

"I take it almost every time I go to New Jersey. It costs more money than driving the whole way, but it's a nice way to get out on the ocean for a while."

The ferry service was well run and they were able to get on right on time. After making sure Noel didn't mind the possibility of sea spray, Toni led the way to the bow of the boat.

The sun was low in the sky and very bright. Noel turned her back so she didn't have to squint, but Toni didn't seem to mind. She faced the ocean as though she were born to it, her chin held high as the breeze blew her hair back. Noel marveled at how incredibly straight and thick Toni's hair was. With the sun reflecting off it she saw shades of gold, red, and amber mixed in among the chocolate brown. Toni wore it very simply and Noel had noticed how easily it fell forward when Toni's head was tilted down. But today it blew straight back off her face showing the strength of her jaw and the planes of her face.

Toni was, without question, attractive. She was what many would call androgynous, but Noel preferred to think of her look as handsome. She couldn't imagine her wearing makeup or lipstick, but not because Toni was masculine. She wasn't. But those types of feminine frills wouldn't have fit her personality or her image.

She didn't look as though she cultivated a butch personality, but on the butch/femme scale she was decidedly on the butch side. Noel decided she very much liked where Toni fit on that continuum. No one would mistake Toni for a man, but she was just androgynous enough for Noel's tastes.

One thing Noel was learning to appreciate about Toni was her sense of style. Her cowboy look was clearly a winter thing. In summer she dressed like an old-money preppy, even though Noel was fairly sure Toni didn't come from money. She just effortlessly pulled off that polo-shirt-and-khaki-shorts number so endemic on the eastern seaboard.

Tonight Toni wore a white polo shirt that was tucked into madras-plaid walking shorts. Her brown leather belt matched her Top-Siders, worn preppy style with no socks. Her hands were in her pockets, as Noel had noticed they often were. She stood tall, as always, looking cool and proud, a combination that Noel was sure most of the lesbians in Rehoboth had a hard time resisting. She was fully aware that she was becoming one of their number and found herself not even trying to resist the lure.

Cape May, New Jersey, was small and compact, and they didn't have to walk very far to find the restaurant Toni had selected. She didn't seem to be on a first name basis with anyone at the restaurant, but it was clear she had been there before.

When they were shown to their table she said, "The bartender here makes a great Manhattan. Are you up for one?"

"I'm up for two." Noel watched compliantly as Toni ordered their drinks and asked for a couple of appetizers to go with them.

As soon as the server departed, Toni focused every bit of her attention onto Noel. "Now that we're settled, I want you to answer me seriously. How is it going?"

Noel wasn't in a rush to answer. She could see that Toni was genuinely concerned, and she wanted to be honest but not over blow it. "It's not all that bad," she admitted. "I could see that most people wouldn't think it was a bad job at all. Sadly, I'm not most people."

Their server brought their drinks, and they touched the rims of their rocks glasses together. "Can you be a little more specific?" Toni asked, shivering when she took a drink.

Noel took a drink, too, then blinked her eyes repeatedly. "Now, that's a drink." She took in and let out a heavy sigh. "I think the problem is that I spend most of my year under a microscope. My students, their parents, my principal, the Board of Education, the federal government. Everyone has an opinion about the best way to teach eight-year-olds. During the summer I usually travel and go out of my way to be as independent as possible. Doing this makes me feel like I went from the frying pan into the fire. It's like I'm still at work, and I really need my vacations to recharge."

Her expression was full of empathy when Toni said, "I can understand that. I can't stand to be told what to do, so I wouldn't be able to do your job. I guess I just have a different view of the guests at The Sandpiper. They seem more like house-guests to me, and I enjoy having house-guests." She took another sip of her drink, her eyes still fixed on Noel. "I'm sorry this isn't working out. I guess I thought you'd get into it once you were here."

"Not so far, but it has only been a week. I guess I have to give it a fair try."

Smiling, Toni picked up her glass and clinked Noel's. "To fair tries."

⌒

They were whipping through their appetizers when Noel said, "I've been feeling kind of uncomfortable talking to you about

The Sandpiper. I mean, I know you'd like to buy it, and here I am bitching about how much I'd like to sell it. Am I being a jerk?"

"No, you're not," Toni said, her expression serious. "My dream of owning it was more emotional than practical. It makes sense that you wouldn't want to carry a huge second mortgage for me. You don't know that I'm the most honest person you'll ever meet." Now her teasing smile was back, and Noel found herself unable to avoid mimicking her.

"It's not that I don't trust you," she insisted. "But my brother says a second mortgage isn't a great deal. It's subordinate to the first, and if the property goes into default, it can be hard to collect. Not that you'd default for no good reason," she rushed to say once she saw the look on Toni's face. "But all sorts of bad things can happen. The town could be destroyed by a hurricane or the inn could burn to the ground…"

"You like to see the bright side, huh?"

"You know what I mean," Noel said, fervently hoping Toni did.

"I do. I've been talking to some other people in town, and they all think you'd be nuts to hold a second mortgage." She smiled, and her shiny, white teeth showed. "Now that you're here, I'm not as focused on buying The Sandpiper. My guess is that you're gonna wind up loving it, and my goal is to have it taken care of."

"I hope you reach your goal. I do. I just don't want to be the one you're counting on."

⌒

After dinner they walked around Cape May looking at the stores selling all sorts of touristy trinkets. The town was decidedly upscale, and most of the shops had things that one would actually not mind having in the house. Noel spent a few minutes looking at nautical-themed Christmas ornaments, mentioning that she collected ornaments whenever she went on vacation. Toni was leaning against a wall, patiently watching Noel shop when a couple came in and asked the proprietor where the best ice cream was. When Noel heard it was only two doors down, her eyes lit up and she said, "I'm starving. I have to get some."

Toni smiled and said, "You can't possibly be starved. You ate everything but the plates."

"I'm a growing girl. I need my ice cream. Don't you want to have any?"

"I was just trying to figure out how to unbutton my pants and loosen my belt a notch without anybody noticing. If I eat any more, I'm gonna have to buy a larger size just to get home."

Noel teasingly patted Toni's flat belly. "Then I'll have two scoops to make up for yours."

"Go get in line. One of my nieces has a birthday coming up. I think I'm gonna get her one of these wooden puzzles. I'll be right over, okay?"

"Sure. You don't have to rush. I think everyone in town is waiting for ice cream."

"It won't take me long. I shop fast."

⌣

They sat on the dock and let the ferry leave without them. It was a perfectly lovely evening, and Toni was not in a hurry to get back to Rehoboth. She leaned up against a piling and wrapped her long arms around a knee, looking relaxed and very comfortable.

Noel didn't seem to need to converse, lifting her stock a few more points, and they spent quite a while just listening to the sounds of boats banging against their fenders, lines squeaking under tension, and water lapping at their hulls. The silence was not only comfortable, it was oddly relaxing for both of them. Toni was a little vexed when people started to line up for the next departure, but she tried to ignore their chatter and just enjoy the peace. She was considering suggesting they skip the next ferry and waste another hour, but Noel got up and brushed off her shorts as the boat tugged up to the dock. She held a hand out to Toni and helped her to her feet. "We'd better get back. I've got to get up very early."

"I can sleep in on the weekend, but I rarely do. I guess I'm just a morning person."

They got onto the ferry and again went to the bow. The temperature had dropped, and the sun had set long ago, so the ride was much cooler. Toni offered to go below but Noel said, "If you can manage to block the wind for me, I can stay outside. You do prefer to be outside, don't you?"

"Much. I'd almost always rather be outdoors than in. But I don't want you to be cold."

Noel put her hands on Toni's hips and maneuvered her so she blocked as much wind as possible. She just had to duck a little when Toni's hair blew into her face, tickling it. "This is good. I'm not crowding you, am I?"

They were standing about six inches apart, facing one another. If Toni leaned forward just a little she could smell Noel's alluring, citrusy scent. Her hair, which Toni thought was possibly the most interesting color she'd ever seen, was blowing in the wind, fluttering in every direction. Noel kept trying to rein it in, but she didn't have anything to tie around it, and hanks of it kept escaping her clutch. It would whip across her face, obscuring her pale eyes, then fly away just as quickly letting Toni get a glimpse of them in the moonlight.

She made a gallant effort to try not to sound like she was flirting when she said, "You're perfect right where you are."

They didn't speak much on the ferry ride back, but Noel enjoyed letting Toni shelter her. There was something captivating about a woman who liked to brave the elements, but was considerate of your need to stay warm. And Toni's muscular body wasn't a bad shield. Noel spent a few minutes imagining how those muscles would feel wrapped around her...perhaps while having raucous sex. She was fairly sure they and every other part of Toni would feel just fine.

On the drive home from the ferry, Toni talked about a few of the landmarks they encountered. It was clear she knew the area well, and equally clear she was proud of her community.

When they arrived back at the inn, Noel thanked Toni for the nice evening and started to open her door. But before she could begin to exit, Toni was there, holding out a steadying hand to help her out of the tall truck. She walked Noel to the front door and handed her a small box.

Curious and surprised, Noel opened it to find a curvy mermaid with "Rehoboth Beach" printed on a sash that draped across her substantial chest. "This is adorable!" She gave Toni a quick, rather ungainly hug. "Thanks so much."

"My pleasure. I couldn't let you buy any of those tasteful things you were looking at. I want you to remember the randy side of Rehoboth. That's where all the fun is." She winked and turned to head back to her truck, with Noel looking at how nicely her shoulders filled out the snug polo shirt. Some women were just made to wear knit, and Toni was one of them.

⌇

A few days later, Noel was cleaning up after breakfast when she heard a knock at the back door. Curiously, she walked over and opened the door to find a woman bearing a large smile and a Tupperware cake holder. "Hi," Noel said. "Welcome Wagon?"

"Sort of." The woman handed Noel the container and said, "I'm Gloria Lake. Max and I were friends, and I'd heard that you'd decided to run The Sandpiper."

"That's partially true. Come on in and I'll tell you what's going on." Noel started to walk into the parlor, but realized that there were still guests in there. "We can either stand here in the kitchen or go into my bedroom," she said, laughing at herself.

"This is fine. I don't want to take up too much of your time. I know morning is busy."

"It is, but it's not all that busy. This is a lot more relaxing than my usual job."

"That's…?"

"I teach third grade in Baltimore."

"Fascinating," Gloria said. "I teach sixth right here in Rehoboth." She squinted for a few seconds and said, "For twenty-six more months. Then I retire."

"Cool. I think every teacher knows when she can get out."

"Yeah, I love it, but I'll be glad to retire. During the summers I work at Pages and Pages, one of our many bookstores. I'll probably keep doing that after I retire. My youngest will be in college by then."

"We'll have to have coffee or something."

"I'd love that. Why don't we meet tomorrow afternoon? That's my day off."

"Great. Tell me when and where, and I'll be there."

⌒

The next afternoon, Noel was waiting at a local coffee shop when Gloria entered. Gloria waved, got in line for her beverage, then joined Noel. The shop wasn't very crowded, probably because it was a warm day and most people were at the beach.

Noel looked at her, guessing her to be in her mid-fifties. She looked like a teacher, even though Noel wouldn't be able to explain that shorthand assessment to anyone who didn't see her in that way. She idly wondered if people could tell she was a teacher just by looking at her.

"So how are you settling in?" Gloria asked when she placed her cup of tea on the table.

"I'm doing all right. My goal was to fix the place up and sell it, but when I couldn't get that done in time for this summer, I decided to run it and make my repairs in the off-season."

"Oh," Gloria said, only the slight furrow in her brow adding to her comment.

"Are you like Max's friend, Toni, who can't imagine why I'd want to sell?"

"No, well, maybe a little. I know that Max wouldn't have wanted you to sell."

With a tight smile, Noel said, "Maxine could have left it to me with restrictions, but she didn't. She also could've tried to find me a lot sooner, but she didn't." Her cool blue eyes looked positively frosty.

"I don't pretend to speak for Max. And I'm not at all sure it was a good idea for her to leave you the property. I mean, I know it's worth a lot of money, but it's also a lot of work. I urged her to have her estate sell it and give you the money, but she had her mind made up."

"I don't mean to be rude," Noel said. "I mean that sincerely. But I didn't know Max, and I honestly didn't want to. So, while I appreciate your kindness, I don't want to talk about her." She tried to smile, but her efforts were not very successful. "No hard feelings." She started to get up, but Gloria put her hand atop hers.

"Will you stay if we don't talk about her?"

Noel hesitated for a second, then said, "Sure." She sat back down. "I hope I don't come across as heartless. This has just been very traumatic for me. I've had kind of a tough year."

"Tell me about it," Gloria said, leaning back in her chair. Her expression was open and unguarded and Noel sensed that she could trust her—at least with the long list of reasons she didn't like being an innkeeper.

⌒

An hour later, Gloria held the door for Noel as they left the coffee shop. "I hope I didn't come across as a total bitch," Noel said. "It's just hard not knowing Max or anything about her, and then stepping into her world."

Gloria put a hand on Noel's shoulder and squeezed it. "Not at all. I know Max didn't handle this whole thing very well. I can understand why you aren't interested in her right now, but if you ever change your mind, I can try to give you my perspective on her."

"I'll keep that in mind. But for now, I'm just looking for friends. I have my evenings free, but I haven't gotten out much."

"Have you been over to Jackie's?"

"Jackie's? No. What is it?"

"It's a bar where most of the local lesbians hang out."

"Mmm," Noel looked unconvinced. "I'm not much into bars."

"It's a very friendly place. I think you'd feel comfortable going into Jackie's alone."

"You won't go with me, huh?" Noel asked, a shy grin settled on her face.

"No. My husband and kids demand every bit of my free time. Why don't you call Toni? She hangs out there, and I'm sure she'd be glad to introduce you around."

"That's not a bad idea. After all, she's the one who talked me into this."

⌣

Noel walked outside and saw that the day was fine—clear and warm with a slight, gentle breeze. The cleaning crew was still at the B&B and could handle any emergencies, so she decided to go to the beach and take a walk. She'd been at The Sandpiper almost nonstop since she'd arrived, but talking to Gloria convinced her that she had to make a little space for herself.

She put on her iPod headphones and got lost in her music while she padded along the sand in her bare feet. Distinct groups of beach-goers were gathered every few hundred yards. Some were a mix of gay men and lesbians; some were a college-aged crowd; some were moms and their kids. Only the kids braved the ice cold water, their mothers refusing to go in any further than absolutely necessary.

By the time she turned to head home, most of the crowd was packing up. She slowed down. The sensation of the cold water rushing over her feet, the rhythmic thrum of the waves, the call of the gulls were all calming. She was content and more tranquil than she had been since leaving Baltimore, and when she left the beach, she found that she'd subconsciously chosen the street that Jackie's sat on. It was early evening, just after five, but she went in anyway, to get a feel for the place.

It was fairly dark inside, something she always hated about bars. But the woman behind the long bar smiled and welcomed her, making her forget about the dim atmosphere.

"Hi," Noel said, while making a quick assessment of the bartender. Graying hair cut fairly short, a kind smile and friendly eyes—she looked to be in her late fifties or early sixties.

"What can I get for you?"

"Oh." Noel looked around and saw she was the only patron. "Do you have any cranberry juice?"

"Sure do."

"How about cranberry and sparkling water."

"I can do that." She started to make the drink, saying, "Don't think I've seen you around. Are you here on vacation?"

"Sort of." Noel put a five dollar bill on the bar and took a sip. "I'm running The Sandpiper."

"Oh! You're Max's daughter!"

"Yep." Noel tried to keep her smile free of the rancor she felt whenever the topic came up. "Gloria Lake suggested I come by to rub elbows with the lesbian movers and shakers."

"Great. I don't see Gloria very often…since Max died. They were good friends."

"That's what she said." She determinedly changed the subject. "So, how do I get into the swing of things around here? I'm going a little stir crazy."

"It might not look like it, but this is a good place to start."

As she was speaking, Heidi walked in and dropped her briefcase on the bar. "Why didn't I go into an easier line of work? Like prison guard. Where I could meet nice people." She put her head on the bar and moaned throatily.

"Bad day?" Noel asked dryly, feeling more at ease now that she knew someone.

"Do you two know each other?" Jackie asked.

"A bit," Noel said. "Heidi gave me some good advice when I first came down here."

Heidi looked up and smiled. "Are we still speaking? Toni says you're not the happiest inn-keeper in town."

"Sure." Noel moved down to sit by Heidi. "I'll even buy you a drink."

"Vodka and tonic," Heidi told Jackie. "Don't be stingy," she added in a dramatic voice.

"What's got you down?" Jackie asked.

"Oh, just the usual. I had a buyer lined up for a little apartment building in Lewes, and the seller totally screwed up the deal. Weeks of work…down the drain."

"Ooo, that must hurt." Noel made a face.

"I'll get over it. Still beats dealing with homeowners."

"Do you only do commercial buildings?"

"Almost exclusively. I did residential for a few years, but that got old quickly. Speaking of commercial buildings, how's The Sandpiper?"

The door opened, and they all squinted to see Toni enter, a big smile on her face. "Afternoon, all. Who wants to buy me a drink?"

"I've got this round," Noel said, nearly euphoric to see her. "You're looking happy today."

"Why not?" Toni sat next to Heidi and tipped the beer Jackie automatically poured for her at Noel. "Summer's here and it's a beautiful day." She took a deep drink and sighed. "Life is good."

"Heidi had a deal fall through," Noel said. "She needs cheering up."

Toni put her arm around Heidi and kissed the top of her head. "Tell me all about it, bunny."

"Oh, just the usual. I wasted time on a deal that got screwed up."

Toni looked at Noel from over Heidi's head. "She gets no respect."

"I'd sell The Sandpiper in a minute if you could find me a buyer," Noel said. "Would that make you feel better?"

Heidi sat up and looked at Noel curiously. "Have you dropped your plans for upgrading the place?"

"No, but I'm certainly not opposed to selling it now if I can get a good deal."

"The place looks great," Toni said. "Maybe you should see what people are willing to pay. It'd give you an idea of where you stand."

This was a new tack, and an odd one at that. "What happened to 'don't even think of selling it?'"

"I thought you'd like it once you got here. But if you don't, why not see if there's any interest?"

"What do you think, Heidi? Should we list it?"

"Sure, we can do that if you want to. I don't think you'll get any nibbles, since people don't generally like to take over mid-season, but it can't hurt."

"Great." Noel finished her drink, paid for the others, and patted each woman on the back on her way out. "Give me a call when you have a contract for me to sign."

After they'd all said goodbye, Toni scowled at Heidi. "You should encourage her."

"Encourage her? I thought I was supposed to discourage her."

"Yeah, but things have changed. I think she might really want to get out. And if she does, she might change her mind about taking a second mortgage, especially if I offer more than anyone else."

"Okay, okay. I'll see what the market looks like and talk to Noel. But I'm not going to tell you anything she tells me in confidence. I've got to protect my integrity."

Toni smiled at Jackie. "Isn't she cute when she says things like that?"

Part Three

That Friday evening, Noel had just put her feet up, and was settling in to watch the evening news. She heard what sounded like a tapping on her window, but chalked it up to the wind. When it happened again, she got up to investigate. Through tilted blinds she saw Toni standing outside, holding up a bottle of wine. "Thirsty?" Toni asked.

"Sure. I'll meet you outside." Noel tried to ignore the little jolt she got whenever Toni appeared. But she did pause and check herself out in the mirror, making sure her hair looked good.

Toni was sitting on the swing she had installed inside the arbor. She grinned when Noel approached with a corkscrew and two glasses. "I knew this would be a fantastic place to sit."

Noel sat down next to her, and handed Toni the corkscrew. "Do you think it's okay for me to sit out here? I never know how normal to be."

"Because of your guests?"

"Yeah. I don't want it to look like I'm one of them. That might be a turnoff."

Toni nodded, but didn't add anything. She got the bottle open and poured, then touched her glass to Noel's. "Nice," she said, taking an appreciative sip. "I like a good crisp wine."

"It is good. Thanks for coming by. I get pretty lonely."

"Don't let that happen. This is a friendly place. You need to get out and mingle."

Shrugging her shoulders and feeling a little embarrassed, Noel said, "I'm not good at…I've never had to adjust to being new in town."

"Then I'm glad I decided to come by. I'll continue to chase you down if I don't see you around."

"I'm probably here more than I need to be, but, like I say, I'm flying blind."

Again, Toni nodded, and took another sip of her drink. It was early evening and the day had been warm, but now there was a nice breeze. The clematis that Toni planted were just past their full bloom, and the climbing roses were ready to pop.

Toni's uncharacteristic reserve made Noel dig a little. "I can see that you want to say something, but you're holding back."

Feigning astonishment, Toni said, "Me? I never hold back."

"Yes, you do. You're very polite."

"Thank you. I'll tell my mother that her indoctrination was successful."

"Come on," Noel urged. "What did you want to say?"

"Nothing earth shattering. I was going to tell you how Max did a few things, but I know you don't like to talk about her."

Noel sat quietly for a few moments, testing her feelings. "You know, I'm more amenable to hearing about her now that I've been here for a couple of weeks. I see all of her things around the house and I'm getting curious."

"Well, I can tell you how she ran things, but only if you're sure you want to hear."

"I am. I'm particularly interested in how she interacted with the guests. I'm not a natural at this, and I think I'm probably being too formal."

"I can't see you imitating Max," Toni said, chuckling softly, "but she was a long way from formal. If you would've walked in here two summers ago, you wouldn't have known that she owned the place. She always ate with the guests, and most nights she'd be in the parlor playing cards or just talking with them."

"Really? I try to be as unobtrusive as possible."

"Like I said, you don't seem anything like Max, and her style wouldn't fit you. But the guests who come here are used to a very casual atmosphere."

Noel scooted around until her back was against the arm rest. She put her foot on the seat of the swing and wrapped her arm around her knee, looking more casual than she usually did. "Tell me a little about her."

"I can tell you an awful lot. What do you want to know?"

Having the whole universe of Max presented daunted Noel. She could feel herself backing off, but was determined not to. "Mmm, just tell me whatever you think is important."

Toni leaned back and made the swing rock gently. She put her arm across the back and let her fingers play against the grain of the wood. "Do you know anything at all?"

"Nothing." Noel frowned and shook her head, wracking her mind for the few details she did possess. "No, that's not true. I know that the adoption agency was in California, so I always assumed I was born there."

"Wow," Toni said, shaking her head. "I can't imagine what it's like not knowing anything about your birth parents."

Smiling, Noel said, "I can't imagine what it's like to know your birth parents at all. And since my brother and sister don't know theirs either, it seemed perfectly normal when I was growing up."

"I guess that makes sense. Well, Max was from Oklahoma. She moved to California with a couple of friends and never went back. She eventually joined the Navy, and she was in for twenty-five years."

"Ah-ha! That explains the little trinkets from all sorts of port cities. What did she do?"

"I'm not sure what she did at first, but I do know she was in the group of women who were the first ones assigned to ships. I think that was the late seventies, maybe early eighties. She was on a submarine tender and was stationed in Scotland for quite a while. She did a lot of traveling around in Europe, so she was pretty international for a girl from a small town on the plains."

"I was born before that. Do you know how I happened to arrive?"

"Yeah, I do." She took another sip of her wine and refilled Noel's, but not her own glass. "I found out all about you last summer."

"Last summer? Why last summer?"

"She didn't tell me or anybody else that I know of about you until she got sick."

Surprised and a little troubled by this news, Noel said, "I wonder why?"

"If you knew Max, you wouldn't be too surprised. She didn't spend a lot of time thinking about the past. She didn't spend a lot of time thinking about the future, either. But when she got sick, she changed. She talked about her past constantly. I think it had always weighed on her mind that you were out there, but if I had to guess her motivation for not trying to find you, I'd say she was afraid."

"Afraid? Afraid of finding the baby she gave away?" Her voice was a little louder and her cheeks had begun to color. She consciously tried not to let her contempt show, but it was hard work.

Toni looked tentative, but she continued. "I think that's the right word. Max wasn't very good at talking about her feelings. She liked to stick to facts. She'd only been in San Diego a short while when she and some of her friends met some sailors from the Swedish Navy. Max was a pretty good drinker when I knew her, but she must not have been when she was a young woman."

"So I'm the result of the wrong ship being in the right port?"

"Something like that," Toni allowed. "She didn't know anything except the ship the guy was on and his first name, but she didn't blame him for what happened. She wasn't the type to blame other people for her own indiscretions." Noel visibly winced at the word, and Toni corrected herself. "I didn't mean that like it sounded. But she knew she didn't want to have kids, and she didn't think it was fair to abort you. So she had you and saw you for just a minute or two. She told me you had the prettiest blonde fuzz and blue eyes that she'd ever seen." Even though it was a story about Noel, Toni was the one who started to sniff away tears. "I'm such a sucker for a sob story," she said, her cheeks turning pink as she let out an embarrassed laugh.

Noel's heartstrings tugged at the sight of Toni's tear-streaked face. She was tempted to brush the tears away with a finger, but the first real facts she'd ever heard about her genetic father overtook her more tender instincts. "Do you remember the guy's name?"

"Yeah. It was Stefan. Max asked me if I thought it was possible that your parents had named you Stephanie. She thought that would've been cool."

"Huh." She sat completely still, letting the facts merge with the emotions that roiled her stomach. When she spoke again she felt strangely resolved, knowing the answer to her question before she asked it. "So, she didn't regret giving me up for adoption?"

"No, she didn't. She wasn't very religious, but she thought abortion was wrong. I don't think she thought it was a sin as much as it was too easy a way out. She believed in facing up to your responsibilities, and she thought that giving birth to you was an important one."

Offput at the idea of being an obligation, Noel soldiered on. "I assume she didn't have any other children?"

"No, just you. Right after you were born she joined the Navy. I always thought she might have wanted to…" She stopped, shifting her eyes nervously.

"I get it. She wanted to start a new life and forget about me. I just assume the Navy would be a good place to meet a husband."

"I knew her for twenty years, and she never had a man in her life. She always talked about how much she wanted one, but I don't know if she honestly did or not."

"What do you mean?"

"I always thought she might be gay. But that's just a guess. If she was, I don't think she ever acted on it. But she seemed a lot more comfortable around women than she did around men." Toni laughed. "Of course, it might be that she had her fill of men when she was in the Navy."

"This has been…interesting," Noel said, not having a better word for it. "I'm glad we talked about it."

"Had enough?"

Noel smiled and nodded. "I think I need to digest what I've just learned. So let's talk about you."

"Me? I'm boring."

"You don't seem boring to me. Actually, I've wondered why you're not with someone."

Toni made a face and shrugged. "I'm not particularly good at being in a relationship. I seem to do better on my own."

"Have you been in many?"

"A couple, and my ex-lovers agree that I suck at it." She laughed, not seeming embarrassed in the least.

"So you're happy with your status quo?"

A loud siren startled them both, but Toni reacted faster than Noel did. She handed Noel the wine bottle and her glass, and started running for her truck. "Gotta go," she called over her shoulder.

"Gotta go where?" Noel stood and stared, stunned at Toni's abrupt departure.

"Fire alarm. I'm on the force." She jumped into her truck and roared away, leaving a weak-kneed Noel to contemplate getting into her own car to follow along to get a glimpse of Toni in a uniform. Was there no end to the surprises that made her more and more attractive?

⌒

The next afternoon, Noel reached Toni on her cell. "Hi," she said when Toni answered. "I was just calling to check up on you."

"What do you know that I don't?" Toni answered, sounding happy and relaxed.

"Oh. I meant because you raced off last night. I've never known a fire fighter, and I found myself wondering about you all day. That's a dangerous line of work."

"It can be. But most of our calls are for minor stuff. Last night was just a fire someone started in a trash can on the beach. Not very exciting. I'm sorry I ran out on you, though. I should've called when I got home."

"No problem. Like I said, I was just checking." She desperately wanted to ask Toni to come by again or to meet her somewhere, but she didn't have the courage.

"That's sweet of you. We'll have to get together again and finish off that wine."

"Anytime," Noel said, hoping Toni suggested the next five minutes.

"I'll call you. Or maybe I'll just drop by again. You didn't mind that, did you?"

"No, I like surprises." She said that even though she didn't like them in the least, but having Toni show up at her door was a surprise she was willing to learn to like.

"That's good, because there's nothing I like more than being extemporaneous."

When Noel hung up, she stared blankly at the phone for a few moments, thinking that she'd be well served by being more extemporaneous herself. But she knew that there was nothing she liked more than a firm schedule.

⌇

At around nine o'clock that night, Noel found herself with a surprising supply of energy. She'd been going to bed by ten every night, but it was a lovely evening, and there were a lot of people out. Oddly, she felt like a child who wasn't allowed to go out on a school night, so the thrill of doing something a little wrong prodded her to act. She got up and checked herself in the mirror, nodding in partial satisfaction at her look. She'd had her hair up in a ponytail all day, and she took the band off and ran her hands through it, pleased with the outcome.

It was a bit of a walk, but she took off to get an ice cream, something that everyone in Rehoboth seemed to do every night. As always, she had her ear buds in and was listening to music. There were several ice cream places in town, but one of them always had a long line. Guessing that people wouldn't wait for something that wasn't superior, she waited and was finally served a fantastic mint chip cone.

It was still warm out, but not warm enough to make her eat the ice cream as quickly as she did. That was due only to the taste. She was concentrating so hard on not losing a drop that she almost didn't see her favorite firefighter.

Toni was leaning against a building that housed what must have been a very popular gay and lesbian hang out. A pretty young woman was leaning against her and Toni was giving her a dose of undivided attention, as she was wont to do, so she didn't see Noel staring at her. But stare she did—boldly.

Noel couldn't see the young woman very well because her back was to the street. But she got a clear message about the nature of their relationship from the presence of Toni's hands on the young woman's ass. Noel felt her body heat flare. There was something very erotic about the way Toni looked at the woman, not to mention the way she touched her. It was those dark, intense eyes, fiery even from a distance, that made her pulse pound harder. But it was fairly clear that Noel was not going to be the one who captured Toni's attention this night, and her chest ached at that fact.

⌒

Noel was a little down the next day, even though she knew she had no reason to be. She had already cleaned the kitchen after breakfast and was tiptoeing back in to get a cool drink when she heard a few of her guests in the parlor. They were trying to be quiet, but one of the women had a voice that carried, and what she said caught Noel's attention.

"I'm not sure we're gonna be back next year," the woman whispered loudly. "I still like The Sandpiper, but it just doesn't feel as friendly as it did when Max was here. I'm going to search around and see if I can find a place where I'll meet more people."

"Yeah," another woman agreed. "Max always made sure that everybody who stayed here knew each other. My girlfriend and I would be walking out the door to dinner and Max would stick us with somebody who didn't have any friends." She laughed. "Maybe I don't miss that part."

"It's still nice here, but it's just not homey."

Noel hated to eavesdrop, but even more than that, she hated what she was hearing. She was trying as hard as she could, but she knew she wasn't carrying this off. Dejectedly, she snuck out the back door and spent a long time picking faded blossoms from the arbor.

⤙

As the day went on, the weather went south. By four o'clock it was overcast and gray. Noel's mood hadn't improved, and she considered calling some of her friends from Baltimore and seeing if she could arrange to meet them halfway for dinner. But she knew she wouldn't be very good company, so she decided to just get some air before it started to rain.

She walked down to the beach and started off on a long stroll. To her surprise, the more she walked the better she felt. There was something tranquilizing about the ocean and she decided she wouldn't let another day pass without a visit. It was after six when she found herself in a diner near the boardwalk. She was just about to order when Toni sat down at the stool next to her at the counter. "Mind some company?"

"No, of course not. I'm always happy to have company."

Toni cocked her head and looked at her quizzically for a second. "Is that true? I haven't been able to figure you out yet. I keep thinking that you might like a lot of time alone."

"I like my own company. That's true. But I'm pretty social."

"I guess I just thought you'd come down to Jackie's or give me or Heidi a call if you wanted to hang out."

"I know I should do that." She shrugged. "I just don't think of it, and then it seems too late in the day." She wasn't about to admit that she was too shy to make a call to either of them, nor that she was mooning over Toni's recent hook-up.

Toni gave her a luminous smile. "Well then, I'll just have to pursue you a little more doggedly."

"I don't think anyone would honestly say she didn't at least secretly like to be pursued," Noel said, trying not to look too coquettish. She wasn't crazy about being another notch on Toni's likely well-worn belt, but sometimes a woman had to swallow her pride.

⟿

After they finished their sandwiches, Toni said, "Would you like to see where the tourists hang out?"

"Sure. I'm up for anything."

Toni looked at her for a few moments, then grinned. "With that attitude, you sound like a tourist."

"I'm not that bad. It's not like I'm doing beer bongs on the beach. Yet," she added. They started to walk down the street, and Noel surprised herself by saying, "I saw you last night."

Toni's head swiveled sharply. "When?"

"I'm not sure. Maybe ten o'clock?"

Toni made a guilty face. "Was I alone?"

"Not a bit."

"Was I with my new friend Amy? About this tall?" She said, holding her hand up to shoulder height.

Her smile was teasing when Noel said, "It was hard to tell. When I saw you your friend wasn't standing up fully."

Looking shocked, Toni said, "Were you looking in my windows?"

Noel slapped at her weakly. "Of course not. I didn't say you were horizontal, just that she wasn't standing up. She was leaning against you, and you were leaning against a building."

"Whew!" Dramatically, Toni ran her hand across her forehead. "It coulda been worse."

"You're a naughty girl, aren't you," Noel said, finding herself charmed by Toni's cavalier attitude.

"Whenever I have the chance."

⌒

Noel wasn't surprised that they wound up in front of the bar that she had seen Toni at the night before. It was early, but there was a slow, steady stream of people heading into the club. Toni didn't seem to know the people at the door, and Noel smiled at her when Toni pulled her wallet out of her jeans and paid the cover charge for both of them.

The room was good-sized, and not very crowded, despite the way it'd looked from the outside. Toni guided Noel to a table at the far corner of the room and said, "The bartenders here don't know what they're doing, and their wine would take the varnish off this table. So I'd recommend a simple mixed drink or a beer."

"Think they can handle a cranberry and vodka?"

"We'll find out," Toni said conspiratorially. "I'll order two just to test them."

She returned in a few minutes. Noel had watched her from the moment she'd left the table, surprised that Toni didn't seem to know anyone. "Well, here goes," Toni said, eyes wide as she took her first sip. "Ahh. Success."

"This isn't bad at all. Thank you."

"My pleasure."

"So, this is the tourist trap, huh? Was Amy a tourist?"

"Yep. She's probably back in Washington now. Hey," she said, smiling brightly. "Maybe you could look her up. You live close, right?"

"Thanks so much," Noel said, wrinkling her nose. "It's not that I don't appreciate the offer, even though I don't, but I think I can find my own tramps…I mean dates."

Toni put her hand over her heart. "How dare you call a woman a tramp just because she blows into town one afternoon, picks up the local handywoman, screws the socks off her, and takes off before they exchange last names? That's very judgmental of you."

"I meant you," Noel said, giggling at Toni's shocked expression.

"I'm just friendly. I'm part of a committee designed to welcome strangers." She took a sip of her drink, eyeing Noel over the rim of her glass. "How about you? Are you planning on making any 'friends' while you're here?"

"One never knows. That was the last thing on my mind when I first got here, but I think I might be changing my view. A summer fling might be just the thing."

"Ahh. I love a good summer fling." Toni looked like she was reminiscing about a favorite song.

"Given what you just told me, a fling might be kind of long term for you."

"Don't get the wrong idea about me. Just because I don't want to eat at the same restaurant every night doesn't mean I don't like to go to a good place repeatedly." She leaned closer and spoke almost directly into Noel's ear. "When I find something tasty, I want it again and again. I can be a real glutton."

Toni pulled back and Noel knew she must look like she was going to jump into her lap. It was a fight to compose herself and try to adopt a more casual mien.

"How about you, Noel? You said something one of the first times we talked about liking sex more than you liked women, or something like that. I'm not sure what it was, but it caught my attention."

"Oh, I was probably just complaining about my ex. I had decided that women just weren't worth the trouble. I kept thinking that what I missed was the fun part."

"Versus…what? The relationship part?"

"Yeah. It's been a very long time since I was just looking for fun."

"It's been hours for me," Toni said, grinning sexily.

"It's getting crowded in here," Noel said, feeling like she had to change the subject or slide onto Toni's lap.

"Yeah, it is. Wanna dance before it gets too crowded?"

"Dance?" Noel asked, her eyes bright. "I love to dance. My ex hated it, so I hardly ever got to."

"There are few things better than dancing," Toni said. "Actually, almost nothing that I can think of that's vertical." She took Noel's hand and started to lead her to the dance floor. Noel held on loosely, allowing herself to feel the callused skin on Toni's strong hand.

As soon as they found a spot, Toni put one hand on Noel's waist and clasped her hand. Toni moved very smoothly. She didn't do anything professional or attention grabbing, she just led Noel around in a small circle, moving with the beat of the music.

The two women were roughly the same height, especially now that it was summer and Toni didn't wear her boots. Their bodies pressed against one another repeatedly, each bit of contact making Noel's temperature rise. They danced for a long time, through all sorts of music. Oddly, they didn't talk at all, but Noel didn't feel any need to. She was just in the moment, letting Toni lead her around the dance floor, feeling good to be in her own skin. Something that she hadn't felt for quite a few months after her breakup.

Noel could've stayed until the place closed, but just before ten, Toni checked her watch and said, "I've got to get over to the station. Wanna walk me home?"

"I didn't hear a siren."

"If you had, I'd already be gone." They walked toward the door, and when they got outside, Toni turned to the left. "Those of us without families stay at the station one night a week."

"All by yourself?"

"Yep. It's usually pretty boring, but somebody needs to be there.

Besides Rehoboth, we help other towns when they need it. That doesn't happen often, but we've gotta be here to get the alarm."

"I think it's cool that you're a firefighter," Noel said, knowing that her smile was goofy looking.

"To be honest, I think it's cool, too." Toni's smile was lethally charming, and when she reached out to take Noel's hand, there was no resistance. In fact, Noel considered starting a diary to mark the first time they'd held hands. Then she realized that was an urge she should have satisfied thirty-five years ago.

They didn't have to walk far to reach the station. Toni stood at the side entrance and took out her keys, which were many. She snuck another look at her watch, and said, "I've got to get in and relieve my buddy, Rusty. I had a great time tonight."

"I did, too. We'll have to do it again."

"That's a very good idea." Toni reached up and slid her hand across the neat French braid that Noel had fashioned. "I love your hair. No matter what anyone tells you, don't cut it. Long hair rules."

"I'll remember that," Noel said, gazing into Toni's dark eyes, hoping she'd kiss her.

Toni closed the distance between them and when she was just an inch away she whispered, "Don't be a stranger," then pressed a gentle but surprisingly heartfelt kiss upon Noel's lips. Noel stood, motionless, hoping for more, but all she heard was a soft chuckle, then the firehouse door opening and closing.

⌒

Rusty was waiting right by the front door. "I was just about to stick my head out and see if you were coming. Who's the chick?"

"The woman," Toni said, enunciating clearly, "is Max Carter's daughter."

"Wow. I couldn't see her very clearly, but she's tasty looking."

"Yeah, she is. The more often I see her, the more she reminds me of Max."

"I know you're getting old, Hoop, and you probably need glasses, but she doesn't look a thing like Max. Is she single?"

"Yeah, she is."

"Straight?" He laughed, shaking his head. "You've always got to ask around here."

Toni was used to his sense of humor, knowing his teasing was benign. "I don't think so, but you could probably change her mind."

"It's not worth the trouble. You've probably already cast your net."

"No, I haven't. And I hate to break it to you, but I'm really not all that successful with the ladies."

"Whatever you say, Hoop." He was chuckling to himself when he left the firehouse.

⌒

Every day for the next week, Noel trolled around looking for Toni. She'd figured out that Toni didn't take her truck to go most places around town, so not being able to search for the distinctive vehicle made things a little more difficult.

It had been years…perhaps never…since she had a crush like the one she'd developed on the fire-fighting handywoman. Still, she didn't feel comfortable calling. She was a fairly confident woman in most situations, but she'd never had to chase someone, and it felt so unnatural that she wasn't sure how to start.

Her breakup had knocked her off her pins in many ways, one of them hurting her self-assurance. While she wasn't devastated any longer, she wasn't sure enough of Toni's interest to track her down.

But if their paths happened to cross…

Sadly, that didn't happen. She knew Toni would likely be hanging out in one of her two favorite bars, but she felt a little odd going into either alone. Stopping by in the late afternoon for a soda was one thing. Going on the prowl at nine p.m. was another.

So she went on three walks a day, figuring she'd run into Toni eventually. It was just that eventually wasn't coming fast enough to suit her.

⌐

Toni had been engaged in the very same activity as Noel had. She usually knocked off work by four thirty or five, went home to shower and change, then left for dinner. Most of the popular restaurants were on one busy street, and each night she'd start at one end of the street and casually make her way down to the other end, looking for any sign of Noel. But a full week passed with their never being in the same place at the same time.

The following week, Toni and her friend Roxy went to Showtime, as they often did on Wednesdays. Roxy kept pointing out women that she thought would appeal to Toni, but Toni refused to bite.

"Why are you so picky?" Roxy asked. "You're not gonna find much better than that cutie over in the corner."

"No, I'm not interested. I think I'll head home early tonight, and I'd just as soon go alone."

Roxy gave her a suspicious look. "What's going on with you? If you were in the majors, they'd send you down to Triple-A with your pitiful batting average."

Toni smiled and rolled her eyes at her old friend. "I don't think of this as a game. If I see somebody I'm attracted to, I'll try to meet her. But I'm not into trying to score with someone just to prove that I can."

Roxy elbowed her and laughed. "Since when?"

"Since always. It's not that hard to convince some drunken tourist to go home with you. If I'm gonna spend the night with someone, I want to make sure we both have fun."

"I always have fun when some sweet thing is cuddled up against me. You over think things."

"Maybe. Maybe not. Maybe my tastes are changing."

"Not mine. I'm always gonna like as many pretty women as I can get."

"I think quality has to come into play too, Roxy."

"You have your rules, I have mine. And if you're not gonna take her, I'm gonna try to separate that brunette from the herd."

"Happy hunting," Toni said, slapping her friend on the back.

⌒

On her way home, Toni stopped in at Jackie's, ostensibly just to say hi but also to see if Noel had been in. Toni made her way around the room, speaking to a few friends and checking out the scene. After she'd made her rounds, she went up to the bar and took a stool in the corner. Jackie looked for her signal, and when Toni shook her head, Jackie brought her some sparkling water. "On duty tonight?"

"Yep. What's been going on?"

"Since last night?"

Realizing her line of questioning wasn't getting her anywhere, Toni decided to be blunt. "Has Max's daughter been in again?"

"No, haven't seen her. I sure wouldn't mind if she'd hang out here, though. She'd be good for business," Jackie said laughing fiendishly. "She probably goes over to Showtime and hangs out with girly girls."

"I don't think so. I'm afraid she's feeling a little isolated over at The Sandpiper. She doesn't seem like she's used to having to entertain herself."

"I'd gladly entertain her. Any night."

Smiling at Jackie's fanciful offer, Toni said, "I don't think you're alone there, but she doesn't seem like she's all that interested in going out."

"Have you tried to interest her?"

Feeling a little defensive, Toni said, "Not very hard. She had a bad breakup just a few months ago, and I think she's still licking her wounds."

"I'd be more than happy to lick her—" Jackie began before Toni hoisted herself up by standing on the lowest rung of the bar stool and clapped her hand over Jackie's mouth.

Part Four

*F*or the first time that summer Rehoboth Beach was hit with a wave of enervating humidity. Everyone in town whined about it, which seemed funny to Noel, coming from Baltimore where summer humidity was an everyday occurrence.

She walked to a local restaurant and had dinner outdoors, having a salad and a glass of iced tea while she read a novel she'd picked up from her new friend Gloria. Her table was near the sidewalk, and she looked up sharply when someone gently tugged on a lock of her hair.

Toni was standing next to her, grinning happily. Judging by the gleam in her eye, Noel figured she was out for a night of lady killing.

Toni had obviously just showered since her hair still looked damp. She was wearing a white sleeveless linen shirt, and there wasn't a wrinkle in it. The shirt was tucked into sky blue shorts, which were similarly pressed into sharp creases. Toni looked long and lean and cool—in both attitude and temperature. Noel eyed her carefully. "Are you just out pulling girls' hair? Or do you have a purpose?"

"I don't have much of a purpose. I don't have air conditioning, so as soon as I got home from work I took a shower and thought I'd better head out." She conspicuously eyed Noel's book. "Could you tear yourself away to share some of your wine with me?"

"I don't have any wine."

Toni easily stepped over the low barrier and took a seat opposite Noel. She caught the waiter's eye, and when he stopped by she ordered a bottle of Pinot Grigio. The smile she shared with Noel was both sexy and impish. "All set. I guess I should've waited for you to say whether you would've rather kept reading, huh?"

"There's no need. My book will be here later, but you're like a firefly. I've got to catch you as soon as it turns dusk"

"That's a good one," Toni said, her smile extending its grasp to reach her eyes. "Am I really hard to hold onto? That's not how I see myself. Actually, that sounds more like you."

"Right. Sure."

The waiter delivered their wine, and Toni spent a moment going through the formalities of the testing and approval. Then she and Noel clinked their glasses together, and each took a sip. "This is delicious," Noel said. "Just the thing for a hot night."

"And I can have more than one glass because I'm off tonight." At Noel's raised eyebrow, she continued, "I get two nights a week off. If a cat gets stuck up a tree tonight, I don't have to go." She took another sip of her wine. "So tell me about how elusive I am. I think I've been kind of a pest."

"Hardly. Why would you think that?"

"You've still never called me. Every time we've seen each other it's because I've seen you somewhere or come by your house."

"Yes, I have. I called you when you ran off to answer the fire alarm."

Toni merely raised an eyebrow.

Noel's smile showed just a hint of guilt. "It's been a long time since I've been single. I think I've forgotten some of the rules."

"There aren't that many rules. All you have to do is show that you're interested. Are you?" She wiggled both of her eyebrows now, making Noel laugh.

Noel leaned back in her chair and carefully assessed Toni, letting her eyes slowly scan her face. "If it's just a matter of physical attraction, there's no doubt. Yes, yes, and more yes." She giggled, her blue eyes nearly closing with the effort.

"I don't have a record, and I don't mind if you run a credit check on me, so physical attraction should do it."

"Yeah, it should." Her forehead was wrinkled in thought. "I'm just very tentative about what I want."

"In terms of women? Or is that just a general tentativity? Nice word, huh?"

"Very nice." Noel sipped thoughtfully at her wine, then put the glass down and looked into Toni's eyes. "No, I'm not usually very tentative. But, as I said, it's been a long time since I've been out on a date."

Toni's eyes were sparkling in the glow of the table candle . "I bet women ask you out," she said, nodding with conviction. "I bet you never had to ask anyone out."

There was just enough of the fading sunlight to be able to see the pink glow that infused Noel's cheeks. "I think…I might have…"

"Just as I thought," Toni said triumphantly. "You've got beautiful-woman disease. You've never learned how to ask anyone out because you've never had to. Sad," she said, shaking her head mournfully.

"I wish I had beautiful-woman disease. I think I'm just lazy."

Toni grew animated, sitting up alertly in her chair. "No, no, I'm onto something. And you're definitely beautiful. You're the talk of the town, you know."

"I am not," she said, laughing nervously.

"You are too. A bunch of women were at Jackie's the other night trying to decide who you look like. The winner was Heidi Klum."

"Heidi Klum!" Noel's mouth dropped open. "Heidi Klum's third grade teacher, maybe."

"No, no, I had to agree, even though you don't have Heidi's dark eyes. Your hair looks a lot like hers, and your face has some of her structure." She reached out with a fingertip and gently brushed it under Noel's cheek bones. "Right around there in particular. You have the same apple cheeks that she has."

"There must not be much going on this summer if I'm the talk of the town."

"There's plenty going on. And I told everyone else that I called dibs, so you might not get any more proposals until I tell them that you shot me down."

Noel reached out and interlaced her fingers through Toni's. "What makes you think I'd shoot you down?"

"I'm not sure. But you've got to admit you haven't been falling all over yourself to get in touch with me."

Starting to trace along the tendons on the back of Toni's hand with her thumb, Noel said reflectively, "I'm very attracted to you. I guess I'm trying to decide if I'm ready to start dating. My breakup was pretty bad."

"You haven't told me much. Do you want to? I'm interested."

Neither Noel's posture nor her expression matched her words when she said, "I don't mind talking about it. It's a pretty common story. We were together for ten years. I thought things were fine; she acted like things were fine, too. But she started traveling more and more with a young woman named Heather. At first it was Heather this and Heather that. They were on the same team, so it made sense they were together a lot."

"Can I interrupt? I don't think you ever told me her name, or what she did for a living. Did she play professional basketball or something?"

Noel gave her quizzical look, then shook her head, chuckling. "No, she's in marketing. She travels a lot—all over the world, as a matter of fact. She worked with this older man for many years, but about a year and a half ago she got promoted into his job and a woman took her old job."

"Heather."

"The very one. I should've started worrying when she stopped talking about her, but Janet, that's her name by the way, didn't let on that a thing was wrong. Actually, I thought things were better than they had been for quite a while. That's why I was a little surprised when she told me that she couldn't go on faking it." Noel was obviously trying to keep her tone light, and she was partially successful in looking like she was merely annoyed. But there was a deep sadness that suffused her eyes, and the most obtuse person would have seen it.

Toni didn't say anything at first; she looked down at the table and let her hands slowly chafe Noel's. When she finally looked up, she looked as though she might cry. "Whenever I feel myself getting jealous of my friends who are in relationships, I remind myself of stories like this. I don't think I'll ever understand how you can love somebody and be committed to them and then just... what? Get tired? Bored? How does that happen?"

"I don't know. I certainly wasn't tired of her. It doesn't help that Heather is almost twenty years younger than I am."

"Twenty years! Is she even legal?"

"Yeah," Noel laughed softly. "I think she's twenty-five or twenty-six. She started to work with Janet right after she got her MBA from Wharton."

"Oh, great," Toni said sarcastically. "So she's new and young and smart. That's a kick in the teeth." She took a drink of her wine. "We have a lot of nerve for making fun of men with their trophy wives. I've heard more than enough stories like this in the last few years. It's just sickening. People act like the only thing that's worthwhile is tight skin."

"That woman I saw you with the other night was a long way

from getting Social Security," Noel said, trying to keep any rancor from her comment.

Even though Noel didn't know her very well, it was clear she had offended Toni. "There's nothing wrong with dating a younger woman," she said hotly. "I'm not involved with anyone."

Grasping the hand that Toni tried to pull away, Noel said, "I was only teasing. There is nothing wrong with dating a younger woman."

"There is something wrong with cheating on someone you're committed to. That's inexcusable. Cowardly." There was a vehemence to her words that made Noel think she spoke from experience.

"I didn't accuse you of that. Honestly."

Toni swiped her hair behind her ear and took a breath. "Sorry."

"It's okay. I want to be perfectly honest with you—I'm afraid of dating someone who doesn't do relationships."

"I can understand that," Toni said, her anger having evaporated quickly. "If you're looking for what you had with Janet, you've been smart to avoid me."

Noel grasped her by both of her wrists and shook them. "Come on," she pleaded, smiling. "I haven't been avoiding you. I just haven't been chasing you." When she saw the look in Toni's eyes, she added, "I think somebody's used to being chased."

"We've already established that. It's you." She grinned slyly. "But no matter who chases whom, I know myself well enough to know I'm not relationship material."

"What is it that makes you not want to be in a relationship?"

"Don't most relationships wind up the way you and Janet did?"

"I don't think so. I know a lot of couples who've been together for a long time and are very happy together."

"I know some," Toni admitted. "And that's not the only reason, of course. I need a lot of freedom. I like to spend time with my dad, working on cars; I like to hang out with my fireman friends; and I don't like to have to account for my time. It seems like the people I know in relationships always have to do that."

"I think that's true, but that's just being polite, isn't it? Janet was usually gone ten days a month, and I never complained. Of course, she would tell me that she was going to Japan," she said, smiling. "I didn't just wake up to an empty house."

"Very funny." Toni's warm fingers tapped Noel on the cheek. "You've already told me I'm polite, so I think I could handle that part. It just seems like people want more than that. They seem to want to control the other person, and I can't tolerate that."

"I'm certainly not telling you how to live your life, but I think you might find that you could be in a relationship and still have your freedom. You just have to find someone who's looking for the same kind of relationship you want."

"What I really want," Toni said, her voice dropping into a seductive purr, "is someone to have fun with this summer. No strings attached. Any interest?"

"Yeah, there's a lot of interest. There's a lot that I miss that has nothing to do with being in a relationship." She gave Toni the same type of sly, sexy grin that Toni had just used on her.

Noting that their glasses were nearly empty, Toni filled them then rested her chin on a fist and looked at Noel expectantly. "Tell me what you miss."

"Oh, so much. Where do I start?"

Toni reached across the table and grasped one of Noel's hands. She placed it atop one of her own, and used the other to stroke it, following the contours of its anatomy.

"That's one thing," Noel said, gazing at Toni's hands. "I love to be touched. Friends, family, a masseuse…they all touch you in different ways, but there's something about a lover's touch that can't be replicated. It doesn't even have to be sexual," she said, looking into Toni's dark eyes which were now trained on her. "It's a different kind of intimacy."

"Don't you love getting to know someone sexually?" Toni asked, now looking back down at Noel's hand as she lavished it with affection.

"Of course I do. There wouldn't be any divorce if that wasn't such a powerful draw."

"I suppose that's true," Toni said, glancing up to gauge Noel's expression.

"Of course it is. There are lots of benefits to being in a relationship, but you don't get that excitement that you get from a new lover. Even though I was happy with Janet, there were times I wanted that jolt."

"You could have it now," Toni teased.

Noel gave her a look that probably worked very well on her third grade class. "I'm still working on my list. Don't rush me."

Playfully, Toni held a finger up in front of her lips, showing Noel that she would be quiet.

"I miss feeling that someone finds me attractive," Noel said reflectively. "Having Janet dump me has messed with my mind a little bit. It made me feel...used up...oldish." Her eyes were focused on the label on their wine bottle, and they were suffused with sadness.

"That's just crazy. You're ridiculously pretty. Janet's new girlfriend might be younger than you are, but that's not why she left." Noel stared at her, stunned. "I know I've never met her, but I'm sure about this." She took Noel's hand and leaned over to be able to maintain eye contact. "She wanted a change or she just clicked with this new woman. Things like that happen. But that's her stuff. It doesn't have anything to do with your desirability. Please try not to think that way."

"It's hard not to," Noel said, chewing on her lip.

"I get that. I do. But you're very, very attractive. Don't let Janet's betrayal change how you feel about yourself. Don't let her do that to you."

Her little speech was so impassioned that Noel spent a few moments trying to get her mind around Toni's words. "I know you're right," she said. "I think…I hope this is temporary."

"I hope so, too. Because I'm being very serious when I tell you that you truly have been the talk of the town. You're the cutest woman to move here since…probably me," she said, grinning brightly.

"Oh, I'm nowhere near as cute as you are."

"I know that," Toni scoffed. "But you're a distant second."

Noel relaxed in her chair and gazed at Toni, her smile growing warmer by the minute.

⌒

They were nearly finished with their wine when the weather turned. The humidity began to dissipate as a breeze off the ocean grew stronger. It was dark now, and Toni gazed up, watching heavy cumulus clouds obscure the moon as they flew past. "Looks like we're gonna get the rain they've been predicting."

"If it gets rid of this stickiness, I'm all for it." Noel grasped her shirt by the placket and pulled it away from her body. "But the heat did convince me to go into the ocean for the first time this season."

Looking shocked, Toni said, "The first time? It's June!"

"I suppose you're one of those people who goes in with an ice ax?"

"No, I'm not that much of a diehard. I actually don't spend that much time at the beach any more. But I do go running most mornings. I like to take off my shoes and run barefoot in the sand."

"I've been walking along the beach as soon as I've cleaned up after breakfast every day. I'm going to miss it when I have to go back to Baltimore."

"You can always stay here."

"No, I couldn't. I like it here, but I love my job. I wouldn't think of leaving before I had my twenty years in, anyway."

"When's that?"

"Hard to believe, but it's only three years away. I don't have any intention of leaving, but I could leave then and still get my pension."

"Must be nice. I'll probably be on the boardwalk begging for quarters to fund my golden years."

"You'll get Social Security," Noel said, then added tentatively, "Won't you?"

"Sure. But that doesn't provide for a very opulent lifestyle. Not that I have one now," she added, chuckling. "I love what I do, but you don't see a lot of sixty-year-old roofers. I'll probably have to get into estimating or go to work for a construction firm before I get too beat up to be of any use."

"You look like you're a long way away from being useless."

"You haven't seen my scars."

Noel took a quick look up at the sky when she felt a fat raindrop land on her arm. "No, I haven't. But I could take a look if we want to go wait out the storm together."

"Oh, boy!" Toni said, her face filled with excitement. "I love a good summer storm."

⌒

They went to Toni's place since it was a little closer. They started out walking, progressed to a jog, and sprinted the last hundred yards. Nonetheless, they were both soaked by the time Toni got her key into the lock and threw the door open.

They were hit with the heat that had built up in the place, and, with the front door still open, Toni dashed to open four windows and the back door. "Do you mind if I leave the lights off? I don't want to add any more heat."

"I wouldn't mind at all," Noel said, closing the distance between them and putting her hands on Toni's hips. "You're very sexy when you run," she said, smiling at her in the shadowy dimness.

"Thanks. I practice in front of the mirror." She tilted her head and placed a brief kiss on Noel's lips. "Would you like a towel?"

"Sure. A comb wouldn't hurt either."

Toni came back a few moments later and extended a wide toothed comb to Noel. She took it and ran it through her hair, commenting, "I must look like a wet Afghan."

"You're a little pale for an Afghan." Toni laughed at her own joke, then said, "Oh, you mean the dog."

Noel just rolled her eyes, then took the towel and blotted her face and arms dry. When she handed it back, Toni did the same, roughly running the towel through her hair also. She threw her head back and her hair seemed to fall into place of its own accord.

Noel walked over to the front door and leaned against the jamb while she watched the rain come down. "This is an adorable place. Have you been here long?"

"I think it's been seven or eight years. It looks like an apartment, but I own it."

"Interesting. I thought it was a carriage house for the place in front."

"I think it was their garage," Toni said, laughing. "But the couple who owns the house converted this into living space and sold it. They must've known somebody on the city council, because I can't imagine how they got the zoning through. I love it, though. It's just my size."

Noel walked from the front door to the back, pausing to take in all of the elements of the long room: a sofa and a comfortable looking chair, a dining table, and a nice L-shaped kitchen. The ceilings were high, and even though they'd only been there a few minutes, the room was now cool and comfortable. With Toni watching her, she continued to poke around, finding a small bedroom and a good-sized bath. Even though the building was old, all of the fixtures were new and modern.

To Noel's surprise, the bedroom walls were decorated with hanging quilts, a style she never would have assigned to Toni. "I can't see them very well, but these quilts look nice hanging up. Are they heirlooms?"

"No. I made them myself." She pointed to one over her bed. "I just finished that one this year."

"Huh." She looked at Toni critically. "I wouldn't have pegged you as a quilter."

"One of the guys at the firehouse taught me how. After you polish the engine, there's not a heck of a lot to do. You'll have to come by the station and see the ones we've done. We have a cool one with flames shooting all over it." She laughed. "Not what you think of when you think of a quilting bee."

"You're just a litany of surprises. I never quite know what you're going to do next."

Toni stood very close to her and grinned expectantly. "I bet you could guess right now."

Noel squinted and acted as though she were thinking hard. "I bet you're going to show me a magic trick."

"Absolutely right! Now close your eyes…"

As soon as Noel did, Toni slid her arms around her and pressed their lips gently together. Opening her mouth slightly, Noel purred with delight when Toni's tongue slid in. Noel wrapped her arms around Toni's shoulders and pulled her close, maintaining the kiss for a long time. Toni eventually pulled away, but then peppered another dozen kisses all over Noel's face. "There's nothing better than kissing the fresh rain off a beautiful woman's face."

"Yes, there is," Noel said breathlessly. "Being kissed is much, much better."

Toni playfully rubbed their noses together. "Kissing is better," she insisted.

"Show me again. Maybe I'll change my mind."

Toni twirled her and pressed her up against the warm plaster wall. This time she kissed her forcefully, letting Noel feel the strength in her body and hands. Toni flexed her knees and pressed against Noel as she stood up, grinding against her sensually.

When she finally pulled away, Noel looked stunned and was clearly at a loss for words. She tried to speak, but nothing coherent came out. Finally, she laughed at herself, opened her arms and pulled Toni back in for more. She was waiting for what she hoped would be a quick strip and a long visit to Toni's bed, but was surprised and a little disappointed when Toni led her over to the sofa. Toni sat down first, then pulled Noel onto her lap, mitigating Noel's disappointment.

Toni placed her hands on either side of Noel's face and looked into her eyes. "Are you sure you're ready?"

"Well, I could stand a few more minutes of kissing…"

Laughing, Toni said, "You know what I mean. I want to make sure we're both on the same page."

"I'm on the I-want-to-have-sex-with-a-beautiful-sexy-woman page. What page are you on?"

"I'm on that page, too. But I'm not on the let's-see-if-we-like-each-other-enough-to-get-married page. I don't want to lead you on. I want to make sure you don't get hurt."

Noel sat up as well as she could and looked into Toni's eyes. "Please don't take this the wrong way, but if I were looking for another spouse, I wouldn't start with you. I've learned the hard way that you have to take people as they are."

"I'd like to take you as you are," Toni said, her voice low and sexy. "Right here. Right now."

"Let's go," Noel said, holding on for a fiery kiss. "You drive."

⌒

Noel felt her orientation change, finding herself lying on her back, looking up at a smile that was almost feral. Toni paused above her, energy radiating from her lithe body. "You're so delicious looking," she said, licking her lips hungrily.

Stroking Toni's face, Noel said, "Then come down here and taste me."

"I like you." Toni settled her weight, distributing it as evenly as possible. Their faces were just inches apart, and Toni held her position, spending a few moments studying Noel. "I really do. You like to have fun."

"I do." Straining, Noel could just reach Toni's lips, and she managed a quick kiss. "Does that surprise you?"

"Yeah. A little. You're kinda quiet—reserved."

"Not when you get to know me. I'm wild," she said, giggling. "Wanna see?" She puckered up, closing her eyes tightly.

Toni sucked her lips into her mouth, making Noel snort and pull away. "Ick!" She wiped her mouth on Toni's shirt. "You slobbered on me!"

Unrepentant, Toni kissed her gently, then a little more aggressively, then a lot more aggressively. By the time she came up for air, Noel looked like she'd been hit between the eyes. "You change gears fast!"

"You can have boring sex with anyone. See me for fun and variety." She licked along the side of Noel's face, laughing when

Noel once again wiped her face and shivered with disgust.

"Were you raised by dogs? Stop licking me!"

"Okay. But you're gonna have to beg me if you change your mind."

"Do something productive with that pretty mouth. Be nice," she soothed, stroking Toni's back. "Nice girl."

"Sometimes I get silly when I have sex. Can't help it. Sex makes me happy."

"I think it makes me happy, too. But it's been so long…" She rolled her eyes, finally looking at Toni and laughing. "You're making me silly now."

"Maybe we're a little drunk."

"I'm happy, not drunk. Having a sexy woman lie on top of me makes me happy. Of course, I'd be happier if she was making me wet…other than my face," she hurried when she saw Toni start to interrupt.

"Oh. Well, I guess I'll have to change my tactics." She shifted around and settled in between Noel's legs. "Nice."

Noel slipped her arms around Toni's back and pulled her into a long, leisurely kiss. When Toni lifted her head, she didn't say a word. Her eyes were still shining, but now they shone with hunger. She slid her hands into Noel's hair, fanning it out against the cushion. Her arm reached out as far as it could, and she turned on a small lamp. "I have to see you," she whispered. She went right back to her serious study of Noel's mouth, pausing every few minutes to look at her golden hair splayed out. She didn't comment again, but it was clear she was taken by the long, shiny strands.

Noel was just as mesmerized by Toni's body, particularly her lean, muscular back. As they kissed, she made a mess of Toni's once neatly ironed shirt. Eventually she managed to tug it from her shorts. Now she was able to let her hands wander all along the swells and valleys of her shoulders. It didn't take long to unhook her bra, but Noel didn't reach for her breasts. She was content to let Toni kiss her into a state of bliss while she slid her hands up and down her body.

"Do you want to?" Toni asked, breaking Noel's rapt concentration.

"Want to what?"

"Go to bed." She smiled and placed a tender kiss on Noel's forehead. "I asked you three times. I thought you'd gone deaf."

"I could stay right here all night," Noel said dreamily. "You're a very, very good kisser."

"I can do a few other things. Wanna see?"

Noel returned her smile. "I guess I could be convinced." Toni pushed herself up, almost falling when Noel tickled her exposed waist.

"Come on, you little tease." She got to her feet and helped Noel up. As they walked, Toni shed her bra by shaking her shoulders and reaching into her shirt. "Did I do this?" she asked, holding it up.

"I did." Noel leaned against her like she was tipsy. "I had to feel your back without any encumbrances."

"After you." Toni let Noel pass and enter the bedroom. She turned on a ceiling fan, opened two windows, and the air started to move freely. Noel lay on the bed and watched Toni unselfconsciously undress. She stared right at Noel, slowly unbuttoned her shirt and dropped it to the floor. Her breasts stood high on her chest, nipples erect. With her eyes still locked onto Noel, she casually undid the button on her shorts, then lowered the zipper.

Noel's eyes widened and she sat up when Toni let the shorts pool around her feet. "Where are your panties?"

Showing her teeth, Toni said, "Too hot out. I had to allow for a breeze."

"Come here, you naughty girl." Noel held her hands out and twitched her fingers. "Come on."

Toni leapt for the bed, making the metal frame shriek when she hit it with her full weight. "Here I am," she said, smiling happily.

"And you're naked. That's just how I like my women."

"Wanna look at my scars now?"

"Later. Much later." Noel started to unbutton her own shirt, but Toni flipped her hands away and took over.

"Let me," she said, her voice growing husky.

Noel lay back and smiled, watching Toni's eyes focus as she worked at freeing the buttons. When the shirt was open she tugged it off and draped it over a chair next to the bed. Toni reached behind Noel to find the clasp of her bra, pausing when she realized it didn't have one.

"Want me to do it? I have to kinda wriggle out of it."

"No, I can do it." Toni grasped the band and drew it over her head, smiling when Noel held her arms up like a kid. "Do you run?"

"Huh? Oh, you mean because of the sports bra?"

"Yeah," she said distractedly.

Toni sat back on her heels and gazed at Noel's breasts, now free of their constricting covering. The expression on her face showed that she'd found a place that captured her interest. Her eyes roamed over Noel's breasts, focusing so intently that Noel wasn't sure if Toni wanted an answer to her question. Nonetheless, she soldiered on. "Sometimes I run. I go to the gym on my way home from school most days. If I wear a sports bra I don't have to change before I work out."

"Mmm." Toni's distracted response showed she hadn't heard a word. She focused on getting Noel's shorts and panties off, and the second she did she put her hands on Noel's shoulders and pressed her into the bed, then filled her mouth with one soft, firm breast.

"Mmm," Noel hummed, pushing herself into Toni's mouth. "That's nice. I love having my breasts played with."

"Mmm-hmm." Utterly focused, Toni devoured Noel's breasts, moving from one to the other as Noel continued to hum her pleasure. Toni, obviously not satisfied to merely play with what were clearly the objects of her arousal, started to nip and bite at Noel, making her squeal.

Noel wrapped her arms around Toni, trying to roll her onto her back to gain a little more control. But Toni was not to be moved. Her body felt as solid as a rock, and she barely budged despite Noel's tugging. In fact, she grew more focused, pulling an entire breast into her mouth and sucking forcefully.

Opening her legs, Noel wrapped them around Toni's thighs and pulled her against her body. Her soft murmurs became growls of pain mixed with exquisite pleasure, and with each gasp Toni redoubled her efforts until they were thrashing around on the bed, tangled in the soft quilt and sheets.

Noel grasped Toni by the shoulders and begged hotly, "Fuck me. Come on. Fuck me now."

Toni pulled away momentarily and collapsed onto her back. "Oh, I'll fuck you," she panted. "I'll fuck you right." She rolled onto her side and tossed her hair, sending it flying back into place. She kissed Noel hard, then pulled back and watched her face as she slid fingers into her. "Ooo, you're so hot and wet."

"Yessssss. That's the way. Just like that."

Nuzzled against Noel's neck, Toni whispered, "I'll lick you if you beg."

"Oh, no, you're not getting away from me now." She held on to Toni's arm with both of her own. "Keep going just like that."

Toni slid an arm behind Noel's neck and held her firmly, pistoning her fingers in and out with a slow, steady pressure. Noel guided her wordlessly, thrusting her hips when she needed to quicken the pace. After a few minutes she parted her own lips with her fingers and slid them through the wetness, letting them lightly skitter across her clit until she pressed down onto Toni's hand and quietly moaned through a long climax, her flesh milking Toni's fingers for long minutes.

"Nice." Toni's soft voice purred into her ear. "Hot, too. I'm about to do myself."

Her motor skills were a little vague, but Noel managed to pat Toni soothingly. "Give me a few seconds and I'll get right on that."

"Give me your hand," Toni said. She knelt astride Noel and took her hand, placing the fingers against her vulva. "Just rub me a little. I'm ready." She leaned over and put her breast into Noel's waiting mouth, then moved her hips, forcing Noel's fingers to hit her just right. "Yeah," she said after a few moments. "That's good. Perfect."

Noel's mouth was so busy that she couldn't speak. She tried to figure out a way to penetrate Toni, but couldn't quite manage it. She needn't have worried. Toni knew just what she wanted, and she ground herself onto Noel's fingers, roughly panting, her eyes tightly closed.

Noel sucked firmly, guessing that Toni would like her breasts treated the same way she had treated Noel's. That firm, forceful sucking sent Toni over the edge, and she groaned and twitched away from Noel's fingers, falling onto the bed next to her. "Sweet," she said, her voice soft and weary. "You know your way around a clit."

Noel rolled onto her side and propped herself up on one arm. Her blue eyes were shining with desire. "I need to touch you some more. I didn't get enough."

"That's the best idea I've ever heard." Toni threw her hands over her head, leaving herself fully exposed. "Don't rush. Take your time," she said, chuckling. "No need to hurry. I don't have another thing planned."

⌒

"What's this one from?" Noel asked, running her finger down a mark on Toni's back.

"Which one?" Toni was lying on her stomach and tried to turn her head to see her lower back, but was completely unsuccessful. "I have a scar there?"

"Yeah. It looks more like a bad scrape. Maybe it's new?"

"No, I don't think so." Toni crossed her arms and rested her head upon them. "It's probably from my younger days." She was quiet while Noel continued to investigate her body. "Oh, I remember now. That's from surfing. I got carried over too close to some rocks and took a pounding. The lifeguards came out to get me and everything. It was quite dramatic."

Noel traced the outline of the scrape. "When was this?"

"Long time ago." Toni yawned and stretched. "I don't surf anymore. Don't have time to work on my technique and I refuse to look like I don't know what I'm doing."

Noel lay down beside her and saw that Toni's eyes were rimmed with red. "Tired?"

"Yeah. I got up early today." She met Noel's eyes and added, smiling, "And a gorgeous woman just screwed my brains out."

"Just returning the favor." She looked at the clock and saw that it was eleven p.m. Struck with a strange feeling of unease, Noel said, "I guess I should get going." She waited for what she hoped would be the usual invitation to spend the night.

Toni turned onto her side and lay there quietly. After a long pause she said, "When do you get up?"

"Six, if I've made the batter for muffins or pancakes the night before. Five-thirty, if I haven't. I guess tomorrow's gonna be a five-thirty day."

"That seems awfully soon. I hope it was worth it."

There was just a flash across her face that made Noel wonder if Toni wanted to be reassured. But it appeared so quickly and disappeared just as rapidly that it made her think she imagined it. She wanted to touch Toni, to share the easy familiarity they'd just spent the last few hours enjoying. But the mere fact that they'd begun talking about their everyday lives seemed to have broken some sort of spell. She tried to make her smile appear warm and friendly. "I had a fantastic time."

Toni moved to swing her legs off the bed, but Noel touched her shoulder and said, "Stay. I can find my way out."

"Tempting," she said with a slow, tired grin.

"I mean it." She bent over and kissed her on the cheek, feeling strange to limit herself to such a chaste show of affection. She took her clothes into the bath, wincing when she caught sight of herself in the mirror and saw that she was a little rough looking after their exuberant evening. Finding the comb she'd used earlier, she pulled her hair into a ponytail and splashed water on her face, managing to look a bit more like herself.

Toni hadn't moved, and Noel saw that she was sound asleep. Quietly, she closed and locked the back door, then locked the windows in the living room. She found Toni's keys, locked the front door from the outside and dropped them back into the house through the mail slot.

It was still raining, but she didn't mind. She protected her book as best she could and took solace in the fact that the rain would make everyone look like they'd been ridden hard and put away wet. The march of shame was never pretty.

⌒

The next morning, Toni sat in her truck, having parked it over a block away from The Sandpiper. She had a notebook propped up against the wheel and was trying, unsuccessfully, to compose a note. Every few seconds she looked down the street to see if there was any activity. Noel finally emerged at about ten o'clock and Toni hurriedly wrote the following:

Do you ever feel a little uncomfortable seeing someone you've just had sex with? That's funny, because I never have. Ha!

Seriously, I just wanted you to pass on a message to Janet from me. She is a complete and utter fool! Any woman who would let you get away should be committed. I'm glad I don't live in Baltimore, because people like her shouldn't be free to roam the streets.

Toni

She took the bouquet of Gerbera daisies she'd bought and folded the note up so she could fit it into the tiny envelope the florist gave her. Then she got out of her truck and walked down the street, knowing that The Sandpiper would be open and she could leave her gift in the kitchen.

Part Five

Noel was walking to the beach when her cell phone rang. Her heart beat increased and she realized she was hoping it was Toni on the phone. With only the slightest bit of disappointment she answered her sister's call. "Hi, what's up?"

"The boys are at an overnight camp and we thought we'd come spend the night. Do you have room?"

"How did you get Ed to take a day off?"

"He begrudgingly agreed to take the afternoon off if we can crash at your place."

"All of my guest rooms are filled, but I have plenty of room for you in my apartment. I have a nice sofa where I wind up falling asleep half the time anyway. When can you be here?"

"Oh, Ed won't want to do that. You know how he is about putting anybody out." She paused for just a second and said, "I think I'll come by myself. Then he can have what he truly wants, a night alone."

⌒

While Noel walked, she ruminated over the previous evening's activities. It had been a long time since she'd had casual sex, and she found the whole experience still resonating with titillating excitement. She'd been in three medium- and long-term relationships: one for three years, one for six, and the ten years she'd spent with Janet.

Those relationships had consumed her entire adult life. But she'd come out as a lesbian when she was a freshman in college, and she'd taken her mother's advice and hadn't gotten tied down while she was in school. So she had more than a passing acquaintance with casual sex.

It was odd, at this point in her life, to consider dating again. She'd honestly thought she'd be with Janet until death parted them, and there were still many days that she wished death had parted them…Janet's death. But being with Toni was making her consider the freedom that being single could provide.

There was something nice about having a period when she could consider only her own needs. She worked hard during the school year, and there had been many nights she didn't wanted to listen to what was going on in Janet's world. There were also times when she wasn't at her best, but didn't want to discuss it. That was difficult when you were in an intimate relationship, and having the freedom to keep your thoughts private was oddly compelling.

In fact, Noel was beginning to wonder if she and Janet truly had the depth of feeling for each other that they claimed. They never shared the same interests, so most nights found them either in different rooms in their house, or with one of them playing on the computer while the other watched television. That worked out well, but given how much Janet traveled, they spent an awful lot of time apart.

So, even though she missed being loved, she had begun to question whether Janet ever loved her, or if people were even capable of loving one another. Maybe Toni had the right idea. Have a lot of good friends, and have sex when you found someone you click with. Weren't things a lot cleaner that way?

⌐

By the time Noel finished lunch with her friend Gloria, then ran a few errands, April was calling her from The Sandpiper. "Where are you? Shouldn't the innkeeper be here at all times?"

"I'm just about two blocks away. Hold your horses." She hung up and walked a little faster, looking forward to seeing her sister.

April helped her carry the supplies into the inn, commenting, "You should go to one of the big box stores to buy all of this stuff."

Noel put the bags of toilet paper, tissues, and various cleaning supplies on the kitchen counter then saw the flowers, artistically arranged in a water glass. "What's this?" she asked, grinning happily. She took the card from among the stems and read the note, blushing girlishly as she did.

"Let me see," April said snatching the note right from her hands.

Noel grabbed for it, but April turned and fended her off while she read it aloud. "You little slut!" She giggled maniacally. "I thought she wasn't even your type."

Finally yanking the note from April's hands, Noel adopted a stern look. "She's doing work around my house. Just a little gift to thank me for the business."

"She says you had sex last night!"

"No she doesn't. She asked me if I ever felt embarrassed after I had sex with someone. She's obviously doing some sort of research project."

April put her arm around her little sister and hugged her. "I'm so excited! I bet she's phenomenal in bed. Is she?"

"She's not bad. Not bad at all," Noel said, looking very pleased.

"Come on! I need more details."

"Oh, all right." Noel gave her sister an aggrieved look that they both knew was put on. "It was…fantastic." She grasped her shirt and pulled it away from her body a few times, fanning herself. "It was a little funny having sex with someone new, but she was so hot that I got over my nervousness incredibly quickly."

"Mom and I both think you should stay single for at least a year. Live it up a little! There might be a dozen women around here who are just as cute as Toni."

Scoffing, Noel said, "I doubt that. And you and mom just want to live vicariously through me. But I didn't see either of you volunteering to have your hearts broken."

"We just want to have the fun parts of being single," April admitted. "Plus, we were both sick of Janet. Toni's right, Janet wasn't nearly good enough for you."

"That's nice of you to say. I tend to agree. Of course, I don't currently think Janet's good enough for a rabid dog…with mange. And fleas and…"

⌐

Noel and April spent the afternoon going through some of Max's personal effects, something Noel had been consciously putting off for weeks. By the time they showered, went out to dinner, walked around for a bit and had ice cream, it was time for bed. Noel was in the kitchen, making batter for the next day's pancakes when she looked at her watch and realized it was too late to call Toni to thank her. She had meant to leave herself a note to call, but she thought that the flowers would be a handy reminder. She bent over to sniff them, even though she'd done so several times that day and knew they had no aroma. Still, there was something very attractive about the bouquet, and even without a scent, they brightened the whole kitchen. She just wished she'd let Toni know that.

⌒

Toni finished her club soda and checked her watch, seeing that it was almost time to go to the firehouse. Her friend Roxy was sitting next to her at Jackie's and Toni said, "Have you ever sent a woman flowers?"

"Sure. Usually when I've done something I'm in trouble for. Why?"

"I don't do it very often, but I did it this morning. Is she supposed to call me and say thanks or something?" She looked adorably confused, and Roxy had to stop herself from laughing at her befuddlement.

"She should definitely thank you. Are you sure she got 'em?"

"Yeah. I delivered them myself."

"Who is this woman who deserves a hand delivery?"

Toni shrugged, then got up and paid for her and Roxy's drink. "Nobody you know."

"Is she why you're not interested in other women?"

Her eyes were bright with interest, but Toni wasn't in the mood to discuss the issue. She leaned over and kissed Roxy, saying, "I gotta get going. See you." She waved at Jackie as she left, her posture not as erect and confident as it usually was.

"Who's she mooning over?" Roxy asked Jackie. "It's been a long time since I saw her let a woman get under her skin."

"Got me," Jackie said, even though she had a pretty good idea who Toni had been tracking for weeks now.

⌒

The next morning, April and Noel worked as a team, serving breakfast to seventeen hungry guests. April spent most of the morning in the parlor, with Noel cooking and listening to NPR in the kitchen. It was a beautiful day, so most of the guests left the inn by eleven. April washed and Noel put away the dishes, and they were finished by noon.

"I think you should reconsider and not sell," April said. "I can't think of a better way for you to retire. You could run a place like this until you were ninety, and even though it won't make you rich, it would give you a darned nice place to stay. You've got to admit it's nicer than Baltimore."

"I don't admit that. I like it here, but my family and friends are in Baltimore, and I wouldn't want to be that far away."

"This place is paid off, Noel. It's a cash cow!"

"It's a ninety-year-old cow that's falling apart. Just to fix it up to get to a place where I can sell it is going to take every dime that I get from Janet for my half of the house…if that scum-sucking slut ever does sell it. To modernize would take me another five years of just breaking even. Believe me, Andy's done the math."

"Andy told us that he thinks it would be a great investment for you."

"The big tattletale! Yes, he said that, but I can make other investments with the money I get from selling, and then I'm not forced to be an innkeeper."

"What don't you like about it? I loved meeting all of your guests today. It's a real nice mix you had."

"I wouldn't mind meeting them, either, as long as it wasn't here. I don't like being in their house. I know it's my house they're in, but it doesn't feel like that. I tiptoe around here like I'm vandalizing the place."

April snapped a dish towel at her sister. "Just because you're mental is no reason to give up on this."

"If you want to keep it in the family, I'll happily sell it to you. I'd even carry the mortgage."

"No," April said thoughtfully. "Ed wouldn't like doing this. He's more like you are. Crotchety." She dashed into the parlor before Noel could return the towel snapping.

"Get back in here!" Noel whispered harshly, giggling the whole time.

"You don't have to whisper. There's no one here. And even if there was, you don't have to whisper." April sat down on the sofa. "I grilled a few people this morning, and I got some info for you."

Looking a little hesitant, Noel sat down. "Hmm," she said, fidgeting around on the chair she'd chosen. "This is more comfortable than the chair I have in my apartment."

"That's one of the things I learned. People like it when you're out here talking with them. They miss that. Max was apparently out here all day."

"That's just not me," Noel said. "I'm not that kind of person."

"Well, the good news is that the people I talked to are still happy to be here. They say you're a better cook, and the things you make are lighter and a little healthier. Max made bacon and eggs and hash browns, and you had to be up by nine or she'd go upstairs and roust you."

"No!"

April laughed. "They said she ran the place like a rooming house."

"But they really liked her."

"Yep. But they only tolerated her style because they liked her so much. They also say the place is a lot cleaner, and they love the wine and cheese. So, you're doing a good job, little sister. But you could be doing a great job if you'd hang out more."

"I think they'll have to settle for sleeping in and eating when they want. This tiger can't change her stripes."

⌐

95

April wanted to meet Gloria, so they walked over to the bookstore, which was, because of the beautiful weather, almost empty. Noel did the introductions, then let April grill her new friend.

"What do you think of The Sandpiper?" April asked. "Don't you think it would be a great investment for Noel to have for her retirement?"

"It worked that way for Max. Most people she knew went right into another full time job after their military service, but she felt like she was on vacation all of the time. She loved being an innkeeper," she said, fondly.

"It sounds like she had a lot of friends," April said.

"She sure did. You could get on her bad side, but very few people did."

"What do you think of her friend, Toni?" April asked, making Noel wince at her sister's obvious subterfuge.

"What do I think of her? In what way?"

"Oh, I don't know." April looked around the store, and Noel could tell she was trying to think of a reason that she needed to know anything at all about Toni. "We were going through some of Max's things, and we wanted to make sure that they went to her dearest friends."

"There's no doubt that Toni and Max were close. Max watched over her like a mother hen."

"Did she need watching after?"

Gloria laughed. "Nobody but Max thought so, but that didn't stop her. She was always trying to get Toni to settle down with a nice girl."

"Really?" Noel wanted to grab her sister by the back of her shirt and drag her out of the bookstore, but she knew that once April got going that was difficult. "But Toni didn't want that?"

"She's been in a few relationships, but she claims to prefer being single."

"Was she in relationships with women from around here?"

Gloria's puzzled look shifted from April to Noel and back again. "Yes, they were from here. Why do you want to know?"

Noel couldn't stand it anymore. She had to intercede. Putting her arm around April, she smiled and said, "My sister sounds a little like Max. She's always trying to scope out the field and decide who I should partner with."

Gloria started to laugh, shaking her head. "Toni's not one to waste your time on. Others have, and they've been burned."

Noel tried to mimic Gloria's laughter, but it was hard going. She had no intention of trying to pin Toni down, but the thought that her friend had broken a couple of hearts disquieted her.

⌒

April was having such a nice day that she didn't want to leave. She talked Noel into having an early dinner, and they were sitting outdoors in the balmy evening when Noel saw Toni sauntering down the street. She was a full block away when Noel caught sight of her, coolly checking out the crowd at each restaurant she passed.

Tonight Toni wore faded red walking shorts, a short-sleeved white oxford-cloth shirt, and navy blue deck shoes. Her hair blew around in the breeze, settling right back into place when the wind stopped. She caught sight of Noel and her smile was immediate, but a little guarded.

"Hi, there," she said when she reached them. "It's good to see you again, April."

"Come join us," April said. "We just ordered."

Toni didn't answer immediately. She waited for a beat or two, then her eyes shifted nervously for a second. "I'm sure you two have a lot to catch up on. But it was good to see you again." She put her hand on April's shoulder and patted it. "Have fun." Then she was gone, walking much quicker than she had been.

Noel watched her leave, wondering what was going on with her. She wanted to thank her for the flowers, but Toni had seemed in a very big hurry. She glumly reasoned that she probably had a woman waiting for her and couldn't waste a moment.

⌒

After April left, Noel walked down to Jackie's, pleased and a little surprised to see Toni in the back, playing pool. Noel ordered a drink and chatted with Jackie, who was, in keeping with her profession, expert at making small talk.

Toni eventually walked over to the bar and sat down next to Noel. "Hi," she said, still looking a little uncomfortable.

"Can I buy you a drink?"

"You can buy me some sparkling water. I already had my beer for the day."

Noel put in the order and, when Jackie turned away, she leaned over and said, "I loved the flowers. I would have called you yesterday, but April showed up unexpectedly and the day got away from me."

"Oh, that's okay. No problem." In seconds, Toni seemed substantially more relaxed. Her smile was easy and full as Noel had come to know it. "What did you two do? Go anywhere?"

"No, but we did go through some of Max's things. If you would, could you come up with a list of her friends in town? There isn't much that has any monetary value, but I'm sure a lot of it would mean something to you...and her other friends."

"Thanks," Toni said. She looked genuinely touched. "That's very nice of you."

"I know how important you were to her, so I want to make sure you have anything of hers that you want." Her drink was finished, and she was a little tired, so she stood up and took her keys and wallet off the bar. "Come by some time and take a look around." She wanted to kiss Toni, at least on the cheek, but she felt odd doing so. She didn't know if Toni liked to keep her private life private, and for all she knew, Toni had designs on the woman she was playing pool with. So, she just smiled, said goodnight to all, and left.

Furtively, Jackie had watched the entire interaction, and now she smiled knowingly, watching Toni stare at the closed door for a long time, a puzzled look on her handsome face.

⌒

A few days later, Heidi called Noel with a business proposition. "I've found someone who's very interested in The Sandpiper. He can be in town this afternoon if that works for you."

With no action whatsoever, Noel had almost forgotten she'd put the place up for sale. But now that she was reminded in such a surprising fashion, her palms felt sweaty, and her inclination was to say she didn't want Heidi to show it. But she knew that was irrational, so she agreed.

She helped the cleaning crew get the rooms in shape, and they were ready by the time Noel and her client, Rod Strahorn, a hedge fund manager from Manhattan, arrived. He seemed like a nice enough fellow, but when he started to walk through the house, Noel immediately got her back up.

"Heidi tells me that I can be frank with you," he said. "She says you're not attached to the property like most owners are."

"That's probably true," she cautiously agreed, not liking the tone he used.

"I'm looking for a sturdy frame that I can gut and turn into a nice summer house for my family. I'd rather go to the Hamptons, but there's a lot of bad feeling there towards Wall Street." His smile was vaguely feral, and Noel found it quite unattractive. He looked at the corners and the doorways, ignoring the rooms themselves. "This place might need a little shoring up, but it's got the benefit of being a complete dump." He grinned at Noel, and she decided that grin probably got him most of what he wanted with women. But she was immune to his charm, and felt more than a little offended. She didn't comment, however, mostly out of deference to Heidi.

"That's a little harsh," Heidi said, narrowing her eyes. "Noel's fully booked for the summer. The Sandpiper is a nice, mid-level B&B."

"What's the low level?" Rod joked, but only he laughed. "I'm sorry, but you've gotta admit this place hasn't been updated since World War II."

Noel privately thought it had been longer than that, but Rod looked like he was in his midthirties, and probably didn't know when World War II had occurred. "That must not matter to you if you want to gut the place," she said, trying to be nice.

"Oh, yeah. It doesn't matter a bit. I'm looking for space. I want to put in five bedrooms and a big master suite. A real party house." He grinned again. "I can just see myself out in the back with one of those huge gas grills. I've heard they make one that you can put a whole side of beef on."

That sounded rather disgusting to Noel, but, once again, she didn't comment. Rod and Heidi kept going through the house, but Noel dropped out of the tour. After he'd taken pictures with his stunningly expensive camera, he and Heidi found Noel in the kitchen, making up some cheese platters for cocktail hour.

"I'm interested," he said without preamble. "If we can strike a deal, I'd like a thirty-day close."

"Thirty days?" Noel was sure she was gawping, but she couldn't help herself. She turned to Heidi. "I've got reservations for the rest of the summer."

"They can be cancelled," Heidi said, but she didn't look happy about it.

"My guests have planned and paid for their vacations. You should have seen the letters I got when I told them I wouldn't be open. Some of them threatened to sue!"

He laughed, completely unfazed. "There's no constitutional right to vacation plans. If you sell the place, all bets are off. That's not an issue."

"It is for the people who've made plane reservations."

"Well, yeah, but that's not your problem. A lot of my clients lost their life savings when the market crashed, but I didn't have to pay them back out of my money. Shit happens." He looked a little puzzled, but didn't dwell on the issue. "Good to meet you," he said, shaking her hand. "I'll be in touch."

Noel couldn't even make herself reply. She just watched them leave, thinking that Rod might be the most irritating person she'd met in years.

Several hours later, Heidi called to ask if she could stop by. Noel was in her apartment, and Heidi came to the door and knocked. When Noel answered, she said, "You're the first person to come to my door."

"You haven't had anyone over?" Heidi looked both surprised and puzzled.

"No, you're the first. What's going on with Mr. Charm?"

"He's something, isn't he?" she said, making a face. "New money can buy anything but tact."

"Not everything," Noel said, reserving judgment.

"He's offering a good price." Heidi pulled out a purchase offer form and laid it on the desk Noel had set up. She looked at the number and whistled.

"That's a very good price." Immediately, she wondered if Toni could match it if she carried a second mortgage. "But I'm very hesitant to sell right now. The people who made reservations would be screwed if I didn't honor them."

"True." Heidi didn't elaborate, and Noel couldn't tell where she stood on the issue.

"I need some time to read this over and think about it."

"Well, you don't have much of that. He made the offer contingent on a response by nine tonight."

Stunned, Noel stared at her. "Can he do that?"

"He can do anything he wants. You don't have to accept, but he can propose that you have to run through town naked while singing."

Noel was scanning the offer. She absently shook her head, saying, "He'd regret that. I don't sing all that well."

⌒

Noel reached Heidi on her cell phone at eight that night. "Hi," she said, feeling like she had to shout. "Can you hear me?"

"Yeah. I'm having dinner at a restaurant that didn't seem that noisy until now. Let me go outside." Noel waited several minutes, listening to the random sounds of a live phone being transported. "Okay. That's better."

"I'm sorry to interrupt your dinner. You can call me back."

"Why not come over to Jackie's and let me buy you a drink. Then we can chat in person."

"Are you sure?"

"Yeah, I'm sure. I was just going to pay the bill. I can meet you in about fifteen minutes. Is that good?"

"That's perfect. I'd like to talk a little bit."

"See you there."

Noel hung up and allocated five of her fifteen minutes fixing her hair and putting on just enough makeup to look like she wasn't wearing any. Before she left, she spritzed a little perfume on, just in case a certain firefighter was in attendance. She didn't know if Toni would want to be with her again, but, just in case, she wanted to look presentable.

⌣

Noel had to wait a few minutes, and she spent her time chatting with Jackie, who seemed to be at the bar every minute that it was open. Heidi blew in, looking a little harried. "Sorry I'm late. I was having dinner with a potential client, and she nearly talked my ear off."

"Oh, I'm sorry I made you rush."

"Rush? We met at five o'clock! I think we would have closed the place if you hadn't rescued me. Thank you." She took Noel's hand and kissed it.

"Glad to help. Any time you want out of something, I'm glad to interrupt."

"I might take you up on that. Now, what do you think of the offer?"

"I think it's very good," Noel said, her lack of enthusiasm showing clearly. "But I'm not ready to...give up." She scratched her head, her expression confused. "I don't know why I used that phrase, but that's what it feels like. I'm...I guess I'm beginning to get invested...both in the inn and my guests. I don't feel right ruining all of those vacations." She put her chin on her hand, after resting her elbow on the bar. "Dumb, huh?"

Heidi leaned over and kissed her cheek. "I was hoping you'd start to like being an inn-keeper."

"Really? I feel bad for turning down a good offer. I know that's gonna hurt your bottom line."

"Buy me dinner some night. I haven't spent much time on this deal. But let's take it off the market until you've decided whether to improve it or run it, okay?"

Noel looked like she'd been pinched. "Oh, no! I'm not going to run it. But I might sell it at the end of the season. I've got to do some research and scope out the competition. I haven't been treating this as an investment, but I'm going to start."

"I think that's a good idea. And if I get a vote, you'll keep it."

"You get dinner," Noel said, "No vote."

Part Six

*N*oel lay in bed that night, ruminating about her decision. She knew she'd made a financial mistake, had known that so clearly that she hadn't even called her brother Andy to ask his advice.

She was still clear she wasn't interested in running The Sandpiper full time. And she just wasn't comfortable with the glad-handing she had to do to enjoy having guests. So, she had to admit that the simple truth was that she wasn't willing to leave town when she had a chance at having a torrid summer affair. It had been many years since she'd put attraction and sex above a well-thought-out financial plan, but she kind of liked this devil-may-care attitude. April always told her that she acted more like the older sister, and she had to concede that was true. But maybe it wasn't too late to start to be more impetuous. And she had a feeling Toni could help in that regard. She just had to hope that Toni felt the same way.

⌐

Noel spent the next mid-day creating and repeatedly revising comment cards that her guests could use to give her feedback. She knew that it would actually be more effective to talk to them, but she figured the comment cards would appeal to the guests who, like her, preferred to write a comment over saying something that might be deemed critical.

By the time she was finished, it was early afternoon, and she was famished. On a lark, she called Gloria, knowing it was her day off. Luckily, her friend didn't have anything important going on, and they decided to meet for coffee. Noel had designs on the raspberry scone that the coffee shop made, and she hoped they hadn't run out.

When Gloria arrived, they took their snacks outside and sat at a table facing the sidewalk. Noel surprised herself by saying, "I'd like to talk about Max."

⌒

An hour and a half went by in what felt like moments. Once she'd started, Noel found that her questions were legion, and she learned everything Gloria knew about Max's family and her early life. Gloria seemed very happy to be able to talk about her friend, and at one point, Noel asked, "Why did you like Max so much?"

"Hmm, that's a tough one. She had a lot of good qualities." She looked contemplative, then said, "I think I liked her moral code."

"That surprises me. Everyone talks about how friendly and welcoming she was. I thought you would have liked her for her personality."

"Oh, she had a good one. But I knew that Max could be trusted with a secret, a husband or a life's savings. If I'd found her taking my money out of the bank, I would have believed her if she said she was doing it because she heard the bank was gonna fail."

Noel laughed, seeing how sincere, yet playful Gloria was being. "You must miss her."

"I truly do. But seeing people go in and out of her home, enjoying themselves, makes me feel like she's still here. And getting to know you has been a true blessing. She would have been so proud of you." She wiped at a tear, shaking her head. "I'm such a crybaby. Ever since Max died I cry at the drop of a hat."

"You're grieving her. Can you think of anything worse than having no one cry when you die?" She shivered, feeling a little distressed. "I hope that doesn't happen to me."

"I don't think there's any chance of that. I don't know you well, but I can tell you've got a good heart. That's what draws and keeps friends. Maybe you got that from Max."

"Maybe," Noel allowed, "But my mom has a good heart, too." She realized she was still being defensive and added, "Maybe I got a double dose from both of my mothers."

⌒

That night, Noel had just set out the wine and cheese when she heard a brief knock on the back door. By the time she was halfway across the small kitchen, Toni was walking in. "You don't mind, do you?" She looked indecisive as she pointed at the door, indicating her entry.

"What? Do I mind you coming in? Of course not. I'm glad to see you."

Toni stood just inside the doorway, giving the impression that she was ready to run back out if necessary. "Really?"

"Of course. Would you like some wine? Or…are you in a hurry? You're not…" Feeling tongue tied, she tried once again. "Can you hang out for a while?"

Appearing a little more at ease, Toni nodded. "I don't have anything planned. But if you do…" She put her hands into the pockets of her khaki shorts and rocked back and forth nervously. "I don't want to get in the way if you're making dinner or something."

"Oh, I've never had dinner here. I go out for my meals."

Toni took the glass of wine that Noel handed her and leaned against the counter. "You really don't like to cook, eh?"

"Oh, no, I love to cook. I'm just afraid to have the whole house smell like my dinner. It seems kind of rude to me."

"You're not serious. What do you like to cook? Oily fish? Lots of curry?"

"No," Noel said, laughing. "Nothing too exotic. But people are right there," she said quietly, pointing at the parlor which adjoined the kitchen.

Toni imitated her volume, but it was evident she was doing so in a teasing fashion. "I know they are, but you've gotta eat. You must be sick of all the restaurants."

Noel moaned. "You have no idea. I've been eating a lot of junk. I hate to go to nice restaurants by myself, and the casual ones give you fries or chips, which I can't ignore."

"You certainly haven't put on any weight."

She looked oddly embarrassed. "No, I never do. But I feel sluggish when I don't eat the way I normally do."

"What do you normally eat?"

"Oh, pretty simple stuff. Since it's been hot out, I'd normally have a salad and some chicken or fish. Maybe a steak."

"Are you finished here?"

"Yeah, pretty much. I have everyone checked in, so the only thing I have to do is keep the wine and cheese stocked until seven."

Toni poked her head around the corner and saw the sideboard, which had a bottle of white and a bottle of red resting on it. "How much wine do you usually go through?"

"Three or four bottles of white, and usually only one of red. What's with all the questions?"

"I'm going to make you dinner, but I'm starving and I want to get going." She grinned, making Noel's heart race when she saw

Toni's cocky self back in full force.

Noel opened the refrigerator, took out three bottles of white wine, went into the parlor and lined them up. Then she filled an ice bucket and put one of the bottles in it. She walked back into the kitchen, slapped her hands together, and said, "All done. Let's go."

A half hour later they were in Toni's backyard, lighting the charcoal in her grill. "When you said you sometimes have a steak, I just had to have one. And there's nothing like having it on the grill."

"I miss my grill." At Toni's raised eyebrow, she said, "Janet bought…is buying me out of the house, and she got custody of the grill."

"They're not very expensive," Toni said, teasingly.

"No, but buying a house by myself is. I'm living in an apartment and I don't think my landlord would like it if I started barbecuing indoors."

"You wouldn't like it either. Carbon monoxide is not your friend. I learned that in firefighter school," she said, smiling cockily.

"Maybe one day I'll have a yard again."

"You're always welcome here." The look Toni gave her was surprisingly sincere, absent of any hint of a tease. "Let's go inside, and I'll make you my favorite summer salad. I bet you'll like it."

Noel watched Toni bustle around putting out plates, napkins, silverware and some candles on her outdoor table. "My father would never allow us to have dinner outside. He always said he didn't put food on the table for the flies."

"Flies? What are these creatures? Things that live in the city?"

"You know, come to think of it…I haven't seen many flies around here."

"We get them, but not that often. We've usually got such a good breeze that I think they head for calmer air. I'll be back in a flash with the salads."

Noel sat down and waited for Toni, who appeared seconds later bearing large plates full of a colorful mix of greens and fruit. "This looks fantastic!"

"I could eat this every day." Toni sat down and put her napkin on her lap and they both took bites. "Mmm-mmm."

"Oh, wow, lots of good things in here."

"Orange slices, pomegranate seeds, pine nuts, a little red onion, goat cheese, and a citrus vinaigrette."

"You're quite the cook."

"I like to cook, but I don't do it for myself all that often. If I'm alone, I usually go out."

"I got on this self-love kick earlier this year." Noel laughed at herself. "I set the table, lit candles, made myself a difficult and delicious meal, and listened to music while I ate. I thought it would make me feel like I was worth going to a lot of trouble for, but it just made me feel like a loser who was all alone."

Noel caught sight of Toni's hand start to reach out, then stop abruptly and rest on the table. Her face was full of empathy when she said, "That must've been so hard for you. I hope you're feeling better now."

"I am. I really am. I wasn't very happy about having to come down here, as you well know, but it's working out well. It's like a much-needed vacation."

"I knew you'd like it," Toni beamed.

"Did Heidi tell you that someone made me an offer?"

Toni couldn't have faked her reaction. Her eyes grew wide, her mouth dropped open, and she turned pale in milliseconds.

"I rejected it," Noel said, hurriedly. "I'm still not sure why I turned him down, because the money was excellent. But he wanted to gut the place, and he wanted to start right away."

Carefully, Toni took another bite of her salad, looking like she was avoiding eye contact for a few moments. Finally, she said, "Maybe you're just not ready to leave."

"That's what I decided," Noel said. She waited until Toni looked at her and added, "I haven't had a long enough vacation."

⌒

After dinner, Toni cleared the dishes but they stayed outside, polishing off a bottle of wine. Toni was clearly charmed to hear about Noel's conversation with Gloria, and she spent a few minutes praising Gloria and all of the kindnesses she'd shown Max.

With regret, Noel took a look at her watch, and said, "I guess I'd better go."

They hadn't touched each other all night, and when Noel stood up Toni did too. They both made a move to kiss goodnight, but it didn't go smoothly—with both of them wincing and rubbing their noses. "I didn't see..."

"Yeah. That wasn't very smooth."

"Maybe we'd better try again," Toni said. She made a move towards Noel, who this time stood still. Their lips met for just a second, then Toni started to pull away. But Noel still had her eyes closed, her lips slightly puckered, just waiting for more.

Obviously unable to resist, Toni went back in for another kiss and found herself smiling through it when Noel's hands went to her shoulders and pulled her close. That set off a chain reaction that had them kissing each other with astonishing passion. It was as if they had days' worth of unquenched desire they were at last able to dispel.

When Toni felt Noel's hands slide under her shirt and unhook her bra, she pulled away briefly. Her eyes were slightly unfocused and she blinked slowly. "We should go inside."

"I thought you'd never ask."

Dutifully, Toni picked up their glasses and the wine bottle and led the way inside. She started to lead Noel to the sofa, but Noel grinned at her and tugged her towards the bedroom, saying, "Unnecessary stop."

"I love a girl who knows what she wants."

Noel punctuated her sentence with kisses. "I. Want. You."

Toni's smile was nearly beatific, and while they stood next to the bed, she started to undress Noel kissing her the whole time. Once she had her blouse off, she stopped to admire what was likely a brand-new bra. This one was designed to make Noel's modest breasts appear immodest, and from Toni's reaction it was very successful. She left the bra on, while she finished undressing Noel. Then she ripped her own clothes off in seconds and they tumbled onto the bed.

Toni seemed unable to get enough kisses to satisfy her. She reluctantly left Noel's mouth and started to move down her body, kissing her breasts through the lacy bra. "I love this," she said, sliding her fingers across the fabric, feeling Noel's hardening nipples.

"Thanks. I decided that I have to start dressing sexier if I want to feel sexier. I'm saving my sports bras for the gym."

Toni pushed herself up to an elbow and gazed at Noel curiously. "Is that really an issue?"

"Yeah, it is. I told you that Janet's leaving kinda messed with my mind." She grinned. "I meant to tell you that I loved the note you left me. That was the nicest thing anyone's said to me in a long time."

"I meant it," Toni said. "Every word." She braced herself

over Noel's body and gazed directly into her eyes. "You're a very beautiful woman, and hot, hot, hot to boot. She's an idiot." She acted as though she were spitting, making a face as she did. "You're smart, and pretty, and kind. The only way her new girlfriend could be better is if she was all that and really, really rich." She tilted her head, as if the thought had just occurred to her. "Hey, wait a minute. You own The Sandpiper outright. You're rich, too! Joke's on her!"

Noel put her arms around Toni's neck and pulled her down until they were nose to nose. "I wouldn't have blamed Janet if she'd left me for someone irresistible. Someone like you," she said, grinning seductively.

Toni closed the distance between their lips, measuring Noel's receptivity. Even though they'd only had sex once, Toni had learned a good deal about Noel. One thing she'd noted immediately was how exquisitely sensitive her breasts were. There were few things Toni enjoyed more than a woman's breasts, but the experience of kissing and suckling them was increased exponentially when her partner enjoyed the sensation as much as she did. And Noel clearly enjoyed having her breasts played with in any way Toni chose. Having a sex partner who was open to just about anything was a huge plus, and so far, Noel had hung right in there and taken everything Toni had to offer. Looking at her slim body made her mouth start to water, and she spent a moment reconsidering her long-held belief that generous curves were what most attracted her to a woman. Maybe the woman behind the curves was more important than she'd thought. There was only one way to find out.

⌒

It was late when they both fell onto their backs, breathing heavily. Toni's voice was so thick it poured from her lips like syrup.

"Fantastic. Absolutely fantastic."

"I've got to get some water. Do you want anything?"

"More energy. I want to do you again and again and…"

Noel scratched her belly, feeling the heat that rose off her damp skin. "You have done me again and again and again. Really well."

"You're absolutely killing me," Toni said, looking strangely puzzled. "I don't know what you do, or how you do it, but I could honestly go at it all night. It's just this old body that keeps betraying me." She teasingly tried to lift an arm, shaking her head when it refused to move.

"You're adorable," Noel said, kissing her sweetly. "Be right back." On the way to the kitchen, Noel stopped in the bathroom, found Toni's toothpaste and put some on her finger to give herself a hygienist-unapproved brushing. She washed her face and fluffed her hair up, not looking bad for having rolled around in bed for over an hour.

She poured herself a big glass of ice water and stood at the kitchen sink drinking most of it. Then she filled the glass again and went back into the bedroom. She was just about to make a comment when she saw that, once again, Toni was sound asleep. Torn, she debated her options. Now that she knew she wasn't just a one night stand, she felt more confident about getting back into bed. But the thought of getting up and walking across town before dawn wasn't very appealing. And she had no idea of Toni's sleep habits. She might be the kind of woman who needed to have the whole bed to herself, and if that was true, Noel didn't want to learn that by being kicked in her sleep.

So, she started to get dressed, hoping that Toni would wake up and ask her to stay. But that didn't happen. She repeated her escape plan from their previous coupling, and listened with a pang of unquenched longing as the keys dropped onto the wooden floor.

When Noel got home she could tell she was going to have a

hard time relaxing enough to sleep. Lovemaking—or rather, sex, she reminded herself, careful with the nomenclature—tended to energize her. She was reading a book that she wasn't particularly interested in, so she picked it up and headed for bed, hoping it would bore her into sleep. On the way, she looked between two heavy books to see how the Gerbera daisy was doing. She didn't usually save keepsakes and mementos, but she had decided to make an exception for Toni's gift, and now a pink blossom was carefully being pressed.

⌒

The next morning, Noel was replenishing a tray with fresh muffins when she heard the back door open. She turned and smiled when she saw that it was Toni. Her hand went to her mouth and she started to giggle when Toni held up Noel's recently purchased bra by the straps and made it dance. "You sure were in a hurry to get out of my house."

Noel went over and snatched it from her and stuffed it into the pocket of her shorts. "I wasn't in a hurry. I was bored. There was nobody to talk to."

"Don't blame me. You're the one who knocked me out."

Noel let herself take in Toni's summer work attire. She wore a chocolate brown tank top tucked into cream-colored painter's pants that she had turned into shorts. White socks just managed to peek out from the tops of her ankle high brown work boots. "That's a nice look you've got going on there. Where are you off to today?"

"I'm helping Roxy with a paint job."

"I hope it's indoors. You'll get burned with your shoulders exposed like that."

"It's not only indoors, it's on the second floor of a place right down the street. No air-conditioning," she added, wrinkling her nose. "As soon as I'm done, I think I'll go run into the ocean."

"Call me if you're gonna strip on the way. I love a good show."

Noel heard someone clear her throat and she turned around to find one of the guests standing in the doorway. "Are there any more muffins?" she asked timidly.

"Coming right up." She saw Toni start to back out of the door. "Stay cool," she said.

"Do my best." Toni smiled warmly, making Noel's heart melt a little. "Have a good day. And try not to leave anything important at anyone's house. Next time someone might have a very nice keepsake of a very nice night."

Noel spent the rest of the morning thinking about Toni. She crossed her mind frequently on any given day, but today, knowing that she was right down the street, made it worse than normal. The day was warm, and by two o'clock The Sandpiper was starting to get a little stuffy, so she made a pitcher of lemonade and set it out on the sideboard for her guests. That gave her an idea, and she called Toni on her cell.

"Hi, it's Noel. I'm not disturbing you, am I?"

"No, not at all. What's up?"

"I just made some lemonade for my guests, and I thought I might bring you guys some. It's hot here, and I'm not doing anything strenuous."

Toni laughed. "We're not doing anything as strenuous as we should be. Roxy's getting paid by the job, but she's paying me by the hour. She's getting screwed."

"Would you like some lemonade?"

"Of course. I love lemonade. We're just six houses to the south, on your side of the street."

"Cool. Then I can meet Roxy."

"See you soon. Oh, you don't have any muffins left, do you? I've been thinking about them all day."

"It just so happens that I have a few. I'll bring them."

"Later."

Noel made another pitcher, found some plastic glasses, and wrapped up the muffins for Toni. She walked down the street and found the house, an easy task since there was a sign in the front yard that said "Roxy Montana, Whole House Painting."

The house was an inn much like hers, and she knocked before she entered, even though most people walked right into places like theirs. A man about her age met her in the hallway. "Hi, can I help you?"

She extended her hand and when they shook she said, "I'm Noel Carpenter. I just took over The Sandpiper up the street. I brought some lemonade for my friends who are upstairs painting."

"Go on up. They're probably about to faint. I should've thought to give them something. I'm Tom, by the way."

"It's good to meet you." She went upstairs and encountered Roxy first. "Hi," she said. "We haven't met yet. I'm Noel Carpenter. I brought you some lemonade."

Roxy looked very surprised to see her, making Noel guess that Toni hadn't mentioned her call. "Well…hi. How'd you…know I was here?"

"I ran into Toni earlier, and she told me you two were painting here. It's so hot out that I thought you might need something cold."

Roxy got off her ladder and shook Noel's hand. "I've heard a lot about you. I'm surprised we haven't met yet."

Noel wasn't a student of the species, but from just a few moments in her presence she could tell that Roxy was a player. She was a pretty woman, with straw-colored hair, pale blue eyes and tanned skin. She looked a few years older than Noel, but Noel reasoned that might be because of the damage the sun had done to her fair skin. "We must just not run in the same circles," Noel said.

Roxy accepted a glass of lemonade and took a big drink. Her eyes were glittering with interest when she said, "Then I should change my circle."

Toni walked into the room and said, "What's this? A snack delivery?" As usual, she was her playful self. She didn't let on that she knew Noel was coming, she didn't even let on that she knew her well.

"When I saw you earlier today, and you said you were going to be right down the street, I thought it would be a good time to come by and meet Roxy. I never got to thank her for doing such a good job on my house."

"I can't take all the credit," Roxy said. "I made Toni do all the trim."

"Isn't that the hard part?"

"Toni thinks so," Roxy said, laughing. "But I believe in making my day laborers do the hard things."

"Day laborer," Toni scoffed. "You make it sound like you picked me up in front of a paint store."

Roxy gave her a sly grin. "As I recall, I picked you up in a bar."

"I don't think Noel wants to hear our sordid history. Let's leave it at the fact that we both came to our senses."

"You two seem like you get along pretty well for having a history," Noel said. "I'd like to see my ex again…under the wheels of my car." She laughed, looking unrepentant.

"I've got a few of those kinds of exes," Roxy said. "But Toni's not one of them. I never make enemies with anybody who can paint."

"I'd better let you to get back to it," Noel said.

"I'll drop the pitcher off on my way home," Toni said.

"I can do it," Roxy said. "I go in that direction when I leave."

Toni didn't say a word, so Noel said, "Whatever works. Try to stay cool."

"We will. It was good to meet you," Roxy called out.

As soon as Noel was out of hearing range, Roxy said, "Where has she been hiding? I thought people were bullshitting when they were talking about her looking like Heidi Klum. She doesn't actually look much like her, but she's damned cute."

"Yeah, she is." Toni poured another glass of lemonade and drank it slowly.

"She's single, right?"

"Yeah. She's still recovering from a bad breakup."

"Just because you haven't hooked her yet doesn't mean she's not ready."

"I didn't say she's not ready. I said she had a bad breakup."

"Hmm." Roxy looked at her friend for a minute, assessing her. "You tried to get into her pants and she slammed the door."

"I wouldn't admit that if it'd happened, which it didn't."

"There's something there," Roxy insisted, grasping Toni by the shoulders and holding her so they were nose to nose. "You're hiding something."

"Nope."

"I think you tried and found out she doesn't like you. That's why she was nosing around here, looking for me."

"Don't count on it," Toni scoffed, taking the muffins and walking back to her assigned room.

⌒

Noel was mildly surprised and supremely disappointed to have Roxy knock on her back door a little after five p.m. She walked in and put the pitcher on the counter. "It was sweet of you to bring us lemonade. The guy who runs the place would've let us die of heat exhaustion."

Noel didn't have a polite way to ask why Toni wasn't standing in front of her, so she forced herself to be pleasant and make small talk. "I don't know any of the other innkeepers. What's that place like?"

Roxy hoisted herself up onto the counter, letting her feet dangle. "It's a pretty low-rent place. He gets mostly young guys. Kind of a gay frat house."

"I'm trying to decide if I should modernize The Sandpiper or try to sell it as it is. Do you have an opinion?"

"I have an opinion about everything," Roxy said, chuckling. "I don't know if it's worth it to do a lot. You're midmarket, and you'd have to spend hundreds of thousands to get into the upper tier. I don't think you'd get that back."

"It's hard to know what to do. Heidi tells me that she thinks I'd get my money back by redoing the bathrooms, but Toni doesn't seem to think I need to do anything."

"They both have their perspectives skewed a little. Heidi always thinks the market is going up and any money you put into a bathroom or kitchen is a good investment. Toni thinks this place is a shrine, and she'd like it to stay just like it was when Max ran it."

"That sounds about right," Noel said, smiling at the thought of The Sandpiper being visited by pilgrims. "It sounds like you lean more towards Toni's view."

"I haven't seen most of the bathrooms. Want me to take a look around?"

"This isn't a good time. I'm fully booked, and a lot of my guests are home right now. Maybe later in the season?" Roxy looked at home enough that Noel thought she might still be there in October to see the last guests out.

"Sure. Anytime. I've been in most of the places in town, and I know a lot of the innkeepers. Maybe we should get together and talk about the market. Are you busy tonight?"

Noel wasn't, but she didn't want to spend the evening with Roxy. She seemed like a pleasant woman, and she was cute, but she wasn't Noel's kind of cute. Noel's kind of cute was Toni, and she thought she'd rather spend the night alone than settle for less. "Tonight's not good for me. Take a rain check?"

Roxy slid off the counter. "Sure. I'm always around. We'll see each other again. Soon, I hope."

"Yeah, me too. Thanks for coming by."

"Thanks again for the lemonade. Take care." With that, she was gone, leaving Noel to ponder Toni's enigmatic behavior earlier in the day. She wasn't sure if Toni wanted to keep her life private, or if Toni just thought of her as another one of her many conquests— someone not special enough to mention to a friend. She sincerely hoped it wasn't the latter.

Part Seven

*A*week passed and Noel was tempted, very tempted to give in to her need to see Toni. But she was careful to remind herself that Toni had been clear from the start that they were having a summer fling. The one who had the fuller dance card always controlled the action, and Toni's card was obviously very full.

Since she wasn't having much luck waiting Toni out, Noel decided to keep her promise to treat Heidi to dinner. They agreed to meet the next night at one of the nicer places in town, even though Heidi tried to convince her to pick a less expensive place.

Noel walked into the dark, intimate bar area of the contemporary, surprisingly elegant place. Rehoboth was full of inexpensive spots that appealed to families, but was a little thin on upscale restaurants. Judging from the bar, Noel thought this was definitely one of the upscale ones.

She ordered a drink and turned when someone touched her back. Heidi smiled at her and Noel took a second to really look at her. They'd never intentionally been alone together, and the soft mood lighting brought out the highlights in Heidi's hair and made her green eyes glow attractively. "Hi. Would you like a drink?"

"Sure. Whatever you're having."

Noel ordered and Heidi sat next to her. "I hope you like

Manhattans."

"I do. Not too often, though, or I'd have to go to rehab. They pack a punch."

"I don't drink much at all when school's in session. But I've been acting like I'm on vacation all of the time down here."

Her drink was delivered and Heidi nodded her thanks. Her eyes nearly bugged out when she took a sip. "Wow," she said, making a face. "Will you walk me home?"

"Sure. I don't know where you live, but I can get your address off your driver's license."

"You have a nice sense of humor," Heidi said. "At first I thought you were pretty serious."

"I was. I was also freaked out by the whole ordeal of finding out who my birth mother was, et cetera. But I'm back on my feet now."

"I'm glad. You seem to be enjoying yourself more."

"Yeah, I am. This is a nice town, and I feel like I've been accepted pretty readily. It's been good."

"I love Rehoboth. I came here right after college"—she covered her mouth and mumbled a number—"years ago. They'll have to carry me out."

"I could definitely get used to it. After I sell The Sandpiper I might buy a little condo. I'd love to spend some time here every summer."

"No desire to be full time, huh?"

"No. I'm not an innkeeper. Plus, I love teaching. I also think Rehoboth might be too small for me full time." She took a sip of her drink. "Isn't it hard to meet new people?"

"People to date?"

"Yeah. It seems like everyone has been here forever."

"No, a bunch of new people come every year. A lot of people my age are retiring early and coming to the beach. That hasn't helped me," she said, rolling her eyes, "but Toni sure seems busy."

"I bet her friend Roxy keeps pace with her."

"Oh, yeah." She smiled. "Roxy's a hound. Has she hit on you yet?"

"Mmm, I don't like to get hit and tell."

Heidi laughed. "'Nuff said. She's a lot of fun, but she goes through town like the flu. No one is safe."

"I guess a resort town is good for people who like to date around. I think I'm more of a relationship kind of girl. At least, I always have been."

"Me too. I've been single for a while, and I'd like to make that a thing of the past. But in the meantime…"

"I'm not ready to jump back in yet, I don't think."

"You're just out of a long relationship, right?"

"Right. Ten years. My ex was killed." When Heidi's eyes widened Noel said, "Wishful thinking. She dumped me for a younger woman."

"Oh, that's bad. Very bad." Heidi took a drink. "I hope her teeth fall out. All at once."

Noel smiled. "Keep going. That's not punishment enough."

"No clues? Caught you flatfooted?"

"Clueless. She was very, very anxious about turning forty. Maybe she thought being with a young woman would rub off on her."

"Since when is forty old? For God's sake, we have a life expectancy of over eighty. That's a lot of years."

"It is. And I hope Janet's new girlfriend is as shallow as Janet turned out to be. Maybe she'll leave her at the first sign of a grey hair." She picked up her glass and Heidi touched hers to it, making a clinking sound.

"Here's to shallow women. May we never meet another."

The next day, April called. "When can I bring the kids down? They're driving me crazy begging to go to the beach."

"I told you that you're welcome any time. But I don't have any rooms available on weekends."

"Ed won't want to bunk with you, but the boys would love it. Are you sure you don't mind?"

"Mind? I'd love it. Haven't I asked you to come twenty times already?"

"Yeah, but you're polite. You'd do that anyway."

"I mean it. Come now. Come tomorrow."

April laughed. "How about Monday? The weather's supposed to be good."

"It's a deal. Bring Andy's kids if you want."

"No way! I want to have fun and I can't do that if I'm watching kids every minute. Mine are old enough to entertain themselves. Speaking of entertaining…how's Toni?"

"Good. I guess. I don't see her very often. I guess she's busy or just not that interested."

"Do you ever call her?"

"No, I don't feel comfortable doing that."

"Why?" April's voice was filled with concern.

"If I'm gonna be honest, I suppose I'm afraid of her turning me down."

"Really? That's not like you, honey."

"I know. I'm still a little gun-shy. This too shall pass."

"Take a risk. What have you got to lose? It's just a summer thing."

"True." Noel paused a minute. "Maybe I'll risk it. All she can say is no."

"Go for it, baby. You're irresistible."

⌐

Steeling her courage, Noel called Toni before she could talk herself out of it. Toni answered on the second ring, sounding bright and chipper. "Hi. What's going on? I haven't seen you in years."

"It hasn't been that long, but it has been a while. What have you been up to?"

"Not much. I've been working on a big job, and working in this heat drains me. I'm not as young as I used to be."

"No one is. Hey, I was wondering if you wanted to have dinner? I'd like to pay you back for having me over."

"Oh, cool. When do you want to do it?"

"Tonight?"

"Ooo." Toni sounded genuinely disappointed. "I've got plans tonight. Tomorrow, too. How about Monday?"

"No, that's not good. April and her boys are coming down for a few days so I'll be busy."

"I'd like to meet your nephews. Can I tag along if you go out?"

Charmed, Noel said, "Of course. We're gonna be in close quarters since I don't have a room available. We'll be out of the house as much as possible."

"How old are the kids?"

"Ten and twelve. Why?"

"Do they like to camp?"

"Yeah. April hates it, but the boys love it. Why?"

"Have them stay at my place. They can camp in my yard and come in and use the bathroom whenever they need it. It'll be fun!"

She sounded so enthusiastic that Noel was taken aback. "You'd honestly like that?"

"Yeah, yeah. My nieces and nephews do it all the time. It's an easy way to make kids very happy."

126

"I'll talk to April and see if she thinks they're old enough."

"They're plenty old. Sometime we should sleep outside," she said, her voice taking on the seductive purr that made the hair on Noel's neck stand up. "We could enjoy nature."

"I like you au naturel," Noel said, allowing her libido to show.

"I think I need to stop by soon. You sound like you're ready for fun."

"I hope that's always true," Noel said, chuckling evilly.

⌒

Later that evening, Noel walked down the street, going home after dinner. It was still early, just seven o'clock, and she saw Heidi standing in front of the restaurant that she had taken her to. She was about to cross the street to say hello when Toni appeared. She was dressed a little more formally than normal, wearing a dark blue blouse and khaki slacks. Noel watched as Toni approached Heidi, kissed her on the lips, and they started to walk into the restaurant. Heidi put her arm around Toni's waist, and anyone who saw the pair would have assumed they were a couple. Noel was one of those people, even though she knew they weren't a traditional couple. But she was certain, certain that they were sleeping together. There was a physical familiarity they showed that couldn't have meant anything else. Noel felt a sense of jealous outrage flash through her body, even though she knew she had no valid reason to feel that way.

Toni had been completely honest with her, and she had assured Toni that she wanted nothing more than casual sex. She reasoned that millions of years of evolution hadn't been able to eliminate the human instinct to control and own a sex partner. The odds were not good at having the process sped up so she was over it by the end of the evening, but there was no harm in hoping.

⌐

At nine o'clock, Noel heard a sharp ping on her window. She ignored the first sound, but there were several more. She got up and walked over to it and, when she pulled the curtains aside, saw a grinning Toni looking at her. "Are you throwing rocks at my window?"

"I had to," she said. "Rocks don't make any noise when you throw them against the screen."

"I do have a front door, you know."

"I know, but then I'd have to walk through the whole house and your guests might see me."

Noel folded her arms and leaned on the window sill. "And you're afraid for your reputation?"

"No. Yours. Mine's ruined."

"So you're protecting me and my guests?"

"I'm looking out for myself, too. This way, if you don't want to see me, you can just tell me to get lost and your guests won't see me crying."

Resting her chin on her hand, Noel gazed at Toni through the screen. "Likely. That's very likely. So, what can I do for you?"

It looked as though Toni were having a seizure. Her expression flipped between her usual cocky confidence and a look that Noel hadn't seen her exhibit often. If she had to guess, she would have said it was vulnerability. But that didn't make any sense. Maybe the darkness or the screen obscured her expression. "Uhm, after I talked to you this afternoon, you sounded like you might like to… you know…get together. I thought it was still early enough…" It wasn't the screen. Toni really did look touchingly vulnerable.

Dozens of feelings surged through Noel. Toni was either coming over after a quickie with Heidi or she hadn't gotten lucky.

Either way, Noel felt like sloppy seconds. But there was something so endearing, something so childlike and innocent about the look Toni was giving her that she had an overwhelming desire to kiss her.

"Do I have to pull you in through the window?"

A luminous smile bloomed on Toni's handsome face. "Get into something more comfortable and I'll sneak in the back door."

"I'm plenty comfortable right now," Noel called out, hearing Toni's satisfied chuckle.

⌒

Toni knocked lightly on the interior door and poked her head into Noel's apartment. "I just realized that this feels odd to me." She walked all the way in and looked around, her eyes scanning the whole place. "It looks very different, even though I can tell you didn't change all that much."

"I put a lot of things away. I like a pretty modern, uncluttered living space." She didn't add that it was disconcerting to be surrounded by mementos from every deep water port in the world. "Are you okay being here?"

Toni sat down on the sofa looking a little like a woman who was shopping at a furniture store. She bounced up and down a couple of times and said, "Yeah, I think so. I was never in Max's bed, so that might be a good place to start." She grinned her semi-lecherous smile.

Noel walked over to her and extended a hand. Toni took it, but instead of accepting assistance in rising, she pulled Noel onto her lap. "I like to have you here," she said nuzzling her mouth against Noel's neck

"I like to be here." They started to kiss, soft and gentle, more tender with each other than they had been before.

Previously, they'd treated each other like they were in heat, but this time it was a relaxed, destinationless journey. It took a while for them to progress, but as soon as Toni started to unbutton Noel's blouse, Noel returned the favor. Soon they were rubbing their bare breasts against each other, both giggling from the sensation. Noel needed to be naked, so she stood up and Toni happily helped her achieve that state. A few seconds later things started to heat up, and they wound up almost wrestling for dominance on the bed.

Noel worked out a lot, and was in good shape. But Toni could toss her around like a toy, and did so. In a matter of moments, Noel was on her back, Toni's head between her legs and Noel's heels sliding up and down the planes of Toni's strong back.

⌒

Much later Noel lay on her belly, legs hanging over the end of the bed. Toni sat on the floor between those dangling legs, her head pillowed on Noel's ass. Her last orgasm had knocked the air from her lungs, and it took a long time for Noel to collect herself enough to say, "Priceless. That was ridiculously good."

There was a beat, then Toni put her hands on the backs of Noel's thighs and groggily said, "Wow, I think I was asleep." She kissed the soft flesh right in front of her and got to her feet. Gallantly, she tumbled Noel onto her side, then swooped her legs onto the bed. "I could have easily passed out on the floor." She gently patted Noel's ass then grabbed her clothes and headed for the bathroom, saying, "I had a fantastic time. Call me when you want to get together again."

Wounded, Noel didn't comment. She couldn't figure out why Toni didn't want to sleep over, but she clearly didn't. It seemed like such a conundrum to her. When they were actually in bed, Toni was loving and affectionate. But once the sex was over, she didn't treat Noel any differently than she did any of her other friends. Noel didn't have to remind herself that might be because Toni was fucking all of her other friends.

⌐

They fell into a pattern of seeing each other two to three times a week. Toni usually dropped by The Sandpiper or she sought Noel out somewhere and suggested that Noel come to her house. They never made plans in advance, and they never went anywhere together. If they met at Jackie's, Toni would whisper an invitation and leave before Noel did, then she'd wait for her on the road to her house.

When they were together, Noel felt fantastic. Toni was complimentary and made her feel more beautiful and sexier than she had in years. Honestly, Noel felt better about her body and her lovemaking than she ever had. Janet could've learned a thing or thirty from Toni when it came to complimenting and encouraging a lover. And Noel tried her best to do the same for Toni. They got along amazingly well, and pleased each other thoroughly. But it was clear to Noel that Toni didn't want it to go any further on any level. She didn't even want to sleep together, so they never did.

⌐

One Wednesday night in late July, Noel was walking home from dinner when someone whistled and she saw Roxy waving at her. She stopped and Roxy said, "You're not going home this early, are you?"

"As a matter of fact, I was."

"Come have some fun." Roxy grasped Noel's hand with both of her own and started to tug her. "Come to Jackie's and let me buy you a drink."

It was early, and Noel had at least an hour before she should get to bed, so she accepted. They went into the bar together and saw Toni, whose head swiveled so quickly in their direction that it must have hurt. Her surprised look was quickly hidden, though, and she greeted both of them warmly.

"What's going on?" Toni asked.

Roxy flipped her hand, pointing at Noel with her thumb. "I saw our newest innkeeper going home this early. I twisted her arm to make her stay up."

Toni's frown evaporated, and she smiled at Noel, quickly looking her up and down. "You look too nice to go home. When you go to all that trouble you should stay out and enjoy all of the attention you must get."

Roxy nodded and Noel felt like she was being judged at the county fair. "She looks great, doesn't she?" Roxy asked.

"She always does," Toni said. "I think Noel and Heidi are the best looking women in town. Don't you, Jackie?"

"No question," Jackie said, grinning at Noel who was now blushing

"I haven't seen you around a lot, Toni," Roxy said. "How's the fishing?"

"You fish?" Noel asked.

"Roxy's being funny," Toni said. "She's referring to our summer visitors, and whether I've hooked any of them." Toni gave Roxy a half smile and said, "I've been working a lot. Not much time for fun."

"Since when do you rank anything higher than having fun?" Roxy shook her head. "I think you're holding out on us. What do you think, Noel?"

Noel gave Toni a long, assessing look. She nodded slowly, adding a sly smile. "I'm almost sure she's holding out on us. I think our friend likes to keep her secrets."

"That's always been true," Roxy said. "Toni never gives you any good dish. I have to catch her red-handed to know who she's going out with." Roxy turned on her barstool and looked at Noel long enough to make her slightly uncomfortable. "Let's give people in town something to talk about. The last time I asked, you said you'd take a rain check. How about dinner tomorrow night?"

Noel felt trapped. She was sure Toni was going out, or more likely, staying in with other people, so she knew she didn't have to be monogamous for her sake. But Roxy was a little too aggressive for her. Nonetheless, she had told her she'd take a rain check and she didn't want to be rude. She shrugged her shoulders and said, "Okay. What time would you like to meet?"

"Whenever you like. I usually quit work at around five and by six I'm presentable."

"Then let's make it six-thirty."

"Great. Let's go to The Seafarer."

Noel's eyebrows rose. "That's a little expensive for my blood."

"I asked you out. It's my treat."

Now Noel felt trapped. She was willing to go out and discuss real estate, but she didn't want Roxy to get the wrong idea. She also didn't want to make a big deal about this in front of the others. So she said, "I know it's early, but I should get home. I've got some things to take care of. Walk me out?" she said to Roxy. Roxy got up and Noel patted Toni on the shoulder. "See you," she said, earning a lackluster nod.

⌒

As Roxy and Noel walked out, Jackie took a look at Toni. If she hadn't known her better she would have worried that Toni was going to follow them out and pop Roxy a good one. But Toni wasn't that kind of person. She kept her anger and her disappointments to herself, something that Jackie thought often didn't serve her very well. Jackie poured a fresh beer and handed it to Toni. "The one you had was getting warm," she said when Toni looked up, startled.

"Oh, it's fine. I should probably go home."

"Are you feeling okay? You look a little down." She stood right in front of Toni and lowered her voice so no one else in the bar would hear. "How are you doin'? I know how hard it's been for you to lose Max. Do you have anyone to talk to? You know…anyone you can trust?"

"You can't replace people like Max," she said, wistfully. "I wish you could."

⌒

When Roxy and Noel got outside, Noel took a breath, and said, "I want to make sure we're on the same page. I'd love to talk, but I don't think it should be a date."

"Why not?" Roxy asked, bluntly.

"I just got out of a long relationship, and I'm not ready to get into another one."

"Neither am I," Roxy said, her eyes wide. "But that's no reason not to go out. We could have fun together."

Smiling at her honesty, Noel said, "I'm sure we could. But that's not what I'm looking for right now. I'd like to have more friends, though. So why don't we go someplace inexpensive and talk about real estate."

"Fine," Roxy said, looking down and kicking at the street like a disappointed child. "But don't tell Toni that you didn't bite. I've got a reputation."

Laughing, Noel said, "You certainly do. And I think it's well deserved."

Part Eight

*T*he first week of August was unseasonably hot and humid. That Friday night, Noel was at Toni's house, and their rambunctious activities didn't do anything to cool the temperature. Noel was lying on her back, trying to catch her breath while Toni lay beside her and drew patterns on her damp belly.

"I'm getting bored with Rehoboth," Toni said. "I need a change of scenery. Want to go someplace?"

Noel thought she was hearing things. Toni was actually asking her to go somewhere! "Sure. When and where?"

Toni appeared to consider her choices for mere seconds. "Atlantic City. Tomorrow. If you can get Barbara to watch The Sandpiper, we could stay overnight." She sat up, grinning with excitement. "Are you in?"

To satisfy that endearing, innocent smile Noel would've closed The Sandpiper down for the weekend. "I'm in."

"Excellent!" Toni jumped out of bed, seemingly full of energy. "I'm gonna take a cold shower and change the sheets so I can sleep. I want to be at my best."

Reluctantly, Noel got out of bed and stood there awkwardly for a minute. Then she put her clothes on and poked her head into the bathroom to say goodbye. "I'll let you know if I can find a babysitter."

"If you can't, we'll just come back tomorrow. But I'd rather stay over."

As Noel walked out of the house, she wondered why Toni would want to stay overnight in Atlantic City when she never wanted to in Delaware. Noel laughed ruefully, thinking that Toni might want separate rooms.

⌒

Even though she tried hard, Noel couldn't find a last-minute babysitter. Toni was a little disappointed, but she didn't let that ruin her excitement. "Don't worry about it. We'll be there in a little over two hours. We can hang out, gamble, have dinner, and be back in time for you to get enough rest to get up tomorrow morning. You're still into it, aren't you?"

"Absolutely. I'll be ready to go by ten."

⌒

They took off in Toni's viper red truck and were soon crossing into New Jersey on the car ferry. There was a beautifully cool breeze that made their hair fly around when they stood at the railing of the ferry. "I love being on a boat, don't you?" Toni asked.

"Yeah, I do. I don't have a lot of experience, though. We aren't boat people."

"We're more car people too, but we had friends and relatives who had boats. I love to go wake boarding and waterskiing."

"That's pretty energetic for me. I like to lie on the beach and read."

Surprising Noel, Toni took her finger and ran it along Noel's cheek bones, and along her jaw. The look on her face was one of rabid interest. "You never lie on the beach. That's why your skin is so

136

pretty. You should compare how you look with somebody like poor Roxy. She's younger than I am, but the sun has thrashed her."

"Yikes! I thought she was older than me."

"No, she's thirty-eight. I keep bugging her to wear sunblock and a hat, but she won't."

Noel looked out at the ocean, relishing the fresh air. She almost gasped when Toni put an arm around her and cuddled up close. "You don't mind, do you?" Toni asked. "I don't want to make you uncomfortable."

"I'm very comfortable. And you're very pretty," she said, looking at Toni's lovely, symmetrical features.

It looked as though Toni were a little embarrassed when she changed the subject. "Do you like to gamble?"

"I teach in the Baltimore public schools. Every day is a gamble." Noel laughed, showing that she was teasing. "My dad loves to play poker, and he taught all of us when we were young. I haven't been to many casinos, but I can hold my own."

"What do you play?"

"Five-card stud, seven-card stud. I can play Texas Hold 'Em, but that's not my favorite."

"Why not?"

"It's too popular. They make it look easy on TV, and everyone thinks they can play. Of course, that's a good way to take money from patsies." She laughed evilly, and Toni squeezed her, resting her head on Noel's shoulder.

"We're gonna have fun. I can just tell."

⌒

Being inside at the casino was a relief. There were large sections that were non-smoking, and the air conditioning was on full blast. Getting out of the heat was very nice after the past few days, and both of them had a lot of energy.

They split up, with Toni going to play slot machines while Noel found a poker table that had low-limit five-card stud. "I'll be right here, so come find me when you get bored," Noel said.

"Or when I go broke, which usually doesn't take too long."

"Either way. I'll be here."

Toni tilted her head and kissed Noel. It wasn't a terribly romantic kiss, but it made Noel tingle all the way to her toes. She watched Toni walk away and the sway of her hips nearly made her swoon.

⌒

About an hour later, Toni came up behind Noel and put a hand on her shoulder. Noel looked up and grinned. "I hope you're not ready to leave."

Toni crouched down and whispered, "I assume that all of those chips means that you're doing well?"

"I am. But as soon as my luck starts to turn, I'm done. Do you mind if I hang in for a while?"

"Not at all. I'm starving, so I'm gonna go to that big buffet. I'll be in there chowing down."

"Cool. I'll call your cell when I'm done."

Before she got up, Toni kissed her cheek. "Good luck."

⌒

Noel's luck lasted for quite a while, and when she called, Toni reported she had left the casino and was sitting outside on the boardwalk. After a brief search, Noel found her munching on some salt water taffy. She sat next to her and smiled, "I'm buying dinner."

Toni looked very excited. "Did you kill?"

"Let's just say that we don't have to go to McDonald's."

⌒

It turned out that Toni had not gone to the buffet. The line was long, so she'd had some ice cream to tide her over. It was five o'clock and they were both famished. They got a reservation at one of the expensive "star chef" restaurants at the newest, nicest casino. When their menus were presented, Toni coughed and made a face, pointing at the prices.

"This is play money," Noel said. "Let's eat like kings."

"Are you sure?"

"I'm positive. Order anything your heart desires."

Toni looked at her hungrily. "I would, but you already told me you can't stay overnight."

Once again, Noel thought that even if Toni said the same thing to six other women, the line still worked.

⌒

They were back in Delaware by ten. A few miles away from Rehoboth, Toni asked, "Would you like to see the place I'm working on?"

"Of course. You haven't told me much about what you've been doing lately."

"Really? I thought I had."

Noel didn't mention that most of their discussions only included the words "harder" and "faster" and "softer" and "oh, god."

"The house I'm working on is probably going to make you jealous. My guess is it's what you'd do to The Sandpiper if you had free reign and a huge bank account."

"Maybe I should go to Atlantic City more often?"

"If you can make that work, I'll gladly be your driver."

They pulled up in front of a rambling, old Victorian that was a few blocks in from the beach and just outside of town. Toni got out of the truck and Noel joined her. As though it were something she did all of the time, Toni grasped Noel's hand as they stood in front of the house. "This place was a total dump. A guy from Philadelphia bought it, and he's going to turn it into a first-class bed and breakfast. I'm not sure he's going to make any money on it, but he's retiring and he and his wife want to live somewhere elegant."

"What are you doing to it?"

Toni laughed. "Everything, and I do mean everything. He hired me to be the site supervisor, and that's why I've been working my butt off. We're putting in everything: new electrical service, copper plumbing, new HVAC, everything. It's the biggest job I've ever done."

Stunned, Noel stared at her. "How did you get this job?"

"I've done some contracting before, and I did a job for a guy this guy knows."

"And he hired you just because of one recommendation?"

Toni smiled, her teeth shining in the moonlight. "It was a hell of a recommendation. I wouldn't like to do jobs like this all the time, but it's nice to have one big project that'll take me all summer. Besides, this is the kind of thing that I'll have to do more often as I get older. As I said, I'm gonna have to learn to use my head more than my hands."

Noel squeezed the strong hand that she held. "You can't go wrong either way. You have great hands, and a very nice head." Toni looked at her and Noel put a hand on the back of Toni's head and pulled her close. They kissed for a long time, standing on the quiet street, with just the moon illuminating them. "You don't happen to have a key to this place, do you?"

"Yes, but there isn't a nook or cranny that'd be comfortable to lie on, and I have to get you horizontal. Your place is three minutes closer. Let's go."

Noel grabbed her hand and ran for the truck, both of them laughing.

⌒

The next afternoon, April reached Noel when she was out in the yard pruning the climbing roses. "Hi," Noel said. "I haven't talked to you all week. What's been going on?"

"I was just explaining to the boys that they can't go to Rehoboth every time the mood strikes them."

"Sure they can. One of the nicest times I've had this summer was when you came down to camp."

"That was my kind of camping. The boys were at a different location, and I didn't have to go near a tent or a stove. I could be an avid camper if it was always like that."

"Well, Toni claimed to have enjoyed it. I'm sure she'd be up for another trip. But this time I'm sleeping at her place."

"I told you at the time that wasn't a problem. You're the prudish one, Noel."

"I know, I know. I just didn't want them to be confused."

"They're boys. They're always confused. How is Toni, by the way?"

"As confounding as ever." Noel chuckled. "I think she's trying to drive me mad, and she's succeeding. Out of the blue, she invited me to go to Atlantic City for the weekend. And while we were gone she touched me, and hugged me, and kissed me in public. So, she must not mind if strangers see her dating me. Or whatever it is we're doing. But we went to the inn when we got back, and after we had sex, we had that strange, uncomfortable silence we always

141

have, and she got up and left, like she always does."

April was quiet for a few moments. When she spoke again the teasing quality was gone from her voice. "What bothers you the most about the way she treats you?"

"It's the same old thing, and I don't have any right to complain about it."

"And that is?" April prompted.

Noel sighed with frustration. "It's what I've been unjustifiably complaining about for weeks now. She treats me like I'm just someone to have sex with, and I want to be more than that to her."

"Now tell me again why you don't think you have the right to complain?"

"Because it's what I agreed to. I was just thinking about the first time we had sex. I actually told her that if I was looking for someone long-term, she'd be the last place I'd look. Rude much?"

April winced audibly. "That's pretty bad. But it didn't stop her from having sex with you."

"No, I think that's what convinced her that she wanted to have sex with me. I don't know what has made her so antagonistic to relationships, but she's obviously the kind of woman who can't commit."

"I know I've said this six times already, but you have to be more forceful. If you're not getting what you want out of this, you need to at least tell her."

"But that's unfair to her. She warned me, she warned me again, and then I try to change the rules."

"We aren't talking about rules, Noel. We're talking about feelings. And how do you know that her feelings haven't changed, too?"

"I don't know." She sounded as frustrated as April had ever heard her. "I don't regret having sex with her. It's been fantastic in every way...except for the fact that I care more for her than she does for me. Oh, well, maybe having two women in a row reject me will give me expert status."

"Well, you did live a pretty charmed life up until now."

"That might be true, but if it was, I'd like to continue that charmed life."

"Wouldn't we all? I know you won't listen, but I truly think you owe it to yourself to talk to her. What if her feelings have grown too?"

"I think I'd be able to tell."

"Noel, I hate to bring up a touchy subject, but you didn't know Janet's feelings for you had changed. You're a little oblivious about some things."

Chuckling ruefully, Noel said, "That's the way to help my self-confidence. Make me doubt all of my instincts."

"You usually have great instincts. This is one tiny blind spot, and you only have it because you've always been so lucky in love."

"I'll think about what you said. I really will. Now put one of my nephews on the phone. I want to tell them they can get on the bus and be here in three hours."

⌒

By Wednesday, Noel still hadn't seen Toni that week. That was the longest they'd gone without hooking up, and she worried that she was being punished for having spent a full day with her on Saturday. She was restless and bored, and after dinner she went to Jackie's, hoping to find Toni.

When she walked in, she saw Heidi inexpertly playing pool. By the time Noel sat down, greeted Jackie, and ordered a drink, Heidi walked over and said, "Can you play pool?"

"I'm terrible."

"I thought the woman who asked me to play was kinda cute, but she's a jerk."

Noel lightly slapped Heidi on the shoulder. "Oh, so you want to unload a jerk onto me?"

"No, no! I just figured you could take over for me and end the misery if you were any good."

"No luck. You could just tell her you concede."

Heidi grinned, her green eyes sparkling when she did. "Great idea!" She dashed across the room, delivered her news and came back to sit next to Noel. "Put your arm around me and act like you're my girlfriend."

"Do you think this will work?" Noel put her arm around Heidi's waist and stared into her eyes, trying to look lovestruck.

Heidi rested her head on Noel's shoulder and Noel caught the scent of her very attractive perfume. "Probably not, but it's nice to have a pretty woman at least feign interest."

"Are things not going well?"

"Oh, they're fine. I've just had a little dry spell." Heidi sat up and took a sip of her drink. "It's kind of a slow night in here. Most of the regulars go over to Showtime on Wednesdays. That's half-price night, and a lot of tourists go."

Laughing a little nervously, Noel said, "Maybe we should head over there."

"Nah. That's Roxy and Toni's hang out. That crowd's a little young for me."

"Don't be silly. You could compete with any of those youngsters."

"Thanks for the vote of confidence." She picked up her drink and touched it against Noel's. "I honestly don't like to date women a lot younger than me."

Noel grinned brightly. "I knew there were a lot of things I liked about you. That's just one more to add to the pile."

Over at Showtime, Toni and Roxy were standing near the bar, checking out the scene. Toni had to get over to the firehouse, so she chugged the rest of her mineral water and leaned close so that Roxy could hear her over the noise. "I've got to take off." She kissed her on the lips and started to head for the door. A very young woman who had earlier tried to buy Toni a drink came up to her again, wobbling a little.

"How about a drink now?"

"No, thanks," Toni said. "I've got to go."

"Don't go. You're really cute."

Toni suspected that the young woman was having trouble seeing anything at all, much less how cute she was, but she tried to be polite. "I have to leave. I've got to go to work." She moved past her, but when she got to the door the woman was right behind her and followed her out.

"Do you know where an ATM is? I must've spent all my money."

Toni sighed and said, "Why don't you pack it in for the night? Tell your friends you're leaving, and head home. You'll thank me in the morning."

"My friend left with somebody." She looked very confused and Toni knew she couldn't abandon her.

"Do you live around here?"

"Philly."

"Okay," Toni said, trying to keep her patience. "Where are you staying?"

The woman fumbled around, searching through her pockets and finally produced a brass key with a tag that read "The Pelican."

"Okay. I have to walk up the street and your place is on my way. I'll walk you home."

Wrapping her hands around Toni's arm, the woman said, "You'll come in with me."

"No, I won't, but I will make sure that you get home in one piece. After that, you're on your own."

⌐

Noel truly regretted the fact that she had to walk past Showtime to get home. It was always noisy, the stench of stale beer wafted out of the place, and it was a little disconcerting to see so many drunken women stumbling around. It was her least favorite kind of bar, but she'd never disliked it as much as she did tonight. Seeing Toni trying to hold up a stumbling young woman on the way to God knows where made her want to erase the place evermore from her memory.

⌐

Noel tried to get to sleep, but she was entirely unsuccessful. Her mind raced for hours, flooded with so many feelings that she could barely keep track of them. She was angry, disappointed, shocked, and most of all, disgusted with herself.

She had been sure she knew who Toni was. Sure of it. But she had been equally sure that she knew Janet, and she'd been completely wrong about that. It wasn't just that Toni was having sex with a stranger, even though that hurt. But there was something so lecherous about leading a drunken young woman down the street that it actually turned her stomach.

She tossed and turned all night long. The sheets felt rough, the mattress dug into her side, the room was too warm, then too cool. She finally got up at five, took a shower, and got dressed. There was no sense in lying in bed when she couldn't sleep. She had everything ready for breakfast, so she went out and took a long walk along the beach, but not even a beautiful sunrise could lighten her dark mood.

⌒

By lunchtime, Noel felt like she was going to crawl out of her skin. She was desperate to talk to Toni, and even though she knew it was unwise, she got into her car and drove around until she found the project Toni was working on.

She wasn't sure what she was going to say, and just being in the vicinity made her anxious. But seeing Toni's red truck convinced her that she had to stay until she saw her. Luckily, she didn't have to wait long. A big lunch truck pulled up and when the proprietor blew the horn, a dozen tradesmen poured out of the building like insects. Toni wasn't one of them, but Noel knew she was around, so she waited her out.

It took another twenty minutes, but Toni finally emerged, walking down the steps with a man who eventually got into a truck that advertised heating and air-conditioning services. As he pulled away, Noel got out of her car. Toni looked up and did a double-take. She looked pleased but very puzzled as she walked across the street to meet Noel.

Toni opened her mouth to speak, but before she could get a word out, Noel said, "Who are you?"

Her tone of voice and the look of bitter disappointment on her face clearly took Toni aback. She stopped abruptly and stared at Noel with her hands raised to either side as though she were being held up at gunpoint. "What's wrong?"

"I saw you last night," she spit out. "I never should have come to a town this small. I can't avoid seeing you lurking around with half of the women in town."

"What are you talking about? I went out for a drink with Roxy but that's— Are you talking about when I walked that girl back to her hotel room?" She looked confused, too confused to be putting on an act.

Noel took a step back and bumped into her own car. Her instinct was to disappear and make the previous three minutes disappear along with her. But April's words came back to her, and she realized that she was, in fact, unable to judge people. "Is this a new service the fire department is providing? Walking drunken girls to their hotels?" Her words were filled with venom, but still Toni didn't look angry. She just looked puzzled…and hurt.

"I didn't do anything wrong. I was at Showtime with Roxy and that girl tried to buy me a drink. I turned her down a couple of times, and when I tried to leave to go to the firehouse, I realized how drunk she was. I walked her home because I didn't think she could find the place by herself, and I didn't want anyone else to take advantage of her. You can go check at the firehouse if you want," she added softly. "You can see that I signed in just after ten o'clock and I didn't leave until six this morning." Her eyes took on a hooded, wounded quality. "We're not allowed to have guests at the firehouse. If we could, I would've taken you there, not some drunken girl."

"Me? You would have taken me? You go out of your way to make sure no one in town knows that we know each other, let alone…have sex."

"Me?" Incredulous, Toni pointed at herself. "I do that? I'm just following your lead."

"Right." Sarcasm encased the word. "I'm sorry I came over here. Who you sleep with is none of my business. But when I saw you, I got upset at the thought of you taking advantage of someone. I started thinking about all of the diseases I could have contracted from having sex with you, and it really, really upset me." She grabbed the handle and tried to open the door, but it banged right into her. She twisted around, trying to get away from Toni as quickly as possible, but a gentle hand on her shoulder stopped her.

"Will you have dinner with me tonight?"

Noel stared at her, unable to get her mind around this development. "You want to have dinner with me? After I just accused you of being a child-molesting pervert?"

Toni didn't even smile. She just nodded quickly. "I would."

"Okay. I guess we do have a few things to clear up." She got into her car, with Toni standing there staring at her with those big brown eyes.

She'd shown she was emotionally invested in Toni and knew she'd overreacted badly. But she couldn't stop herself from snapping back when Toni had the gall to say she was following Noel's lead. That was such bullshit! But why want to have dinner? The only logical reason was for Toni to set her straight and clear her good name. She just hoped that Toni was a big enough person to forgive her for assuming the very worst and that, no matter what, they could remain friends.

⌒

They hadn't made any formal plans, but Noel was certain that Toni couldn't be ready for dinner before six. So she made a point to be dressed and ready to go right then. In fact, Toni didn't show up until seven. She came to the front door, which was a first, and she rang the bell, also unique.

When Noel went to answer the door, she was so stiff with anticipation that the muscles in her neck hurt. She opened the door and saw Toni, nicely dressed and wearing a smile that looked far from genuine. "Hi," she said. "Are you ready to go?"

"Yeah. Just let me get my purse." Noel dashed back to her

apartment, got her things and locked up. She walked out onto the porch and stood next to Toni, looking at her expectantly. "Where are we off to?"

"I haven't been to Sapore in a while. Is that okay?"

The restaurant was considered one of the best in town, with prices to match. "It's more than okay, but we don't have to go anyplace that nice."

"I'd like to."

They were only about ten minutes away, but it was a very long ten minutes. Neither of them spoke. Not a word. And Noel worried every step of the way. She couldn't figure out why they were going to a nice restaurant if Toni was going to tell her off for making assumptions about her or for meddling in her private life. But if she just wanted to chat, why go out?

The table wasn't ready, and the hostess steered them towards the bar, where Toni, without asking, ordered two Manhattans. When their drinks were delivered, Toni handed one to Noel and fixed her with one hundred percent of her attention, a trait that Noel loved even though she sometimes felt like she was under the microscope. This was one of those times.

"I'm not sure what's going on, but I've obviously hurt you. I'd never do that on purpose, so tell me what happened."

"I already told you," Noel said, feeling like she had to physically pull her eyes away from Toni's mesmerizing gaze to think clearly. "I know you see other women, and there's nothing wrong with that," she rushed to say. "That's what we agreed to. But it upset me to see you with someone so young, especially someone who didn't look like she was in control. I truly apologize for jumping to that conclusion." She shrugged her shoulders and took a hesitant glance back at Toni. "That's about it."

Toni nodded briefly, and said, "There's more. What aren't you telling me?"

"Nothing," Noel lied. She desperately wanted to tell Toni that she had developed feelings for her, but she couldn't get over her belief that her admission would put Toni in an untenable position. It just wasn't fair to agree to keep things light and then change your mind and expect the other person not to feel trapped. "I'd been over at Jackie's, and Heidi and I were talking about younger women and how we hated feeling threatened by them. Then I saw you and assumed you were with the youngest woman you could be with and not go to jail…" She made a face that she hoped looked apologetic. "I let it get to me."

The hostess came by to tell them their table was ready, and Toni lightly touched the small of Noel's back as they moved through the room. The hostess pulled Toni's chair out and started to move around to the other side of the table, but Toni beat her to it. She pulled Noel's chair out and waited until she sat down to slide it across the wood floor.

As soon as Toni sat down, the hostess handed them their menus, and addressed her comments to Toni. A few seconds later their server delivered their drinks from the bar and told them about the evening's specials, but Noel paid almost no attention to him. She desperately wanted to hear what Toni had to say.

It didn't look like Toni had been listening, either. As soon as the server stepped away, she said, "I'm sorry that seeing me upset you. I wish you would have said something at the time, but it makes sense that you didn't." She took a sip of her drink and started to look over the menu.

There was an uneasiness between them that hadn't been there since their first few tense meetings, but Noel wasn't sure how to break it. In fact, she had almost no idea. Even though she and Toni had been remarkably intimate with one another all summer, she didn't know her that well emotionally, a fact that saddened her.

"If you like bluefish, it's locally caught," Toni said. "Are you hungry?"

"Not very. My stomach's been in knots all day."

"Would you like me order for us?"

"I'd love it." With relief, Noel folded her menu closed and put it on the table, glad that Toni was taking over.

Surprisingly, after their order was taken, Toni looked a little nervous. She cleared her throat several times, then said, "How do you feel about being with me in public?"

"Great. Why wouldn't I?"

"I just had the impression…" she trailed off. "No, that's not true. At least it wasn't at first." Noel must have looked confused, because Toni laughed softly and said, "I've never thought of you like I think of the tourists I see. But I have a reputation, even though I think it's out of sync with how I really am."

"I'm confused. Where are you going with this?"

"People seem to think I'm with a new woman every night, but that's not true. That's never been true. Yes, I do enjoy the company of a pretty woman, but it doesn't happen all that frequently. I'm pickier than people seem to think."

"Why do you think that is?"

"Probably because I don't talk about my personal life that often. I let people think what they want to think. But when I meet someone I like, I worry that people will assume she's just another pick-up." She looked deeply into Noel's eyes. "I never want anyone to think that about you."

Frustrated, Noel felt her hands balling into fists, and she consciously tried to relax. "Why didn't you say something?"

"I don't know," Toni said, looking surprisingly stumped. "That's kind of an odd conversation to have."

Noel couldn't help herself. She had to reach across the table and hold Toni's work-scarred hand. "You started to say that things were one way at first and then they changed. What changed?"

"I thought you didn't want people to know you were seeing me."

"Me? Why would I not want people to know I was seeing you?" She shook her head, feeling a little dizzy. "Are we seeing each other?"

"I thought we were," Toni said, looking shy and a little hurt.

Noel squeezed her hand. "No, no! I felt like we were seeing each other, but I thought you thought we were just having sex."

"We have been. I keep trying to date you, but you don't reciprocate."

"Me? I don't reciprocate?"

"No, you don't. I asked you out to dinner when you first got here, I had you over to my house for dinner, and I asked you to go to Atlantic City. You've never asked me to go anywhere."

"That's not true," Noel said, clearly agitated. "I called you and asked you out for dinner."

"And when I couldn't do it that night, you never asked again."

Noel made a face and cringed. "That was so rude of me!"

"I didn't know what to make of you. I got such conflicting messages." Toni looked like she might cry, and she took in a few deep breaths. "I missed Max so much this summer, it was painful. She always helped me figure things out. She was such a good sounding board. Now I don't have anyone." She bit her bottom lip as a few tears ran down her cheeks. "It's been so lonely without her, and I feel lost not having her advice."

Noel let herself speak the words that came straight from her heart, not letting herself censor her feelings. "I want to skip dinner and go to your house and hold you." She squeezed her hand so hard that Toni winced.

When Toni smiled, it was shy and very vulnerable looking. "I'd like that. I just wish you would have told me before I ordered."

⌒

They were waiting for the check when the most dreaded sound seeped into the building. The fire alarm could not have come at a worse time. Toni jumped up, took her wallet out, tossed her charge card to Noel and said, "Forge my name." Then she bent over and kissed her gently before race-walking out of the restaurant.

⌒

Toni called the next morning, the background noise on her cell phone making it hard for Noel to understand her. "Hi. I just stopped to get some coffee on my way to the job. It was a long night."

"Poor thing. You must be exhausted. How late were you up?"

"All night. It was a big warehouse fire in Georgetown and all of the neighboring companies were there. It was one of those hot, potentially toxic fires. The kind every firefighter hates."

"People who care about firefighters hate them, too. Why was it dangerous...besides the obvious?"

"They weren't sure what was in one part of the warehouse. There were conflicting reports and, at one point, we thought it might be flammable chemicals."

"That must have been terrifying!"

"No, not really. We're very well trained, so we just do our job. But I must admit it does get your heart racing. I volunteered to stay around since I knew I had too much adrenaline pumping to fall asleep."

"You could've come over here."

"Now you tell me." Toni laughed softly, and Noel could easily imagine the faint lines that bracketed her lips when she smiled. "The next time I'm looking for fun at four a.m. I'll head right over to The Sandpiper."

With a deep sense of longing, Noel said, "Only for another week."

"Aw, damn. I knew it was soon, but I didn't realize it was that soon."

"I wish it was still June."

"I wish the ground was still frozen and I was just heading over to The Sandpiper to meet you for the first time. I think I could do a better job if I had another whack at it."

"That's such a sweet thing to say. I hate that we wasted all that time too."

"I wish I didn't have so much going on with this job. I've been there past dark every night for two weeks."

"My brother and his wife and kids are coming down tomorrow for three days, but I've got the weekend free. Can we spend some time together then?"

"No," Toni said, sounding grumpy. "I have to go to a seminar on hazardous materials in Wilmington. It sounded like a good idea when I signed up, but now I wish I could get out of it."

"You can't, huh?"

"No. The city wants someone to go and it's too late for me to find a substitute."

"Want me to make you dinner tonight?"

"I'd love that. But I'm having dinner with the guy I'm working for. He has to come over from Philadelphia and it's easiest for him to meet for dinner."

"Come over here if it's not too late when you're finished."

"If I get a second burst of energy, I will."

Noel felt a rush of protectiveness, and said, "No, no, don't come over. You didn't sleep at all last night. You go home so you can get some rest."

"Sometimes I miss being twenty," Toni said, yawning. "Actually, I miss it every time I have to climb up on a roof."

Part Nine

Noel still didn't know exactly where they stood, but she felt that some major barriers to discussing their relationship had come down. She was happy that Toni made it clear that she wanted to date her—not just have sex with her. But with so few days left in the summer, she didn't feel that they had the time to develop any emotional attachment, if that's even what Toni wanted. But just knowing that she was, in some way, special helped her recover bits of her faltering self-confidence. For the first time she felt they were on equal footing, and that significantly buoyed her spirits.

⌒

Even though Toni was too busy to spare any time to meet Andy, Amy and their kids, she called Noel to check in and make sure she was having fun with her family. That small gesture felt better than receiving a dozen roses, and Noel wished she could press the phone message the way she pressed the first flower Toni gave her.

⌒

Noel spent her last weekend in Rehoboth saying goodbye to the friends she'd made. School started on Tuesday, and she needed at least one day to get her apartment in order and focus on the year ahead, so she planned on leaving on Sunday. Barbara, the bed and breakfast babysitter, was going to take over Sunday morning, freeing Noel to spend her last day exactly as she wanted.

She arranged to have dinner with Gloria on Friday night and with Heidi on Saturday. Toni had to sleep at the firehouse on Friday night, but they made plans for Noel to go to Toni's after she and Heidi finished dinner on Saturday. She was pleased that Toni rearranged some family commitments so they could spend not only Saturday evening together, but also Sunday. Noel was tempted to invite Toni to dinner with Heidi, but she still felt a little odd being with both of them at the same time. Heidi was very clearly fond of Toni, and their physical familiarity was too much to witness.

She and Heidi met fairly early, so it wasn't even ten o'clock when she arrived at Toni's. She knocked, but didn't hear a sign of life. Knocking again, she started to feel a little anxious. She took out her cell phone and called Toni, her anxiety building when she could hear the phone ringing inside. On the fifth ring, Toni answered. "Hello?" Her voice was rough and heavy with sleep.

"Hi. Did you forget about me?"

"Noel?" Toni sounded like a child just woken up from a long nap. "Where are you?"

"In front of your house." Noel smiled when she heard a significant amount of noise coming from inside. Toni threw the front door open, and Noel couldn't help but laugh at her. She was neatly dressed, but her linen shirt and cotton shorts were a mass of wrinkles. Her hair was in place—it was so thick and straight, it was always in place. But her eyes reminded Noel of a newborn kitten's. Unable to resist, she walked inside and kissed each sleepy eye. "I think somebody took a nap."

"I never would have if I knew I'd fall asleep that soundly." She went to turn on a couple of table lamps. The TV was on, tuned to the Orioles game, and the pillows and cushions from the couch had been kicked or thrown onto the floor. Given Toni's neatness, the place was a wreck, but thirty seconds of straightening up had it in shipshape again. "Whew! I'm gonna get some iced tea to help me wake up. Would you like some?"

"We can just get together tomorrow," Noel offered, even though she did so only to be polite.

"No, I'm fine. I intentionally let myself take a little catnap so I'd have some energy. But the game had just started when I lay down, so that's been a while."

Noel looked at the TV. The graphic showed the game was in the bottom of the seventh. "That's been about three hours. The games start at five after seven, right?"

"Right," Toni said, looking pleased that Noel was up on the team enough to know their exact starting time. She finished pouring her tea, took a few drinks, then walked over to Noel. She put the tea down and slid her arms around her waist. But for a change, she didn't kiss her. She wrapped her tight and held her for a long time. The feeling of being encased in Toni's embrace was one Noel knew she would have a very hard time giving up. She felt enveloped by Toni's body, and everything—from her scent to the beat of her heart to the warmth of her body—was perfect. If they'd stayed just as they were until she had to leave for Baltimore, she would be happy.

All too soon, Toni released her. But Noel didn't move away. She looked into Toni's eyes and said, "I wish things hadn't gotten so…"

"Me too. I wish I hadn't been so busy this summer. But I've got to take some jobs being a site supervisor or a general if I want to build a clientele."

"Don't worry about that. You've got to work. I'm just sorry we didn't spend more time together…standing up."

Toni's smile was gentle and warm. "You've only got yourself to blame for that. I have all these things I want to talk to you about, but when you're standing this close to me it's almost impossible not to start kissing you. And when I start kissing you, it's almost impossible not to..." She playfully looked towards the bedroom, twitching an eyebrow.

"I guess there are worse problems. I'm never going to wish I had less sexual chemistry with someone. But sometimes, with you... Whew!"

"I know," Toni said, her handsome face reflecting her puzzlement. "I've never had this kind of sexual chemistry with a woman. It knocks me off my feet."

Noel was drawn to put her arms around Toni and hug her tightly. "I love to knock you off your feet." She kissed her tenderly, feeling the warm softness of her lips. "Sometimes you look like you're not even sure of your name."

"I'm not! You've got me completely mesmerized. That's why I wish I hadn't been working so much. If we could have met for dinner more often, it would have given us a couple of hours where we had to behave."

Noel looked away, not wanting to bring up the sore subject they'd already discussed. But Toni obviously didn't want to let it drop. "I'm very, very sorry that I didn't ask you how you felt about people in town knowing we were seeing each other. I just assumed..." She shook her head. "I thought I knew what you were thinking."

Noel took her by the hand and led her over to the sofa, sitting next to her instead of on her lap, which always led to an express trip to the bedroom. "Do you want to know what I was thinking?"

"Very much."

Taking a big, deep breath, Noel said, "Okay. Here goes. At first, I was mostly interested in having sex. It'd been almost a year, and it felt fantastic to have someone I was so attracted to find me attractive. But after a few times together I started to feel like I was only someone you had sex with. I started to feel a little objectified."

"Oh, Noel." Toni looked like she wanted to cry. "Why didn't you say something? I was feeling the same way. Well, not objectified, but I started wishing that you wanted to hang out with me. But you didn't show any real interest."

"How can you say that? If you just looked in my direction, I came like a well-trained dog."

Toni stared at her clasped hands. It was clear she was struggling with what she wanted to say, and Noel waited patiently, giving her the time she needed. "It's true that you were always ready to get together. But, like I told you the other day, you never reciprocated. You never asked me out."

"I know, but—"

Holding up her hand, Toni continued, "That's not the bad part. The part that hurt was that you never asked me any questions about me. At first, I thought you were self-involved. It didn't bother me too much, since you certainly weren't that way when we were having sex." She laughed, her eyes taking on the sexy tease that Noel was ridiculously attracted to. "But over time, I realized you weren't self-involved. There's a lot of give-and-take when you're talking to Heidi or Jackie or Roxy. And Gloria told me how much she liked you and how interested you were in finding out about Max. So I started to think you just weren't interested in me as anything other than a bed partner. I thought you didn't find me interesting enough to get to know."

Noel put her hands on Toni's shoulders, squeezing them. "Nothing, nothing could be further from the truth. I was sure you wanted to keep things very topical, so that's what I did. I kept trying not to let myself get too attached to you, since you made it so clear you didn't want to be in a relationship."

"I did," Toni said, dropping her head. "But I was just protecting myself." She looked up and let Noel see the deep sadness in her dark eyes. "I should've taken more risks." She put her arm around Noel's shoulders and let their heads rest against one another. "You haven't changed your mind about taking a risk, have you?"

"Which risk is that?"

"A really simple one. You give up a job you love and leave your friends and family to do a job you're not suited for. And, of course, you get to try to turn a relationship-phobic, beat-up handywoman into a girlfriend."

Noel chuckled. "I could get that done before breakfast." She shifted and put her arms around Toni, feeling a thrill run up her spine when Toni rested her head on her chest and relaxed into her embrace. Soothingly, Noel stroked Toni's hair, loving the way the thick strands slid through her fingers. "I've got another idea. You could move to Baltimore and build up your contractor business there. I know a very sweet woman who'd love to try to tame you." She kissed her head. "Not that I think you need taming."

Toni's voice was soft and a little tentative when she said, "What do you think I need?"

"I'm not sure. But I would have loved to find out."

"Me too. I bet I could have made you like being an innkeeper in six or seven years."

"That's a little optimistic," Noel teased, laughing along with Toni. "It's gonna be a long time before I want house-guests. I honestly don't think I could ever get used to living in the place I worked. It's just not me."

"That's pretty clear, given that you never had a meal there."

"No, I felt like the night manager at a motel."

Toni started to move and Noel released her. "Max would have been happy that you gave it a try. But she never would have wanted you to be stuck with something you didn't want." She stood up and went into her room, emerging with a tissue paper wrapped package. Her expression was a little shy when she extended the gift. "I made this for you."

Noel took the gift and unwrapped it, feeling her cheeks flush and tears flood her eyes when she gazed at the quilt. "Oh, my god, there's The Sandpiper!"

Toni had crafted the quilt to center around the image of the hotel. Surrounding it were scenes of the ocean, the sun, an anchor, an apple, and a rustic tool box. "The anchor's for Max," Toni said, her voice rough with emotion. "The apple's for my favorite teacher. And I had to put myself in there." She shrugged and wiped her eyes with the back of her hand.

Noel threw her arms around Toni's neck and shook with emotion. When she was able to pull away she kissed her cheeks repeatedly. "No one has ever given me anything so fantastic."

Toni looked shy but pleased, and she eagerly accepted Noel's kisses.

"For my fortieth birthday, Janet gave me a beautiful diamond tennis bracelet." She squeezed the quilt, closing her eyes briefly. "This is nicer. Much nicer."

"I think you're exaggerating a little bit."

"No, I'm not." Noel's gaze was intent when she stared into Toni's eyes. "Janet had a great job, and she made a lot of money. I'm sure she spent a lot on the bracelet, but I don't wear much jewelry—especially not to work. So, even though I appreciated it, it didn't reflect me or who I am. And it didn't show me anything about her." She rubbed the quilt against her cheek, grinning. "This does."

Toni gazed at Noel for a long time, looking perfectly happy doing just that. Her smile grew when Noel wrapped her arms around her neck and stood so close they were nearly nose to nose. "I wish we could start over. I'd love to have another chance to do this right."

"I know." Toni's dark eyes fluttered closed. "We let the summer get away from us."

"How are you feeling? Still sleepy?"

Toni's slow smile made a chill chase up Noel's back. "What've you got in mind?"

"Like you don't know." She kissed her gently. "We've gotten to know each other pretty well in bed. Let's go do what we're good at."

Toni's long lashes batted seductively. "We do have a certain flair, don't we?"

"No doubt." She took Toni by the hand and led her to the bedroom.

⌐

As she almost always did, Toni took over as soon as they crossed the threshold of the bedroom. Noel hadn't realized how much she appreciated a lover who wasn't afraid to direct the action, and she wasn't going to spoil a perfectly good thing at this point.

This was the first time Noel had ever known she and Toni were going to get together, so she'd had time to prepare. Toni sat on the bed and methodically undressed her, stopping to admire the sexy bra Noel had picked out for the occasion. She looked down at Toni's hands, admiring the strength as well as the small scars that decorated them. Those strong, yet tender hands caressed her breasts, making Noel's heart race when she saw the hungry look in Toni's eyes. Not surprisingly, she could feel herself start to get wet, even though Toni hadn't yet touched a bit of bare skin.

"I'm already hot for you," she said, a small grin turning up a corner of her mouth.

"Good," Toni said, not moving one bit faster, her attention fully fixed on Noel's breasts. "I love it when I put my mouth on you and you're dripping wet."

"I get wet walking over to your house," Noel said, laughing. "Just thinking about you is enough."

Toni stopped and put her hands on Noel's hips, looking up into her eyes. "Do you think about me?"

"Yes." Forcing herself to be honest, she started to run her fingers through Toni's hair, speaking softly. "I think about you all of the time."

"What do you think about?"

"Mostly I try to figure out how to find you," she admitted. "I try to remember if you've told me when you're going to be on duty, and where you might be."

Looking a little unsure, Toni said, "So, it's usually just a scheduling thing?"

"No. Not at all." She increased the pace of her head rub, smiling when Toni rested her head against her belly. "I think about the last time we were together, and what we did. I think about how you smell, how you taste. But most of all I think about how happy I am when we're together." Toni slowly lifted her chin and looked curiously at Noel. It was hard for her to continue with those big eyes staring at her, but Noel forced herself. "Being with you has been the highlight of my summer, and you had a lot of competition. Someone left me a piece of property worth a load of dough."

That broke the tension, and Toni grasped her by the hips pulling her onto the bed. She kissed her gently, slowly. Then she looked into her eyes and said, "I can't tell you how many nights I walked by The Sandpiper, hoping to get a glimpse of you. I didn't have the nerve to knock on the darned door, but I thought it'd be okay to toss a pebble at the window if I saw you. I'm a dope. A big dope. I wasted so much time."

"I did the same thing, Toni. It's not your fault. We just didn't communicate well."

"Let's try to start now." She held her tightly and kissed her, showing more emotion, more tenderness than she'd ever revealed. Noel responded with the same depth of intensity, and soon their bare bodies were expressing the feelings they both experienced, but never gave voice to.

⌒

Much later, Toni lay on her side, spooned up against Noel, sleepily rubbing her belly. "Will you stay with me tonight?"

"I'd love to." Noel yawned, trying hard to stay awake. "You sure you don't mind?"

"Mind? Why would I mind?"

"I…uhm…assumed you didn't like to sleep with a lover."

"Huh? I love to. I assumed you didn't."

Noel grasped Toni's hand and brought it to her mouth, biting it playfully. "Don't ever say that word again. I'm declaring war on 'assume' and all of its permutations."

⌒

In the middle of the night, Toni had to get up and use the bathroom. There was a cool breeze coming in the windows and she rushed back to bed to warm up. Still asleep, Noel immediately snuggled up, making a soft, whimpering sound that touched Toni's heart. She snuck an arm under Noel's head and stroked her body, smiling when Noel sighed and purred, burrowing against her. She forced herself to lie awake for as long as she could, relishing their closeness, and wishing that it hadn't come so late.

⌒

The next morning, Toni displayed her culinary skills by whipping up blueberry pancakes. She was standing in front of the stove, clad in just an oversized chambray shirt when Noel came into the kitchen and hugged her from behind. "Do you mean that I could have been getting breakfast made for me all those times I stupidly went home?"

"Well, your guests might not have liked that, but I would've." She turned her head and gave Noel a sweet smile. "What do you want to do today?"

"If you don't have anything in mind, I'd like to spend the day in your bed. We can talk and have sex and talk some more. How does that sound?"

"That sounds great." She turned again, but her smile was so sad and filled with longing that Noel wished she hadn't seen it.

⌒

Noel leaned across the bed and licked a drip of maple syrup from the edge of Toni's mouth. "This is fun. I've…uhm…been wondering. Why are you antagonistic to relationships?"

"I'm not antagonistic," Toni said, chuckling softly. "I guess I just hadn't found the right woman, and I'd begun to believe that I wouldn't. So, rather than create false expectations, I tended to say that I'm not relationship material."

"But you don't believe that."

"I'm not sure, to be honest. I think I'd probably have tried a few more times if I lived in a bigger town. But everyone knows your business here." She shook her head. "It's better not to bother. Besides, I like my freedom, and I get most of my needs met."

"Most?"

"Up until this year, I guess I was getting all of them met. But when Max died, I lost my confidant. I have a lot of friends, but

Max's the one I relied on for my emotional home base."

"I know how close you were, but it surprises me that you don't have that with Heidi or Roxy or one of your other friends."

"You know how it is. You rely on people for certain things. Max was great at drawing me out and making me tell her things. That's harder to do with somebody who's a peer or a lover. At least for me it is."

"And it's hard to change after you've known someone for a long time, isn't it."

"Yeah, it is. Maybe it's time I tried to change, because Max's not coming back."

It was a lovely day, and Toni suggested they sit outside for a while.

Noel was lying in bed, leaning up against the headboard, with Toni's head on her lap. "Sounds appealing, but this isn't bad either. I'm pretty fond of being naked…with you, that is. I wear clothes most of the time."

"When we first met, you accused me of not wanting to work inside. I think I denied that, but it's pretty close to the truth. I get antsy if I'm inside too much."

"No problem. I can put some clothes on." She patted Toni's head and started scooting off the bed.

Toni went to her closet and found another oversized shirt. She tossed it to Noel, and said, "This is all you need."

"Really? What about your neighbors?"

"You must not have paid attention when you were out there before. Nobody can see in."

Noel accepted the shirt and put it on. "Then why are we bothering?"

"The sun can still see in." She kissed Noel's forehead, and added, "You've avoided getting a sunburn all summer long. Why ruin your record now?"

Toni poured glasses of iced tea for both of them, and they went out and sat in a pair of rocking chairs. "This is the life," Noel said. She propped her feet up on Toni's bare legs and took a sip of her tea.

"You might not know this, but the weather's always like this here. You ought to think about running the inn just for the weather."

"I'm gonna call you one day in February and remind you of the vicious lie you just told me." She wiggled her toes, poking Toni's breasts through her shirt.

"Well, it always feels nice. I've never been to Baltimore in the winter, but I bet it's lots nicer here."

"You're probably right. I think it's been established that I've had a lot of crazy illusions this summer. My belief that Delaware gets about the same weather as Maryland is probably just one more of them."

A frown creased Toni's forehead and she put her hand on Noel's knee. "Hey, I want to clear something up. During our…whatever it was the other night, you said you were worried that I might give you some sort of STD."

Covering her face with her hands, Noel said, "Please forget that entire day. Seriously."

Tugging her hands away, Toni looked at her. "No, that's not a good idea. I know you were upset, and sometimes when you're angry you say things that you wouldn't ordinarily say. Sometimes that's where the truth is."

"Not in this case. I was just angry."

"Just in case there was any truth in there, I want you to know that I've always been very careful."

"It's not necessary—"

"It is," Toni interrupted. "It's important to me. Whenever I'm with someone I have any doubts about I limit things to hands only. No oral sex."

Noel cocked her head and said, "We had oral sex the first time we were together."

"I knew you'd been with someone for ten years. And you said you hadn't been with anyone since then. Plus," she said, looking a little embarrassed, "I know this isn't what the Centers for Disease Control would recommend, but you just don't seem like the kind of woman who would walk around with an untreated STD."

Noel couldn't stop from laughing. "That's the weakest compliment I think I've ever gotten, but I appreciate it nonetheless."

"You know what I mean," Toni said, giving Noel's belly a scratch.

"I do. And I should learn something from that."

Toni looked very serious when she nodded. "You should. You didn't know me well enough to do the things we've been doing. You need to be a lot more careful with people you don't know." She smiled again, but her smile had that veneer of sadness that it had had for the past two days. "You don't want to mess up some very nice equipment."

"I won't." Noel picked up her chair and moved it so it was right next to Toni's. Then she held her hand and leaned on her shoulder. They began to rock their chairs in sync, neither woman speaking.

⌒

Noel wanted to get going by five o'clock, and she dutifully got into the shower at four-thirty. She'd just gotten the water to the right temperature when an impish looking Toni got in with her. "I got bored," she said, grinning.

"You can help." She handed Toni a bar of soap. "You can wash my back."

Toni soaped up her hands and did as she was told, but other, softer parts called to her. It didn't take long for Noel to turn and begin to rub her soapy body against Toni's, a lascivious smile on her face. "This is a fantastic way to shower. A human loofah."

Tilting her head so that her lips were next to Noel's ear, Toni whispered, "I think you need one for the road."

Noel pulled back and looked at her, seeing the spark in her eyes. "You do, do you?"

"Actually, I need one, so I figured you did, too."

"Oh, what the heck. Schedules were made to be broken."

⌒

Toni walked Noel back to The Sandpiper, but instead of taking the main commercial street they went along a quieter, less traveled one. Noel had packed up her things, so all she had to do was load her car. They went in together and Toni chatted with Barbara while Noel went to her apartment and picked up her suitcases. She'd decided to leave most of what she'd brought, figuring she wouldn't wear most of her summer clothes now that fall was coming. Her new apartment in Baltimore was nice enough, but there wasn't a lot of room and using The Sandpiper for off-season storage seemed like a good idea.

She went out and said goodbye to Barbara, thanking her for all of her help. Then she and Toni went out to the street. "My poor little car might not be up to getting me all the way to Baltimore. She's seriously out of shape after just sitting around on her wheels all summer."

Toni patted the hood. "She's a cute little thing. I've never had a newer car."

"She's post breakup. Janet used to pay for our cars, and when the lease on mine was up, I had to buy my own. Just like an adult," she added, making a face.

"Since we don't have the right to get married, shouldn't we be immune to the pain of divorce?"

"You've got a point," Noel said, smiling at Toni's logic. "I'll write my congressman." She was suddenly overtaken by a wave of sadness and she leaned against Toni, shivering as she was wrapped in a tender hug. "I don't want to leave," she said, crying softly.

Toni was clearly choked up as well. "I don't want you to go."

Noel relished the hug for as long as she could. When she finally pulled away, she said, "I should go now. Traffic is pretty bad on Sunday night."

Toni opened the back door and stowed Noel's suitcases. She cleared her throat and said, "So, is this it?"

"Do you want it to be?"

"No, not at all. But if you'd rather have a clean break, I understand. It seems pretty clear we don't have a real future together, but I can live with that—if you still want to see me." Her chin was quivering when she added, "Even if you don't want to be lovers, I hope you still want to be my friend."

"I do," Noel whispered. "I really do. Why don't we just take things as they come? This probably isn't the best time to make decisions about the future." She tried her best to smile. "Maybe you'll visit Baltimore some time and decide it's exactly where you've always dreamed of living."

Looking as earnest, and as vulnerable as Noel had ever seen her, Toni said, "How about Friday?"

⌐

Noel spent the first ten miles of her drive crying. Crying wasn't her natural response to most troubling situations. In fact, she'd taken more than a little criticism through her life from people who called her unemotional or non-empathetic. While she understood it could look that way, she thought she was just stoic. Nonetheless, she didn't feel at all stoic today.

By the time she reached the Maryland border she felt in control and she called April. "Are you busy?" she asked when her sister picked up the phone.

"A little. Ed's mom and dad came over for a barbecue. I'm in the kitchen cleaning up while everyone else is outside having fun. Why? What's up? You don't sound like yourself."

"I'm driving back home and I wanted some company." She sniffed a little, unable to keep the sadness from her voice. "I'm lonely."

"I'll call you back in two minutes. Is that okay?"

"I can call Teresa or Nancy or Karen if you're busy. Don't worry about it."

"I'm calling you back in two minutes. Bye-bye."

Noel pulled over to the shoulder and found her headset microphone. She had a feeling they'd be on the phone for a long time, and she wanted to be prepared.

April called back a few minutes later. "The decks are cleared. I'm upstairs in my room and the door is locked. I'm all yours. Now, tell me why you're lonely."

"Because of Toni. We had the nicest weekend together, April. I could just kick myself for wasting most of the summer. If I'd only taken your advice…"

"Tell me what happened."

"You were right. Her feelings for me had changed, too. But she thought I wasn't seriously interested in her, so she didn't say anything. Now the summer's over, and I feel like we just had our first real night together."

"Isn't that good? You've got to start somewhere."

"Where? I could see having a long distance relationship with someone I was already committed to. But that's not where we are. She's admittedly phobic about being in a relationship, and neither of us wants to live where the other one lives. Again, that might be different if we were madly in love, but it's too early for that. I'm not going to move away and do something I don't like on the off chance that this could work out, and neither is she." She sighed heavily, still sounding like she might cry. "I think I'm most upset because I let a good chance get away."

"Where did you leave things?"

"Pretty up in the air. I couldn't bear to say goodbye so I suggested she might come to Baltimore some day to visit."

"That's pretty vague, Noel. Why weren't you more specific?"

With a soft laugh Noel said, "I didn't have to be. She volunteered to come next weekend. That's why I'm not more depressed. I can't see how it will work, but she's not ready to give up, and I'm not either."

Part Ten

*T*oni had to work a full day on Friday and she didn't leave Rehoboth until seven o'clock that evening. She called Noel at ten-thirty and asked, "Can you act like an air traffic controller and guide me?"

"I'm more than happy to." Toni was very close, and Noel spent a few minutes directing her to her parking space. She was standing in front of it when Toni pulled in. Rolling the window down, Toni said, "You don't have to give me your parking spot. I can find something."

"I know where the good spots are hiding." She swallowed, and made herself say what she was feeling. "And I wanted you here as soon as possible."

Toni turned off the car and got out. As soon as her feet hit the ground, she had her arms around Noel, holding her tight. "I missed you. I kept reminding myself that this week was just like some of the other weeks we've had. Ones where I worked a lot but knew I'd have time to hunt you down on the weekend. But this was different. Really different. I hated it."

Noel lifted her head and looked into Toni's eyes. "I think we've been more open in the last two minutes than we were in the last two months." She kissed her quickly. "Let's keep that up."

⌐

They went into the apartment building and Noel led Toni up through the admittedly dark stairwell to reach her third floor unit. Toni stopped in the entryway and looked around. "This is cute. I've been to Baltimore a lot, but I don't know anybody who lives here. Until now, that is. I like how people have redone a lot of the older housing stock."

Noel took her hand and led her through the small living room and kitchen, then into the even smaller bedroom. "I grew up in the suburbs, and one of the things I have to thank Janet for is getting me acclimated to living in the city. We lived on Federal Hill, which isn't very far from here." She chuckled softly. "Just far enough so that the odds are not good that we'll run into one another. We bought a ridiculously run-down town house for a hundred and forty thousand dollars and spent almost two years renovating it top to bottom." She walked over to the window and put her hand on the plain, ill-fitting trim that surrounded it. "We did things right. Not like this."

"This is fine for a rental," Toni said. She stood next to Noel and put her hand on the window frame. "Wow. They cheaped out on the windows."

"They cheaped out on everything. But the rent isn't too bad, and I can walk to school."

"That's worth a lot. But I bet your little car thinks you don't love her. You didn't drive her all summer, now you don't drive her to work."

"She's a hybrid. She understands we're trying to save the planet one gallon of gas at a time." She giggled and started to take Toni's shirt off her. "It's late, and I know you're tired. I'd better get you to bed."

"It is late, but I'm not very tired. Having to pay attention to my driving kept me awake."

"You don't mind getting undressed, do you?"

"Not as long as I can undress you. That's one of my favorite things."

Noel gave her a warm smile and kissed her gently. "I've noticed that about you. You like to take all of my clothes off—except my bra. I wonder why that is?"

Toni grinned as she removed Noel's blouse and pulled her against her chest. Moving side to side, she shivered. "I love the way your bra feels against my skin."

Pinching her cheeks, Noel said, "That's a very good line. The fact that my new bras give me some cleavage probably has nothing to do with it."

"I'm weak. I can't help but give in to my animal instincts. I'm crazy for breasts." She leaned over and put as much of Noel's breast into her mouth as she could, making a loud sucking sound when she pulled away. "It doesn't bother you does it?"

"As long as I turn you on, I've got nothing to complain about."

"Then you should never complain again because you make me crazy." She bent down and swept Noel off her feet, making her giggle. She deposited her onto the bed and removed her jeans and panties. "I've been thinking about you all week," she said, bracing herself above Noel. "Especially at night. I think about how you smell and how you taste." She let her eyes roll around in every direction. "Makes me nuts."

"And what do you do about that, you naughty girl?"

Toni chuckled and placed a quick kiss on Noel's lips. "Nothing. I start thinking about you then I fall asleep before I can do anything about it. I obviously bore myself. But I'm wide awake now, and ready for action."

⌒

They stayed in bed until eight o'clock the next morning, a rarity for both of them. After a light breakfast, they got into the shower together, managing to get clean as well as to create a bruise or two from the confined space. "Did they buy that tub at a doll house?" Toni asked. "I've installed a lot of tubs, and I've never seen one that small."

"I think the tub is original. People were obviously smaller in 1900." Noel slid past Toni and opened the door. "I'm gonna dry off here in the hall, or one of us is gonna wind up with a black eye."

"Let me." Toni put her hands on Noel's waist and maneuvered her back into the bath. "There's something I've always wanted to do." She was in too deep to back out now, but she felt like a fool. Noel was looking at her curiously, so she had to leap. "Would you mind if I blew your hair dry?"

Noel looked at her image in the mirror, and smiled. "I think it's adorable that you want to do that. Of course I don't mind."

Score! She was so happy she started to babble. "I never had the chance before, and I felt a little silly asking, to be honest. I'm crazy about your hair. It's one of my favorite things about you." She kissed the top of Noel's head, trying to slow down. Her attention was diverted and she cupped the breasts that once again captivated her. "I could lie and say it's a toss-up, but the breasts win. They always win." She lightly bit Noel's neck. "I'm an animal."

⌒

A half hour later, Noel tossed her hair, settling it against her shoulders. "Well, that was fun! But now I need to get in the shower again." She draped her arms around Toni's neck and kissed her tenderly. "If I'd met you when my hair was longer, we could have been in trouble."

"We're already in trouble. How long was it?" Toni asked, her eyes bright with interest.

"I'd better not tell you. I want to get out of here while the sun's still up."

⌒

The weather was hot and humid, fairly typical for Baltimore in early September. The principal at Noel's school was going to be in her office and Noel had arranged to bring Toni by to show off her classroom. Her school was just about a mile away, and they started off, walking along the very quiet residential streets.

Even though she enjoyed just being able to be with Toni, and she knew there were probably thousands of things Toni would rather do, Noel thought it was time to get a few things out in the open. "Do you mind talking about us?"

"I'd love to. I've been thinking a lot about us."

That was surprising, but good news. "Me too. I've been trying to think of ways we can stay close without driving ourselves and each other crazy, but it's not easy."

"That's about the same conclusion I've come to."

"Have you ever had sex with a friend?"

Toni smirked at her. "Versus an enemy?"

"No. You know what I mean. Have you had sex with someone where you tried to keep things casual? You know. Just sexual."

"Uhm…yeah. That's really not easy though. It's hard for both to be in the same space emotionally. I think it works best when you've had a little bit too much to drink and your friend starts looking surprisingly sexy." She shrugged, grinning. "It doesn't happen all that often."

"Hmm." Noel didn't speak for a few minutes, wondering if Heidi was one of the friends Toni turned to after she'd had a few too many. She conjured up a surprisingly lurid image of the two of them together and forced it out of her mind. "I told you I didn't have any great ideas."

"Why don't we just take things slow and see what happens? That's not ideal either, but I don't think I could be casual about you."

Noel grasped her hand and held it over her heart, smiling at her. "I don't think I could either, and the idea of saying goodbye is…" The mere thought made her ill .

"Hey," Toni said brightly. "I've got an idea. Let's not talk about us."

"Best idea you've had all day." She gave her an intentionally sexy look. "Well, the best idea was to dry my hair, but this is a close second." Everything was fine as long as they didn't talk too much. But how long could that last?

⌐

By the time they arrived at Noel's school, the principal was getting ready to leave, so they were only able to spend a few minutes. They toured Noel's classroom, and took a peek at the teachers' lounge. On the way home, Toni seemed contemplative. They had walked a long way when she said, "I assume most of the kids in your class are poor, right?"

"How did you guess?"

"Well, the building looks like it'll hold up against a storm, but that it'd rather not. And you only have two computers for your whole class. Yuppies would never stand for that. My eldest nephew just started first grade and his school is nicer and has more resources than my high school did."

"Yeah. One of the many challenges of urban teaching. I've been doing it long enough now that I don't have many illusions left. I try to give all of the kids the same level of attention, but I know I'm wasting my time on some of them."

"Even in third grade?"

"Sure. You can tell by pre-school. If the parents won't get involved, it's almost impossible for the kid. And every year I have a few. We've only been in session for a week, and I can already tell which ones they are."

"It's only been a week. Maybe the parents were really busy."

Noel smiled gently. "A good parent is never too busy to make sure that their child is clean. One little guy looks like something the cat drug in. One of the girls told me that no one wants to sit by him because he smells." She shrugged. "He does."

"What do you do?"

"You do what you can. You try to find out if he's getting fed and if there's any abuse in the home. But you have to be careful. Getting the state involved can make things worse." She reached over and took Toni's hand, and squeezed it. "This probably sounds callous, but over time you stop trying to fight losing battles. If I'm confident a kid is being harmed, I'm not afraid to get other people involved. I've had to do it several times. But sometimes you just have to feel bad for a kid and hope things change."

"It must be hard."

"It was harder at first. Much harder. Now I try to make the day as interesting and challenging as I can for every kid. But I can't take all of the sad cases home with me, and we don't have a system that you can rely on to take over for bad parents." She shivered visibly. "I can't imagine how much the government would screw it up if they had more power."

"But you still like it, even though it's frustrating."

Noel smiled, the satisfaction showing in her eyes. "I do. I'm certified to teach a higher grade, but I like sticking with primary school kids. Most of them aren't aware that poor people don't have a lot of value in our society."

"I couldn't do it," Toni sighed. "And not just because I'd want to take a lot of the kids home with me. I don't even like supervising adults. I've got a lot of patience, but not much at all for bureaucracy."

Noel patted her on the side. "Don't ever go near a public school."

They spent a couple of hours wandering along the streets between Noel's school and her home on Butcher's Hill. Noel's body tensed and she took a quick left turn just as Toni spotted a few young men riding low-slung bikes and going up to the cars that inched along. "Drug dealers?" Toni asked, peering down the street. "Right out in the open?"

"Depending on the time of day, yeah, they're very bold about it."

"Time of day? What's that got to do with it?"

"The police can't be everywhere, and the dealers have lots of scouts further up the street. I never see them in the morning, but they're out in force by noon."

"Isn't there a safer street to walk down?" Toni looked hesitantly back over her shoulder. "That makes me nervous."

"It won't last long. I'll call my neighborhood watch group and the police will roust them. Then they'll move a block or two away. It's a cat and mouse game."

"Maybe you should drive to work."

"Toni," Noel said gently, giving her a reassuring squeeze. "I'm alert and I try to stay out of trouble. But if there's trouble, a car wouldn't protect me much. It's better to be vigilant, and I am."

They continued to walk, with Noel noting that Toni had a death-grip on her hand. It wasn't verbal, but that small gesture showed her how much Toni cared about her safety. Maybe they could figure out a way to make all of their communication nonverbal. They turned onto a street full of small restaurants, a couple of jazz clubs, and a few shops filled with baby clothes and fashionable women's wear. "This is quite a change," Toni marveled. "Drug dealers on one street and women pushing six hundred dollar strollers on the next."

"That's Baltimore. Always a surprise."

They went to a café and ordered lunch. While they were waiting for their meals, Noel pulled out an envelope. "I can tell you're bothered by my neighborhood, but there's a benefit to living in the city."

"Besides ready access to crack?"

"Yep." She opened the envelope and pulled out two tickets. "The O's. Tonight."

Toni's eyes lit up as she took the tickets and gazed at them. "I've never had seats this good. Never."

"Andy got them for us. His company owns a box."

"Can I date Andy instead of you?" Toni asked, her eyes so fixed on the tickets that she didn't see the punch coming at her arm until it hit.

⌣

That night they went to a sports bar Noel often went to with her friends. It wasn't far from Camden Yards, and the place was jumping with Orioles fans having a meal before the game. The food was perfect for a hot summer night—juicy hamburgers and cold beer. They left in plenty of time to get to their seats and were both impressed with the tickets that Andy had been able to get for them.

"These seats are awesome," Toni said. "We usually decide to

come at the last minute, and get the dregs."

"I like coming nice and early."

"I do too. Every once in a while we luck out and get good seats. Then we come for batting practice."

"You said your brother got seats the last time you came. His name's Tracy, right?"

Toni laughed. "No, that's my sister. My brother is Terry."

"What's with the T's?"

"We haven't been able to get a good answer on that. I don't know if our parents didn't have a plan or if they're ashamed of it."

"It's kinda nice to have some uniformity. I know your sister works in fashion merchandising, but I forget where she lives."

"She and my brother both live around DC. He's a lobbyist for the pharmaceutical industry, but he never has any samples, so don't ask."

Noel flipped her hand in Toni's direction. "Alcohol is my only drug. Are your siblings as close to your parents as you are?"

Toni spent a moment hoping they wouldn't have to talk about this stuff once the game started. Then she wasted another few moments trying to categorize the various connections, wanting to be accurate. "Kinda, but in different ways. My brother and my mom are pretty close and my sister gets along equally well with both of them. Luckily, all three of us kids get along great." She didn't go into the way her father treated her brother. That would make both of them look bad. If Noel ever met them she could make up her own mind about whether her father disrespected Terry or if Terry intentionally tried to antagonize him.

"Don't take this the wrong way, but if I didn't know better, I'd think that your mom was dead."

Toni winced internally, wishing she'd hidden her real feelings better. She could go for years at a time in Rehoboth without mentioning her family. They were at the Yards, in fantastic seats!

Were they even going to get to watch the game when it started? She focused and tried to cut it short. "I can think of a lot of smart comebacks for that, but I won't use any of them."

"I don't mean anything bad by that. You just never talk about her."

Toni shrugged. "We don't do much together. I don't wish her ill or anything, but I don't think either of us would mind seeing the other less often."

"That must be terrible. When my mom and my sister and I get together, we act just like we're all buddies. My mom's a real hoot. I'm sorry you don't have that same kind of closeness."

"We were never close. I don't know if it's because I was a disappointment in some way or she just didn't like me, but she doesn't seem fond of me. She never has." She shrugged again, trying to keep her expression neutral. "It bothered me a lot when I was young, but I've gotten over it. I wish things were different, but they're not."

"That's very mature of you."

"Not really. It's self-protective. I'm pretty good at that." Being self-protective was a lot easier when someone wasn't trying to pull information out of you.

Noel put her hand on Toni's leg and brushed it across her soft skin. "You might be a little too good at that. I think you have to leave yourself exposed to be in a successful relationship."

"See?" Toni laughed. "That's why I haven't been in one before." She knew this wasn't something she was going to be able to brush off, so she faced the music. She took her eyes off the players warming up and focused her attention on Noel. "Is that something I should add to my New Year's resolution list?"

"Maybe you could try it now. It's quite a while until the New Year."

"I'll give that my full consideration as soon as I go get another beer. What can I get for you?"

"I'd love it if you'd get me a Boog's BBQ beef sandwich to go with a beer?" She batted her eyes fetchingly.

"I can't say no to such a pretty woman. Even though I've got to go all the way out to center field." She held out her palm and used the fingers of her other hand to show how far she had to walk. Then she grinned and planted a loud smooch on Noel's cheek.

As she walked up the stairs, Toni spent a few moments hoping Noel would stop with the questions. Things were what they were and talking about her mom and dad didn't make anything different. That was one benefit of sleeping with strangers. They didn't know if she was an orphan or one of twelve. A one-night stand appreciated the things she was good at, and didn't nose around sensitive areas. Emotional ones, at least. Of course, she'd never had a one-night stand touch her like Noel did. Or make her heart race the way it did when she saw her. Or weigh on her mind nearly every minute of every day. Why was this so damned hard? Shouldn't it be easy to be with someone you liked so much?

⌒

When Toni returned, she handed Noel her neatly wrapped sandwich along with a beer.

"Mmm...I love these sandwiches." Noel opened the foil wrapper and noticed a large bite missing. "This one's defective." She held it up in front of Toni's face. "Will you return it?"

"That's the delivery charge. I was tempted to get one for myself, but I thought there was a pretty good chance of exploding." She shifted her gaze and looked Noel up and down. "You must have a freakishly fast metabolism."

Noel took a bite of her sandwich and nodded. "I guess that's what it is. I've never been able to gain weight, but I'm not going to complain about it since no one in the world has any sympathy for me."

"Does it bother you?"

"Yeah. I know I'd look better if I could put on ten or fifteen pounds, but I can't manage to. It's okay now, since being thin is fashionable, but I hated it when I was in junior high and high school. I looked like one of the boys until I was seventeen."

"Max was kind of the same way. She was thin all over, except for the beer belly that we all teased her about."

"That's weird," Noel said. "After I left Janet, I was depressed and started eating nothing but junk. I was probably eating a thousand to two thousand extra calories a day and not exercising at all. After about a month my pants started to get tight and every ounce I gained was right in the center of my belly. I guess genetics always wins."

"You don't have an extra ounce on your belly now. How did you get rid of it?"

"I have no idea." She shrugged. "It just went away." She took another bite of her sandwich and smiled sheepishly.

"I promise I'll empathize with your inability to gain weight if you'll empathize with my ability to gain it as soon as I sit on my butt for a few days."

"Really?"

"Yep. I broke my hand a few years ago, and I gained five pounds in two weeks. That ticked me off because I didn't change my eating habits. Just not being active all day did it."

"I promise I'll empathize if the need ever arises, but don't go hurting yourself just to test me."

Toni shook her head quickly. "I'm not that competitive."

"Do you mind if I ask a question about your dad?"

"No. Just wait until we stand up for the National Anthem."

They stood and Noel sang along, sounding so sincere and

patriotic that Toni found herself singing along too. They sat back down and waited for the O's to take the field.

"You didn't answer my question," Noel said, tapping her on the leg.

Toni had hoped the sandwich and song would deter Noel from her investigative work. No luck. "What's the question?"

Noel looked slightly uncomfortable, but she pressed on, "Doesn't it bother your dad that your mom doesn't treat you very well?"

"I think it does," Toni said, thinking that was the proper response, even though she'd never considered it. "Maybe that's why he overcompensates," she ventured. She paused for a second to let the thought settle, and it seemed right. "He's always treated me like I'm just about perfect. My mom has always been on him about me being his obvious favorite."

"I meant…I thought that…he might do something a little more direct. Like intervene and tell your mom to knock it off."

Toni laughed and shook her head, finding the mere thought of that too funny for words. "That will never happen." She stood up and applauded with enthusiasm when the team took the field. Chills chased up her spine to be so close to the field. But when she sat back down Noel was looking at her with that keep-talking look she'd perfected. Toni reluctantly got back to work. "I love my dad to death, but my mom is the boss. In everything. I've never even heard them have a fight. When she says jump his only answer is, 'How high?'"

"That's…how does that…make you feel about him?"

Toni wanted to grind her teeth, but she knew Noel would see her and ask why the question made her so tense. Trying hard to sound casual she said, "That's my dad's thing. It's none of my business how he and my mom interact." She didn't add that she'd much, much rather be alone than have her partner ordering her around like a prison inmate.

⤳

On the way home, Toni was proud of herself and her team. The O's had kicked butt and she had learned how to keep Noel from probing too deeply. If Toni went on the offensive and asked question after question solely about baseball and the place it played in Noel's life, the evening passed like a lovely dream. She couldn't imagine having a better night with a better companion. This wasn't hard at all.

⤳

They'd been home about a half hour and Noel was resting her head on Toni's thigh. She was playing with her body, slowly teasing while they talked. "I think it's funny that I don't know your nieces and nephews names, but I know where every sensitive spot down here is."

Toni's lazy, soft voice floated down. "Why don't you prove it? I dare you."

"This little spot," she said, touching a place right next to her clitoris, "is sensitive, but it's not nearly as sensitive as it is on this side." She touched the other side and Toni flinched. "See?" She looked up, beaming.

"We have gone about this in a strange way. I feel like I know your body really well, too. But I don't know your brother's kids names. As a matter of fact, I don't know what your dad does for a living."

"He's retired. Or, I should say, semiretired. He was a stockbroker, and he still manages a few portfolios, but only from home. I don't know what your dad does, either."

"He's a carpenter."

"Cool. Just like you."

"I'm not a carpenter. I'm a plumber."

Noel's head lifted abruptly. "What? You do carpentry."

"I do a lot of stuff. But I'm trained as a plumber. I've got my union card in my wallet if you want to see."

"But why?"

"Why what?"

"I'm not sure," she said, laughing. "Something just doesn't seem right. Why don't you work full-time as a plumber? My dad always says plumbers are the best paid people in the country."

"He's wrong about that, but we make a decent living. I don't do it full time because I enjoy variety. Plus, it's very hard work. You spend a lot of time crawling under and into things, and a lot of the time you're lying on your back working on a pipe that's leaking right over your face."

"If not plumbing, what's your favorite thing to do?"

"I like to frame."

"That's carpentry. Why didn't you do what your dad does?"

"He encouraged me to go to trade school and I chose plumbing. I probably should've gone with electricity, but for reasons I don't remember, I chose plumbing. Being an electrician is usually a cleaner line of work than being a plumber, but I'm stuck now."

"Why didn't you go to school for carpentry?"

"Oh. That wasn't offered at the place I went. Just plumbing, HVAC and electric. In most areas carpentry isn't considered a trade. Don't know why, 'cause it's just as hard to master."

"So, why'd he want you to go to school at all?"

"I think his goal was to have me be expert at something he wasn't expert at so we could do projects together."

"Have you done that?"

"Oh, yeah. We've done a lot of things together. We're doing a media room for my brother over Christmas. But my dad's a foreman for a pretty big construction company, and he likes the job security, so we never started our own gig. He wouldn't be happy being a roustabout like I am."

"How did your mom feel about you going to trade school?"

"She was thrilled," Toni said, sarcasm dripping. "She didn't shed any tears when I moved to Rehoboth right after I finished trade school. I don't think she wanted people in our town to know I worked with my hands." She made an exaggerated licking action. "Or my mouth."

"I thought you were from Rehoboth."

"Nope. Lewes, where we catch the ferry to Jersey. It's close, but not too close."

"So she doesn't like your being a plumber or your being a lesbian."

"Correct on both counts. But I don't hide who I am. I would proudly display both my tool-belt and my lover anywhere in Lewes."

Noel gently pinched Toni's lips. "But you've never had a lover to take there."

"Maybe that will be yet another New Year's resolution." She decided she'd better start keeping a log, since those resolutions were piling up faster than she could keep track.

⌒

The next day they spent a long time looking at Noel's photo albums. After seeing dozens upon dozens of pictures of the happy, towheaded baby, Toni said, "I'm happy you got the parents you did."

"I am too." Noel spent a moment considering life as a child of a single parent who was away at sea for months at a time. Max probably would have stuck her with her parents out in Kansas or

Montana or wherever she was from. She felt an overwhelming sense of gratitude that things had worked out as they had. "My parents aren't perfect, but I wouldn't trade them for anything."

"How did they feel about you finding out about Max?"

"They were fine. I think they would've been okay if I'd decided to try to find her years ago, too, but that's a moot point now."

"They didn't encourage you to try to find her?"

"No, but that's not surprising. I don't think I'd urge my daughter to do that if I were in their position. If she wanted to find her birth mother, I'd support her, but I wouldn't bring it up. It's a very personal thing," she said thoughtfully. "April wanted to find her birth mother, but she's never been able to. My parents tried to help her, but they didn't get anywhere."

"Why do you think April wanted to know?"

"She's just generally curious. I don't think she had any deep dark psychological need to find her birth parents, but she was interested."

"How about your brother?"

"I think he's forgotten that he's adopted," Noel said, laughing. "I'm sure Andy has an interior life, but he doesn't share it."

"Are you guys much alike?"

"In some ways. As you can see from the pictures, we don't look too much alike, but I think we're about the same as most siblings. How about yours? Are you like them?"

"Not a whole lot. My brother has no mechanical skills whatsoever, and my sister likes guys." She made a funny face and Noel put her arms around her and kissed her.

"I'm very glad you like girls."

⌣

Toni spent the late afternoon dawdling, clearly trying to delay her departure. Noel answered the phone and told her brother she'd call him back later in the evening. After she hung up she said, "Oh, I forgot to tell you. Andy was talking to me about what I should do with the money I made this summer."

"Wow. He really is your financial advisor."

"No, silly. He was talking about my tax situation. After I've paid all of my expenses, I'm gonna clear about fifty thousand from the summer, and I don't want to have to pay tax on all of that. He suggested I reinvest some of it and I was thinking it might be a good idea to redo the bathroom between rooms C and D. What do you think?"

"If you have the money to spend, that's a good place to start. I've fixed the shower pan in there at least three times. It'd be much more watertight if you bought a one piece shower enclosure."

"Would you have time to do the work?"

"Of course." She made a lecherous-looking grin. "I'd give you a discount in exchange for services."

"No way. I want to pay you what anybody else would pay."

Toni didn't think that real girlfriends charged each other for favors. She did little jobs for Heidi and Jackie all the time. They never even offered to pay, and she would have been insulted if they had. Why would Noel want to pay? "When does your last guest leave?"

"Now it's the end of October. People keep trying to book. I could probably have left it open year-round, but Barbara is booked elsewhere for November and December, so that won't work."

"Max usually took January and February off, so people are used to coming down for a weekend in the fall. She got a lot of birders."

"Birders?"

"Yeah. Cape May and south is like Mecca for a lot of bird watchers."

"Who knew?"

Smiling, Toni said, "I did." She reached into her back pocket and took out her Blackberry. While making a note, she said, "Okay. I'll put you on my schedule for some time in November. We'll just have to talk about how much you want to spend and exactly what you want to do."

"Great. Andy will be thrilled."

"As long as Andy's happy, I'm happy."

⌒

Noel had parked Toni's bag in a closet by the bedroom. Toni went to get it when she was preparing to leave and noticed cartons of energy bars, fruit roll-ups, and other nutrient-rich food. Next to the cartons were packs of colorful T-shirts and white socks, all looking to be just the right size for a third-grader. She smiled and felt her heart clutch with emotion at the thought of Noel quietly making sure her students had the most basic of their physical needs met. The fact that she hadn't boasted about doing it made it all the more dear to Toni, and just made it that much harder to leave the woman she was growing more fond of day by day.

⌒

Noel walked Toni out to her truck and they spent a few minutes kissing, continuing the goodbye they thought they'd completed while they were in the apartment. "It's so hard to say goodbye to you," Noel whispered.

"It is." Toni's lips were pressed to Noel's neck, and she didn't seem to have any intention of removing them.

"Maybe we could see each other again…soon?"

"You could always come down and we could go shopping for

fixtures for the new bath."

Brightening, Noel said, "Excellent idea. Do you know your schedule?"

"I'm free next weekend." Toni stood up and wiggled her eyebrows playfully.

"I have plans, but I'm gonna cancel them. See you Friday." She gave Toni one last big kiss and practically skipped back to her apartment.

Part Eleven

*N*oel left Baltimore as soon as school was out the next Friday afternoon, so it was still early when she got to Rehoboth. Toni had waited to have dinner, and the two of them went to one of Noel's favorite restaurants. As they were leaving, they ran into Heidi, who was with a woman neither of them knew.

Heidi and Noel both acted a little skittish, but Toni was cool as always. Heidi said, "This is Angela. Angela, these are my friends Toni and Noel. I thought I said goodbye to you a couple of weeks ago," she said to Noel.

"Yeah, you did, but I've decided to do some work on one of the bathrooms. Toni and I are going to make plans this weekend."

"Oh," Heidi said, looking puzzled, but not asking any further questions. "Give me a call if you're bored."

"I will. It was nice to meet you, Angela."

As they walked away, Toni looked perturbed. "Why didn't you just say you were visiting me? I thought we'd kinda…settled this."

"We did." Noel winced, seeing a rare display of pique in Toni's expression. "I just thought you might not want everyone to know."

"Didn't we already have this conversation?" Toni scratched her head and her frown disappeared. Now she looked more perplexed than angry, and Noel felt her heart flutter at Toni's expression. She was so quick to forgive any transgression. What a wonderful trait that was.

"Yes, of course we did, but we didn't discuss how you'd feel about Heidi."

"Feel about Heidi what?"

Noel desperately wished she hadn't said anything, but she had, so she continued, "You and Heidi have a…history, right?"

"Uhm, yeah. I don't think you and I have ever discussed that, but I'm happy to if you're interested."

"I am. Let's go to your apartment."

⌒

They didn't speak on the way home, but Toni seemed perfectly at ease. Noel was a little anxious, mostly because there was part of her that was worried that Toni wouldn't want to give Heidi up. She'd known many people who had a lasting physical or emotional connection to a lover that seemed impervious to change, and she fervently hoped that wasn't how Toni and Heidi were.

It was a lovely evening, still warm but with a nice breeze. Noel borrowed one of Toni's sweatshirts, and they went outside with glasses of wine to sit in the rocking chairs.

When they were settled, Toni held Noel's hand. "I'm pretty sure we've never talked about my relationship with Heidi. How do you know about it?"

"You can chalk that up to my unerring tendency to spy on you when I don't mean to."

"Spy on me? How could you spy on me?" Toni turned halfway around in her chair to look at Noel.

"I saw you two about a month ago. I should've said something…" she trailed off, looking embarrassed.

Toni closed one eye and cocked her head. "I have no idea what you're talking about. What did you see us doing?"

"I saw you going out to dinner. You kissed her and she had her arm around you. It's okay," she said hurriedly. "I don't mind."

"You don't mind what? That I have dinner with people?"

"No," she said, shaking her head. "I don't mind if you see other people."

Toni's eyes popped open wide. "You don't? Are you seeing other people?"

"No, but I don't want to."

"I don't, either. How do you think we can consider having a relationship if we're dating other people? That's kinda screwed up, Noel."

"I just assumed that you had something special with Heidi."

"I do! But we haven't had sex since we broke up."

Amazed, Noel stuttered, "You haven't? But you treat each other like you're lovers. I noticed that the first day we met."

Toni's open expression closed down. Her tone was composed and careful when she said, "I don't treat Heidi that way. I'm careful not to."

Noel had no idea what type of land mine she'd stepped on, but it was a big one. Toni hadn't looked so emotionally impenetrable in weeks. She knew she'd really have to press to get anything else out of her, so she decided to move on.

"I'm really sorry. You just looked like you were going out on a date."

"If we were dressed up and going to The Seafarer, we were. It was her birthday. We always take each other out on our birthdays."

"God, I feel so stupid."

"There's no reason to feel stupid." She settled back into her chair and took Noel's hand. "It's not unbelievable to guess that Heidi and I were sleeping with each other. But don't assume things like that. If you want to know what's going on, I'll tell you." She turned her head, meeting Noel's eyes. "I don't play games. Honestly, that's one of the reasons I haven't been in many relationships. They're so complicated." She looked tired, and Noel wanted to kick herself for bringing the whole thing up.

"I'm very sorry. I just thought you might be like a lot of people I know who continue to have sex with ex-lovers."

Toni made a face, one that Noel had come to learn meant she was embarrassed about something. "I didn't say I've never done that, but I never have with Heidi."

"Wanna tell me about it? You kinda look like you want to."

She showed a reluctant smile. "I don't really, but I should. It's somebody you've gone out with."

"Roxy?"

"Yeah. It hasn't happened in a year or two, but every once in awhile the winter blues overcome us." She chuckled, looking embarrassed. "It's kind of funny. It's like two male dogs trying to mount each other."

Noel grinned. "One, that's kinda hot. And two, Roxy and I didn't actually go out. I made it clear that I just wanted to talk about making improvements on the house."

"Really?" Looking very pleased, Toni put her arm around Noel's shoulders and pulled her close. "That's interesting."

"Which part?"

"Both, really. But I'm curious about what seems hot."

Noel reached over and tickled her waist, making her giggle. "I should have known." She took a breath, thinking. "Well, you're both pretty butch, and I'd imagine you'd have kind of wild, aggressive sex."

Toni's dark eyes bore into Noel. "Would you like to have wild, aggressive sex?"

"I thought we had," she said tentatively. "Haven't we?"

Laughing, Toni said, "Every once in a while. Especially at first. We've been pretty...I'm not sure what we've been lately, but it feels different. When I've had sex with Roxy, it's like we're both trying to get what we want. It's much more selfish than sex is with you."

Noel's eyes were shining with interest. "I'd like to hear about you having aggressive sex. Can you tell me a sexy story?"

"Sure," Toni said, confidently. "Does it have to be completely factual?"

"Of course not. Just make it hot."

"No problem. No problem at all."

She turned her chair around so they were facing each other, then picked Noel's feet up and put them on her lap. Slipping Noel's sandals off she started to gently rub her feet, seemingly using the distraction to allow herself to think. "Okay, I remember the last time. We have a big party around Christmas. The town puts the Christmas tree up on the beach and most people go to watch. It's a lot of fun, and Roxy had some peppermint schnapps we kept sipping from. By the end of the evening we were both pretty gone."

"I haven't seen you drunk. Do you get funny or morose?"

"Neither. I get horny." She grinned, showing her teeth.

Noel tried to tickle her with her toes. "Maybe I have seen you drunk. I'm sure I've seen you horny."

"Funny, I don't remember hearing any complaints."

"You won't. Continue."

"Okay. So we were both a little looped and we went to Showtime. We were both looking for someone to hook up with, but the pickings were slim. It was getting late, and Roxy, who was standing behind me, put her hand up under my shirt and pinched my nipple. Hard."

Noel's feet rapidly tapped against Toni's chest. "I like this story already, and it's barely started."

Toni grinned and continued. "She pulled me against herself and took a nip out of my ear. She was still holding onto my nipple, and I started to twist away because it hurt. But she held on to me with her other arm and wouldn't let me go. She said, 'I'm gonna take you home and fuck you rough.'"

"Whew!"

"That's what I thought," Toni said, grinning slyly. "When she released the pressure off my nipple, I turned around and grabbed her by the hips. I kissed her hard, trying to show that she didn't control me. And I said, 'You're the one who's gonna be fucked. I'm gonna have you naked on the floor by the time we get past the front door.'"

"Good story. Good story!"

"We stayed there for a few more minutes kissing each other so hard and fast that we almost bruised our lips. We left and I tried to go towards my house, but she pulled me towards hers." She laughed, closing her eyes, either trying to remember or making up the details. "We must have been in front of that bar for three or four minutes tugging and pulling on each other. If the police had come by, they probably would've arrested us; for what, I'm not sure."

"Drunk and disorderly sounds like a pretty easy charge to make stick."

"Hey, this is supposed to be hot. Play along. So, jumping ahead, let's say that the cooler head prevailed and we went to her house. As soon as we got through the front door, we started grappling with each other again, while still kissing, of course. It took a while to even get our coats off, but once we did, things started to move pretty quickly. I grabbed her shirt and yanked it so hard that some of the buttons popped off. So she had to do the same thing to me. She's very competitive, you know."

"I don't want commentary. Just the facts."

Toni saluted, and kept going. "Our shirts were off, and then we started trying to get each other's bras off. As soon as we did that, we started to get hot."

Noel was bouncing around in her seat. "Me too!"

"We were kissing and sucking on each other's lips while we rubbed our breasts together. My nipples were so hard that they hurt, and every time Roxy's nipples rubbed against mine it sent a jolt of pain up my back. Good pain," she added. "The kind that gets you right here." She slid her hand down and patted between her legs.

"Damn, you're a good storyteller. You could be on NPR."

Ignoring the praise, Toni continued. "She tried to pull me into her bedroom, but I didn't want to wait that long. I put my arms around her and tried to bull rush her onto the sofa, but we didn't make it. We got our legs tangled and we slid off the sofa onto the floor." She closed her eyes for a moment, and Noel could just see her constructing the elements of her story. "She grabbed a remote control off her table and electronically turned on the fire in her gas fireplace."

Noel nodded, willing herself to believe everything she heard.

"Now we were in a hurry, and we both stripped out of our jeans and panties. Very sexy panties. Roxy has a great ass, you know. All those years of climbing up and down ladders does nice things for your butt."

Noel twirled her index fingers around each other to signal that Toni should continue.

"We were both on our knees, on her luxuriously thick rug, with the flames reflecting off our naked bodies."

"Good. Very good. More."

"We kissed each other hungrily for a long time. Roxy's hands were everywhere, grabbing my breasts and squeezing them hard. Then she tried to tumble me onto my side, but I got the upper hand. I pinned her, but she got her leg up between mine and threw me onto my side. She tried to get me onto my back, but I wouldn't give in. We wrestled, sweat glistening off our bare skin. It took all of my strength, but I got her where I wanted her. Flat on her back in front of the fire. She was trying to wrench away from me, but I got my hands on her shoulders and held her there while I kissed her possessively. She realized that I could overpower her and she slowly gave in. She begged me to let her taste me, so I slowly crawled up her body and settled myself over her mouth."

"That does it for me." Noel tossed her feet off Toni's lap, stood up, and extended a hand. "I willingly admit that you overpower me. Now let's pick up right where your story left off."

"Another fine idea. You have millions of 'em."

On Sunday afternoon, Toni and Noel stood in the street in front of Toni's house. Each had her hands clasped behind the other's back, loosely holding each other. "How can this be so hard?" Toni asked.

"I don't know, but it sure is." Noel put her head on Toni's shoulder, trying to touch as much of her as she could. "It seems like I just got here."

"I know. I had all of these ideas about things we could do, but we didn't get to any of them."

Noel chuckled softly, and Toni felt the rumbling through her own body. "I think we got to one of them."

"Yeah," Toni agreed, laughing along with Noel. "We got to an important one." She turned her head just enough to be able to kiss Noel's cheek. "You might not believe this, but I've never been this sexually…focused…or whatever it is I am. I always thought it was a joke when people said women didn't reach their sexual maturity until middle-age, but I'm feeling a heck of a lot better about turning forty since I'm living proof that it's true."

Noel leaned back and looked into her dark eyes. "Is that true?"

"Yep. Hard to believe it, but I'm going to be forty."

Kissing her quickly, Noel said, "You're a silly one. You know what I meant."

"I don't know if I'm truly hitting my sexual peak or if there's some other mysterious force that's making me horny all the time." She made her eyes as wide as she could. "Maybe I've been abducted by aliens."

Noel smiled, feeling like she could stand right there in the street for the rest of the day and just chat. "Did they insert probes into all of your orifices?"

"Not all of them," Toni said, grinning evilly, "but I think they're working their way up to it."

"I don't attribute my rampaging lust to anything but you." She poked her finger into Toni's chest. "You're very, very good with your hands. And your mouth. And your…everything." She smiled, lost in Toni's expressive eyes. "You're fantastic."

"To be honest," Toni said, lowering her voice as if telling a secret. "I think you have a little something to do with my libido too."

"Both of our libidos stopped us from doing any planning on my new bathroom."

Toni snapped her fingers. "I knew there was something I was forgetting. I should've written it down."

"If you hadn't written it on my body, you wouldn't have seen it." Noel put her arms around Toni's neck and pulled her close to kiss her properly. "We'll just have to get to that another day."

"Next weekend?" Toni asked, looking like she was desperately hoping to receive a "yes." "Even though I'm on call and might have to run out in the middle of the night?"

Noel couldn't refuse. "Yes. Next weekend is perfect."

On Thursday evening Toni sat at the bar, rather glumly staring into her beer. It was just seven o'clock, and there were only four other people in the place. She'd stopped by on her way home, feeling like she needed a little company.

Jackie noticed she didn't seem her usual chipper self and made her way over to the end of the bar to talk. "What's going on? Are you working too hard?"

"I'm working hard, but not too hard. But I have to admit that it's harder to supervise people than it is to do the work yourself." She pointed at her head. "It's harder up here. I'm not able to leave my worries at work like I can when I'm just doing a solo project for a homeowner."

Jackie nodded. "That makes sense, but you look like something else is bothering you."

"No," Toni said immediately. "I'm fine."

Testing a theory, Jackie said, "Somebody said they saw Noel here last weekend."

Toni looked up warily, mumbling, "Mmm."

"Are you keeping in touch with her?"

Doling out her words as though they were thousand dollar bills, Toni said, "Yeah."

"I really like her. She's awfully easy on the eyes, too."

Unguardedly, Toni sighed and said, "She sure is."

⌒

The next night Toni was waiting with dinner when Noel knocked on the front door. It was almost the end of September, but the weather was still nice and she had barbecued, knowing how much Noel liked her food cooked outdoors.

They'd barely gotten the kitchen cleaned up after dinner when Noel tried to maneuver Toni into the bedroom. Uncharacteristically,

Toni deferred the invitation and went back into the living room.

Noel sat next to her on the couch and put her arm around her shoulders. "What's up? You seem like something's on your mind?"

"Nothing big," she said. Noel's ability to read her moods was beginning to get annoying, but Toni felt a little of the pressure release when Noel pulled away and leaned against the opposite arm of the sofa.

"Tell me about the little thing that's on your mind. If something is bothering you, I'm interested."

"Really?" All of the possible ways Noel could shut her down flooded her mind. She wanted to start over and try harder to act like everything was fine.

Noel scooted back across the couch and sat right next to her. Toni felt boxed in again, as though Noel was cutting a hole in her head to see inside. "Absolutely. I'm remarkably interested in everything about you."

"Other than sex?" Her eyes darted toward Noel once again, trying to see if she was sincere.

"Of course!"

"Then why don't you ever call me?" She knew she was pouting, but she couldn't help it.

"Call you?"

Toni stood up and went into the kitchen to get a glass of water. She threw ice cubes into her glass, using more force than she needed. "Forget it." She castigated herself for bringing it up. No good ever came of talking about hurt feelings.

Noel got up and went into the kitchen, cornering her. "Stand still and tell me exactly what's bothering you. I want to know."

Toni's eyes darted from side to side, and she bit her lip for a second. She was so stupid about things! How did she get to be forty years old and know so little? "I don't know how this is supposed to go."

"How what is supposed to go?"

"This dating thing." She flipped her hands around, angry with herself for being so inarticulate, and angry at Noel for her persistence. But it was too late to back out now, and she was too irritated to drop it. "Is it just about having sex?"

"No! Of course not." Noel put her arms around Toni and held on even when she felt some resistance. "But when you first start dating, you're crazy for sex. In my experience that doesn't last that long, so I've been taking every opportunity that's been presented." She kissed Toni gently on the forehead. "Dating is about a whole lot more than sex. It's about getting to know one another."

Shyly, Toni looked up through her dark lashes. "Wouldn't it help if we talked to each other more often?"

"It would. I just assumed you were busy during the week." She kissed each shuttered eye. "Plus, I didn't want to smother you. I know you like your independence."

"I do. But I have plenty of it. I'm not asking you to fill up my nights or anything. Just a chat when something comes up."

"Things come up every single day that I want to talk to you about. I keep telling myself that I have to remember to tell you about this or that. From here on out, I'll just call you. Is that okay?"

"That'd be nice."

"But you have to do something for me." She held Toni's chin between her fingers. "When something starts to bother you, let me know. We can work anything out. Anything," she said fervently.

"Really?" She felt as though she would cry, but valiantly forced the feeling away.

"Anything," Noel repeated. "If we want this to work; it will." Immediately, Toni felt like a fog had lifted. She felt lighter and a surge of energy flowed through her. She kissed Noel with the thrumming passion that she usually displayed, and seconds later she was carrying her to bed.

Noel woke the next morning and stretched her arms out, disappointed when they weren't met by the softness of Toni's skin. She sat up, looking around the room confusedly. She didn't hear a sound, so she got up and put on Toni's shirt from the night before, knowing that the larger size would cover her better. The living room was empty, but the back door was open. Noel stood in the doorway and saw Toni sitting at the outdoor table, several stacks of paper piled in front of her. "Why aren't you in bed?" she asked.

Toni turned and squinted to be able to see her. Her smile was bright and happy. "I love summer."

"Summer?"

"Yeah. Only in the summer would a fantastic looking woman come to my back door wearing my shirt. It's particularly nice if that woman looks like she's been fully satisfied in the not too distant past."

"Oh, I'm satisfied," she said, her voice low and sexy. "How about you?"

"I could barely be more satisfied. But that's no reason not to keep trying."

"Then get in here. I can give you another tumble."

Toni looked longingly at Noel, then took a quick glance at the papers in front of her. "Why don't you take a shower and have some coffee. I went out and bought some fresh muffins this morning. They're right in the warming drawer. By the time you've had your breakfast I should be able to stop."

Noel scanned the property line just to make sure no one could see her. She went out and put her hands on Toni's shoulders and rubbed them gently. "Do you need to work?"

"There are few things I have to do."

"And a few more you'd like to do?"

With a guilty grin, Toni nodded. "If I can get a little bit ahead on the weekend, I feel much more in control."

"Then do that. I have plenty of things to keep me busy." She kissed the top of her head and rubbed her lips across thick hair. "As long as you save time to give it to me good sometime today, I'm happy."

Toni turned her head and looked up at Noel. "I really like dating you."

"I really like being dated. Now get back to work and call me when you're done. I'll go check up on The Sandpiper and maybe I'll try to find Heidi."

Toni turned all the way around and pulled Noel over so she stood between her knees. "I haven't told her we're dating."

"Why?"

"No good reason. We haven't been alone together since you and I decided we were dating, and I didn't want to make an announcement at Jackie's. She's probably going to wonder why you're in town again, so be prepared."

"Do you not want me to…"

"No, not at all. Feel free to talk to her or anybody else in town about us."

"Are you sure?"

"Positive. I just have to be prepared for all of the jealous looks I'm gonna get."

Noel kissed her and pinched her nose. "I think that might go in the other direction. We'll just have to see."

⌒

Heidi was working in her office and agreed to meet Noel for lunch. Noel spent the rest of the morning over at The Sandpiper, chatting with Barbara and carefully measuring the bathroom she wanted to redo. She was so intent on sketching out the room properly that she was almost late for lunch, but she walked quickly and met Heidi just as she was coming up the street.

"Are you sure you haven't moved here?" Heidi asked, kissing her cheek and hugging her.

"No, I haven't. But you have to admit Rehoboth is a nice place to spend an Indian summer weekend."

"I haven't spent much time in Baltimore, so I'll take your word for it. Did you have to kick Barbara out of your apartment?"

Noel wasn't expecting the question, and it took her an embarrassingly long time to answer. "No, I didn't," she finally said, knowing that her cheeks were beginning to color. "I'm famished. How about you?"

"I got up late and only had breakfast an hour ago. I'm just going to get something to drink."

"You should've told me. I could've just stopped by your office to say hello."

"Don't be silly. I wanted to see you."

They walked into the diner and were shown to a booth. Noel knew exactly what she wanted, and when their waitress walked away, she started to feel a little nervous. Deciding it was best to just get on with it, she said, "I don't see myself moving here, but I have been dating someone."

Heidi looked very surprised. "From here?"

"Yeah. Toni and I have started dating."

There was a pregnant pause, then Heidi started laughing. "That's a good one." When Noel didn't laugh, Heidi stopped abruptly. "You can't be serious."

Feeling more uneasy by the second, Noel said, "Why is that so impossible to believe?"

"You mean you and Toni are having sex, right?"

"No. I mean that we're dating."

"What do you mean by that?"

Frustrated, Noel said, "Is it just in Delaware that people don't know what dating means? Toni keeps asking me to define the rules."

Heidi's expression was full of concern. "Don't be offended, but if you're looking for monogamy, you'd better keep looking."

Noel leaned back and stared at Heidi, stunned. "I thought you were her friend."

"I am. But I was her lover too. I know you had a bad breakup, and I'd hate for you to have another one."

"We're just dating, but she's the one who insisted she didn't want to see anyone else."

"Toni has a good heart, and the best of intentions. But don't expect her to be monogamous. It's just not in her nature."

"You're saying she cheated on you?"

Heidi clasped her hands together and spent a moment staring down at the table. When she looked up, there was pain in her eyes. "She broke my heart."

Noel's blood ran cold from all-too-fresh memories of Janet's betrayal. Her heart went out to any woman who'd been cheated on—but to hear Toni was the same kind of vermin... She had to force herself to ask the question that could change everything. "What happened?"

"It's just what I said. Toni's not able to be faithful. She wants to be, and she feels horrible when she cheats, but..." The tears that welled up in her eyes clutched sympathetically at Noel's heart. "She needs her freedom." Heidi seemed irritated with herself for crying, and she quickly used her napkin to dry her eyes. "I feel sorry for her in a way. She wants to have the benefits of a relationship, but she just can't follow through." Heidi shook her head, looking frustrated. "I can't say I wasn't warned, but I believed she wanted to be faithful."

She sighed. "Now I worry about her growing old all alone."

"People can change, Heidi."

The look Heidi gave Noel was full of certainty. "No, they can't. They can try. God knows that Toni tried, but eventually her true nature came out. And Toni's true nature is…" She drifted off, seemingly unwilling to apply a label.

"What? She's naturally a heart-breaker?"

"No, that's not it. Toni's one of the kindest people I know. I swear that," she said, her voice growing stronger and more emphatic. "She doesn't want to hurt anyone. She just can't control her wandering eye." She took Noel's hand and squeezed it gently. "Don't get too invested. She's a wonderful friend but a truly awful girlfriend."

Reflectively, Noel said, "That's what she told me not long after we met. She said her ex-lovers would agree that she sucks at being in a relationship."

"She does. She doesn't want to…but she does."

⌒

Noel was unsettled and cranky when she and Heidi parted. She walked around town for a while, hoping the strong ocean breeze would clear her mind. But the brisk wind couldn't erase her troubled thoughts. What was she missing? Toni seemed so honest, so honorable. But she did have a hell of a hard time expressing her feelings. Not only that, but Noel often had to force her to think about emotional topics. Maybe she couldn't, or wouldn't stop herself when she was attracted to a new woman. It was entirely possible that she'd tamped down her feelings so well that she didn't realize when she was getting bored. Then, when a pretty face blew into town she was caught unawares when she found herself straying. What else made sense?

She knew Toni thought the world of Heidi. To cheat on her,

when she had so much invested, when everyone in town would know about it… There must be some illogical explanation, since the logical ones didn't work.

Whether by unconscious design or happenstance, she found herself by the bookstore where Gloria worked, and she poked her head in to see her friend behind the counter.

"Well, hello, stranger!" Gloria said when she saw her. "What good wind blew you into town?"

Noel hugged her and leaned against the counter. "Full disclosure?" she asked shyly.

"Sure. Although I can't imagine any reason you'd want to hide."

"I might have one," Noel said. She spent a few seconds thinking of how she'd say it, but then just blurted out, "I'm involved with Toni Hooper."

Gloria's eyebrows shot up, and she looked as though she were truly shocked. "Well, that might just be something you want to hide."

Noel slapped her hand onto the wooden counter, making the lone customer snap her head in the direction of the sharp sound. "Sorry," she said to the woman. She rolled her eyes when she turned back to Gloria. "Has she cheated on every woman in town? Have I picked the woman with the worst reputation in Delaware to fall for?"

Gloria put her arm around Noel's shoulders and hugged her. "It's not that," she said, rubbing her shoulder. "It's not that her reputation is bad. In fact, it's fantastic. Everyone loves Toni."

"She's just a slut," Noel groused.

"That seems harsh, but it's common knowledge that she likes to play the field. I personally don't think it's fair to call her names when the same behavior would win her accolades if she were a man."

"Just don't try to form a real relationship with her. Is that the word on the street?"

"Well, yes, that's what I've heard."

"From Max?"

"No, but…" She looked like she didn't want to continue, but she did. "It's common knowledge. Toni and her friend Roxy are well known for their competition to be the most popular woman in town."

The customer departed, leaving Gloria and Noel alone. "What did Maxine think about her?"

"Mmm." A half smile curled the corners of her mouth. "Ahh, Max. She was as proud of Toni as if she was her…" She trailed off, and her cheeks grew pink. "Well, that was a ridiculously insensitive thing to say."

"It's fine. Really, it is. People expect me to be more tied to Max, but it's like finding out you had a twin who died at birth. It's interesting, but it doesn't affect my life very much. So tell me more about how she treated Toni. That I find interesting."

"Okay." She drew in a breath. "She acted like Toni was her… son." When Noel's eyes bugged out she said, "I know it sounds silly, but that's what it felt like to me. Max acted like a proud father when she talked about Toni. And one of the things she enjoyed was boasting about her success with the women in town." Noel was looking at her as if she were delusional, making Gloria say, "I know it doesn't make sense, and maybe I read it wrong, but that's how it felt to me. Max was a salty dog, Noel. She was an old-school sailor and being in the Navy for twenty-five years made her a pretty tough old bird. If I saw her on a Saturday night, she'd say, 'I bet Toni's got some pretty girl talked out of her jeans about now' or something equally colorful." She shrugged her shoulders, as though at a loss for a better explanation. "She was proud of that."

"Do you think Toni behaved that way to please her?"

Gloria smiled. "That seems a little unlikely. I think Toni's just a charmer. Women have been chasing after her since I've known her, and that's been fifteen years."

Noel draped herself across the counter, looking like she didn't have the energy to stand. "So I'm just another tourist who can't resist the local tramp, huh?"

"Toni's not a tramp. She's not," Gloria said emphatically.

"She just cheats."

Gloria shook her head roughly. "No, not true. From everything I know about her, she's a woman of her word."

Noel stared at her. She wanted to ask about Heidi, but didn't want to put the thought into Gloria's head if it wasn't there already. "You really don't know of her breaking any hearts?"

"No, I don't. That doesn't mean she hasn't, but Max never mentioned anything like that. Has she made any promises?"

"Well, not in so many words, but she did say she didn't want to date anyone else."

"Great! I can't imagine her lying about that. I really can't."

"But she might not be able to stay faithful," Noel said, her lower lip stuck out.

"That's potentially true for everyone, isn't it? I'd bet money on Toni being faithful, or telling you if she wasn't able to be."

"Super. So I try to hold onto her while trying not to get so invested that she breaks my heart in the end."

"Again, how's that different from any new relationship? You never know if it'll work out until you give it an honest try."

"But will she be honest?"

"You can't know that about anyone. She might not be able to make a go of being in a relationship, but I'd be amazed to hear that she lied to you. I just can't see that. Toni is honest and very forthright. I can't say enough good things about her character."

"Or her wandering eye."

"Maybe she never had anyone she wanted her eye to settle on."

She gave Noel another hug and a quick kiss on the cheek. "She's not as smart as I think she is if she doesn't recognize what a catch you are."

⌒

When Noel walked into Toni's house, she was met by a naked, grinning woman—fresh from the shower. "Oh, I was hoping you'd be home soon. I was lonely." Toni embraced Noel, enveloping her in her warm body. "I missed you."

Noel turned her head to be able to look into her eyes. "Did you?"

Solemnly, Toni's head nodded. "Very much. I want to spend every minute I can with you."

"Really?"

Why did Noel seem so suspicious? That was weird. Toni thought she'd be pleased to have her tell her how much she missed her. She'd better show her. "Yeah. Every minute." She tipped Noel's head back and kissed her tenderly. "Every minute."

⌒

After Noel left Rehoboth on Sunday afternoon, she spent the first few miles of her drive thinking about Toni. She hated that the enigmatic woman had her so spellbound, but she felt powerless to fight against the pull. Deciding to follow her own advice about calling when she thought of her, she dialed her phone. "Hi," she said when Toni answered. "I know I said this already, but I wanted to say it again. I had a very good time this weekend."

"Me, too. I'm glad you called. I was sitting here on the couch trying to think of what to do with myself." She laughed, the low sexy laugh that Noel had come to need like a drug. "I know one thing I won't be doing with myself for a few days."

"That goes double for me. Besides, having sex alone doesn't have much interest for me anymore. It's kind of like when I used to make a nice dinner for myself. It's just a heck of a lot more fun when you share it."

"It is. A whole lot more fun."

"I loved looking at your photo albums. Make sure you bring some more back from your parents' house. I want to see everything you have."

"I will. Maybe I'll go over there tonight. My dad's working on a car I'll probably wind up driving."

"That'd be fun. Why don't you do that?"

"Mostly because I'm lazy. He always wants me to get under the car and then get up and run to get him a tool that he forgot. He treats me just like he did when I was twelve years old, but I'm getting a little creaky."

"You didn't seem very creaky this weekend. At one point you were in a position that I couldn't quite figure out how you got into. Have you been taking yoga?"

"Not hardly." She laughed. "You just get me so worked up that I find myself twisted like a pretzel. It takes every bit of my work ethic to get my butt out of bed on Monday morning. That's when I really feel it."

Noel's voice was soft and wistful when she said, "I wake up on Monday morning and I reach for you. It's always a huge disappointment when you're not there."

Toni sighed heavily. "It's so nice sleeping with you. I'm sorry we didn't start that earlier in the summer."

"I am too, but we're doing it now. That's what matters."

"Yeah, I guess." Toni was quiet for a second, then said, "You're sure we can work everything out?"

"If both of us want to be together, we can definitely do it."

"I want to be with you, Noel. I really do. But you're awfully far away."

The words struck Noel like a blow. "Yeah, I am. But you're just as far from me as I am from you."

Toni didn't answer for a bit. When she did, she sounded puzzled. "Yeah, I suppose that's true. But that doesn't make it any easier."

"We'll both have to make sacrifices to have a relationship. It's never easy."

"No, I guess it's not." Her voice sounded small and unsure. "But the work week seems awfully long."

"I know. I really do. We'll have to hang in there and see if this can work."

"You just said it could!"

"It can. I'm saying that every relationship goes through different stages. Right now we're in the I've-gotta-have-you period. We'll probably need our space again when this is over, then we'll see if seeing each other on the weekends is enough."

"How long does this last? 'Cause even though it drives me nuts, I'm wild for it."

"Well, I've been in three relationships, and I've seriously dated... maybe three or four others. It's been different with each of them, but I think the frantic part only lasts a month, maybe two."

"We've been in the frantic part longer than that."

"Yeah, I guess we have." They were both silent for a minute, then Noel added, "But we've only technically been dating for a few weeks. Before that we were just having sex, right?"

"Yeah, I guess. I've told you I don't know a lot about this stuff. The rules are pretty confusing."

"That's the good thing about being adults. We can make our own rules."

"I always like that," Toni decided.

"One of my rules is being honest. I'm not going to date anyone else while we're together."

There was a long silence. Noel was about to ask if Toni had heard her when she heard a quiet response. "I thought we'd already agreed to that."

"We have. I was only trying to make it clear how important it is to me to know that you'll be honest with me."

"Isn't that important to everyone?"

Noel didn't have a reply to that. She felt like they weren't quite on the same wavelength, so she switched topics. "Before I forget, one of the reasons I called was to tell you that I had the brilliant idea of going to a home improvement store in Baltimore. You and I can't seem to get our act together to pick out things for that bathroom."

"I don't know about that. We worked pretty darned well together this weekend. I think we make a good team."

"Too bad we can't compete in the Olympics. We'd medal for sure. Now tell me what to look for when I go to the store."

～

Three hours later Noel pulled into her parking spot. "Okay," she said. "My battery's almost dead, but I'm home. Are you sure you want me to call you every time I think of something to say?"

"Well, maybe not every time," Toni teased. "Just when it's important."

"How do I know when it's important?"

"If you think it's important, I think it's important." Toni hoped she'd been clear enough. It was so hard to tell!

～

Noel had barely put her bag down before she started dialing

April's number. When her sister answered, she said, "Okay. You've got to give me a sane perspective. Toni's driving me nuts. Completely nuts."

"Hello, Noel. I'm fine. Thanks for asking."

"Oh, you know I care about you. I'm just so fixated on that woman that I should be ashamed of myself."

"Tell me what happened."

"Toni was wonderful this weekend. She was sweet and loving and kinda vulnerable. Really adorable."

"Trade ya."

Noel emerged from her fog to laugh at her sister's comment. Her voice was softer and more thoughtful when she said, "When we're together, everything is great. Really awesome. But I'm going crazy trying to figure out if she just has a bad reputation or if she's a cad."

"Why do you think she's a cad? Can women be cads?"

"Yes, they can. I think a cad is someone who hurts people without meaning to. And Heidi, her friend and ex-lover, made it clear that Toni has a history of doing just that."

"Eww. That's not good news. Do you think she's just got an ax to grind, or can you trust her judgment?"

"I think I can trust her. She loves Toni, and they've stayed very close. But she claims that Toni's incapable of being in a committed relationship."

"I don't know. That sounds like sour grapes to me."

Noel thought of that possibility for a moment. "Yeah, it could be, but Heidi's very close to Toni. Actually, she knows her history so well I'm surprised she got involved with her."

"It must be those eyes," April posited. "When she looks at you, it feels like there's no one in the world she'd rather be talking to."

Noel sighed heavily. "You should see them when she's making love to you. I swear I've never felt prettier or sexier than when I'm with her. She looks at me like I'm…magic."

"Damn, Noel, don't get all worked up about what other people say. You can only judge her based on your own feelings. And if she makes you feel like that, just go with it."

"I have to," she said softly. "I can't pull away now. She might break my heart, but I can't resist her."

Part Twelve

A few nights later Toni was sitting at Jackie's, enjoying her nightly beer. Her spirits were high, and she spent a while speaking to almost everyone in the bar, which was, at this time of year, populated exclusively by locals. She saw Heidi come in and made her way over to sit next to her at the bar. "Hi. What have you been up to? I haven't seen you in a while."

Heidi took a sip of her drink and replaced it carefully on the coaster. She seemed to consider her answer equally carefully before she replied. "You remember that woman you saw me with a few weeks ago? I've been seeing her. She lives in Jersey, and I've been going over there a lot."

Toni's face lit up. Having Heidi in a relationship would make everything so much easier. "Very cool! But why are you going over there instead of sharing the trip?"

"She has a son who's still in high school, so it's harder for her to get away."

Toni nodded. "Got it. That makes sense. I hope it works out if you like her."

"I wouldn't go out with her if I didn't," Heidi said, a bit of an edge to her voice.

"Well, no, I guess you wouldn't." Toni did what she often did when engaged in a conversation that made her uncomfortable—

she shifted her eyes away from Heidi and tried to look as though nothing untoward had occurred.

Heidi put her hand on Toni's back and scratched it through the jacket, an old habit. When Heidi touched her, that was the same as an apology, one Toni always accepted without comment. "I was a little surprised to hear that you and Noel are…what is going on with you two?"

"We're dating." Toni shrugged her shoulders, not sure what else to add.

"What does that mean for you?"

Slightly annoyed, Toni said, "I think it means what it does to most people. We're going out with each other. We're involved."

"Noel seemed a little vague on the terminology, too. You're not being exclusive are you?"

Now a small furrow had formed between Toni's eyebrows. "Yeah, we are." She didn't say anything else, but she let her irritation show.

"I'm not judging you, Toni." Heidi put her arm around her shoulder and tried to pull her into a hug, but Toni didn't yield. "Come on, now. Don't be mad. You've got to admit it's been a while since you've tried to be monogamous."

Roxy had come in a minute earlier, and she'd heard the last few sentences. "Who's trying to be monogamous? Hooper?" She signaled to Jackie who brought her a beer. "Jackie, did you know about this?"

"I don't know nothin'. Never have, never will." She wore a small smirk which all involved recognized as an acknowledgment that she had known everything that was being discussed.

Roxy stood between Toni and Heidi and put an arm around each of them. "Tell me more."

"I'm going out with Noel Carpenter. I'm not sure if that's the most interesting news story of the day, but there you have it."

Roxy slugged her friend in the shoulder making Toni wince. "You dog, you. Were you boning her this summer when I asked her out?"

Toni gave her a withering look. "I don't have a bone."

"You know what I mean."

Toni took a breath, appearing to compose her thoughts. "It was just a few weeks ago that we decided to start dating. It was right before Noel left."

"You're still a dog. You probably weren't even interested in her until I acted like I was."

Shrugging, Toni said, "I don't think that's the way it played out, but I'm not good with dates."

"I know!" Roxy laughed. "Heidi and I both know Noel's gonna have her hands full trying to date you."

"Thanks for the vote of confidence guys. It's nice to know you can count on your friends."

"We are your friends," Heidi said gripping Toni's arm and squeezing it. "And we know how much you hate to hurt people. I just want to make sure you're not trying to make Noel into a Max substitute, because that would break her heart."

Toni noisily slammed her beer down onto the bar making a dozen heads turn in her direction. "What? I can't have heard you right."

"Don't get all excited. It just seems like a major coincidence that you're suddenly interested in seriously dating Max's long-lost daughter."

It was almost possible to see steam coming from Toni's ears. "I might not be the deepest person you know, but I'm not completely clueless. I wasn't sexually attracted to Max, but I am to Noel. A lot," she added vehemently. "This isn't my mind playing tricks on me. When I think of her my mouth waters. Hell, I don't think of anything else! She's on my mind all god-damned day!" She gulped down the remainder of her beer, then quietly placed the bottle on the bar and strode out.

"Whoa," Roxy said, her eyes wide. "I haven't seen Toni that mad in a long time." She sat down next to Heidi. "Knowing her, you hit a nerve she didn't want to have hit."

"That's what I'm worried about. I don't think she knows why she's so attracted to Noel. I just hope she doesn't get too hurt in the process of finding out."

Toni had only been home a few minutes when she called Heidi's home number and left a message. "Hi, it's Toni. I want to apologize for losing my temper tonight. I actually appreciate that you care about Noel. I just want you to know that I do too, and I wouldn't try to use her. See you." She hung up and paced around her apartment for a few minutes, trying to decide whether or not to call Noel. She finally decided that doing that would only make her feel worse. Noel would make her dig up all kinds of things she didn't like to talk about, especially about Heidi. Noel would never understand the unspoken rules she and Heidi had, and Toni wasn't able to explain them even if she'd wanted to. Which she didn't. The best idea was to forget the whole thing. So she walked over to the fire station to spend an hour or so with whoever was on duty. None of the other firefighters ever wanted to talk about anything more complex than sports, and that was about all she was up to.

A couple of hours later, Toni was walking home when her cell phone rang. She found herself smiling at the simple fact that Noel's name was on the screen. "Hi," she said. "It's nice to hear your voice."

"I'm getting ready for bed and haven't talked to you all day. I couldn't let a day pass without at least a goodnight kiss."

"That's pretty romantic," Toni said, chuckling softly. "Next thing I know you're going to be writing sonnets."

"If I knew how, I'd write them about you. What have you been up to?"

"Same old stuff. I'm just walking home from the firehouse now. How about you?"

"Nothing unusual. I spent the evening grading papers. I always spend a lot of time early in the year trying to find some germ of promise to pin my hopes on." She laughed, but it didn't sound like she found the situation particularly funny. "So far my environment is pretty germ free, but I'm not gonna give up so easily."

"That's one of the things I most…respect about you. I appreciate how much you care for your students."

"I do, but I think I care about you more. I assume you weren't able to trade days off with anyone or you would've mentioned it by now."

"No, I didn't have any luck. I assume your brother-in-law is still insisting on having his birthday on Saturday."

"Yeah, he's hardheaded that way. I'm very tempted to skip the party and come see you. Would that make me a bad sister-in-law?"

"You could be a lot worse, but you should probably stay home. He did buy you a nice arbor this year."

"He sure did. I just wish I were sitting under it with you."

"That makes two of us. Well, I'm home now and I think I'll get ready for bed."

"Okay. Sleep tight."

"I will. Thanks for calling, Noel."

Toni hung up and put her phone down on the table. She was

feeling edgy and guessed that she'd have a hard time sleeping even though she was tired. On her way to the bedroom, she saw the message light on her home phone flashing. She hit the button and heard Heidi's voice, sounding contrite. "How about having dinner with an old friend who owes you an apology. I'm really very sorry for what I said tonight. I know you're not the type to hold a grudge, but I want to make sure you know that I feel bad about what I said. Call me."

Looking at the machine for a moment Toni smiled, thinking it funny that Heidi hadn't had the nerve to call her cell phone.

⌒

That Saturday night, Toni sat across from Heidi at one of the nicer restaurants in town. They'd had a pleasant evening together, their fight seemingly forgotten. Noel's name had come up frequently, but they hadn't discussed her in any depth. They were waiting for their dessert and coffee to be delivered when Heidi said, "I replayed our fight in my mind a few times since the other night."

"Forget about it. I have."

"No," Heidi said thoughtfully. "It didn't come across this way, but I was asking a serious question. I'm genuinely interested in what's going on with you and Noel. I know I butchered this question, but what I wanted to know was what is it about her that's made you want to give up your freedom?"

Toni fidgeted in her seat, briefly regretting her agreement to meet for dinner. But Heidi was her oldest friend, and she had to get past any discomfort where Noel was concerned. "You know this isn't what I'm best at. I have a hard time putting words to my feelings."

"You can do it when you put your mind to it," Heidi said, smiling fondly. "I've heard you with my very own ears."

Even though she'd been very comfortable for the past hour, Toni felt like she was sitting on pins, and almost checked her chair to see if the upholstery had come loose. She moved her chair back an inch or two, thinking that might fix things. "I don't know," she finally said when she realized she hadn't answered the question. "It's certainly wasn't anything I planned." She gave a helpless-looking shrug. "It just happened."

"I can understand that. You got carried away."

"Yeah. That sounds right. Before I knew it, I'd lost interest in going out with anyone else."

Smiling, Heidi said, "It sounds about like the time that ornithologist was here for a couple of months. What was her name?"

"Mandy. Mandy Thompkins. Boy, that's probably been five years ago."

"At least. You were massively crushed on her."

"Not really. Well, not when I think about it now."

"Oh, come on! She's all you talked about."

"Maybe. But that was mostly about sex." Toni laughed at the memory. "If there is such a thing as a nymphomaniac, she was one."

"How is it different with Noel?"

Heidi's gaze was firmly settled on Toni's face. Toni felt as though she could see right into her thoughts. "I'm not sure," she said, irritably. "I just know it's different. I'm really, really attracted to Noel. It's more than just sex."

"That's what I'm interested in. Do you have a lot in common? Do you share the same interests? Hobbies?"

Toni felt as though she were trying to figure out a complex carpentry problem…without a tape measure or calculator. "No… well, kinda…I guess. She doesn't work on cars or anything, but I think we have things in common."

"What do you do when you're together?"

Toni's eyes were scrunched into slits. She sat perfectly still for a few seconds. "Noel says we're doing what most couples do when they first get together. She says this only lasts for a little while though, so we're enjoying it." The chair was acting up again, and her ankle itched. Maybe there were sand fleas in the restaurant.

Heidi charitably came to her rescue. "Having a great sex life can come in handy when things get tough. If Isabel and I had gotten along better in bed, we might still be together."

"We don't have any problems there." Toni's smile was tight, and she immediately tried to change the subject. "I think our biggest problem will be distance. It's hard for both of us to be this far away, and it's hard for me to get weekends off. I hate to make Noel come here all the time, but she might have to."

"That might work out in your favor. Your honeymoon period should last a lot longer if you only see each other on weekends." She made a face. "Then you have to get to the hard work of relationship building."

Toni felt the knot in the pit of her stomach start to build. She wasn't sure what Heidi meant, and the fact that she didn't know made her worry that she wouldn't be capable of doing it. Why did this have to be so hard?

⌐

The Saturday after Thanksgiving found Toni lying in Noel's bed, trying to relax enough to go to sleep. Groggily, Noel reached over and patted her belly. "I've never known you to have trouble sleeping. Want to talk about what's bothering you?"

"I didn't say anything was bothering me."

The tone Toni used was unmistakable. She was bothered by something. Probably something big. Noel sat up and propped some pillows behind her back. "You've been a little distant all day. I thought I might just be imagining it, but I think there's something there. Talk to me." She put her hand on Toni's head and gently stroked her hair. "Come on, tell me what's on your mind."

Grumpily, Toni mumbled, "It's nothing."

"Yes, it is. If something's keeping you awake, it's important enough to talk about."

"I'm just…thinking…worrying that I might be more into you than you're into me."

"What?" Noel jerked up straighter. Had anyone ever said anything crazier? "You've got to be kidding."

"I'm not kidding at all. This doesn't seem funny to me."

"Come on, Toni. You've got to tell me more. If I were any more into you, I'd…" She struggled to think of an example but Toni provided one.

Quietly, in almost a whisper, Toni said, "Maybe you'd have wanted to spend Thanksgiving with me."

Noel's stomach turned. What in the world had she missed? "What? I would've loved to have spent Thanksgiving with you, but you said you were going to be with your family."

"I didn't have any other offers."

Noel slipped down until she and Toni were face-to-face. "I'm so sorry," she whispered. "It didn't dawn on me to invite you, but it certainly wasn't because I didn't want to be with you. I just assumed…"

"I thought we weren't going to do that anymore. Assume stuff…"

"You're right. We did agree to that. But you've got to admit that you didn't invite me to your house for Thanksgiving either."

"I didn't have that option. My mom doesn't like to have strangers come to family functions, and just about everybody is a stranger."

"That's…unique."

"She's always been that way. My mom has to control everything, and having someone around who she doesn't think of as family throws her for a loop. A few years ago I tried to invite Heidi for Christmas. There was a bad storm and she missed her flight to see her family, so it was last minute. My mom acted like I'd asked if I could bring a box full of rats."

"Oh, Toni. You must have felt terrible not having her there."

"No way," she said, shaking her head. "I stayed in Rehoboth. My mom was mad at me for months, but I wasn't going to let Heidi be alone."

"You're such a sweetheart." Noel stroked her face and kissed it repeatedly. "I'm glad you did that. That shows your character." She moved closer and put her arm around Toni, pressing their bodies together. "You're a very, very good woman. And I'm very sorry I was too oblivious to invite you to join us for Thanksgiving. Can you join my family for Christmas? We have a great time together and I know you'd have fun."

"Don't you have to ask your mom?"

"No. Of course not. She's dying to meet you."

Sheepishly, Toni said, "I can't come. My dad and I are doing that addition for my brother. If I took a day off, it'd screw up our schedule."

"Christmas Day?"

"Yeah. My dad has us scheduled for the whole day."

Noel thought that was insane, but she held her tongue, knowing that Toni's opinion of her father was unblemished. "Maybe I could go to Virginia to see you."

Toni shrugged. "You wouldn't have any fun. My mom has to run the whole holiday like it's boot camp. Presents have to be opened at a certain time, the right photos have to be taken." She sat up and kissed Noel's cheek. "Stay with your family. I guarantee you'll have a nicer holiday."

"But being with you would make any day special."

"Thanks." Toni looked weary and she lay down and let out a breath. "We'll see. Maybe we'll be able to see each other for a little while."

⌐

Two weeks after Thanksgiving, Toni, Heidi and Roxy were all at Jackie's, complaining about the fact that they would all probably be there on the weekend too. Noel was taking a class in Baltimore and Toni was on duty, so she couldn't go up. Heidi's new girlfriend, Angela, was chaperoning her son on a school trip, leaving her solo. And Roxy was grousing about the fact that the weather was expected to be cool and rainy, the kind of weekend that made tourists stay away in droves.

The bar was very quiet and Jackie was leaning against it questioning Heidi. "So tell us more about this girl you've been seeing. Is it serious?"

Heidi smiled somewhat inscrutably. "You know how it is. Once you've had two dates with someone, it's serious."

"Are you seeing her a lot?"

"Yeah. It takes a little juggling of our schedules, but I don't think we've missed a week."

Roxy pinched Toni on the back. "She's doing better than you are, Hoop. You've missed a lot of weekends."

"Heidi's new girlfriend isn't a firefighter. I can only change days off so many times." She didn't look angry when she replied, but her tone was a little sharp.

"You don't want to let Heidi beat you to the altar," Roxy said, clearly trying to get a rise out of Toni.

"I'm not in a rush," Toni said, her tone arid.

"You guys have both been seeing somebody for about the same

232

amount of time, right?"

That wasn't true, but Toni didn't want to make a point of how long she and Noel had been sleeping with each other, so she just shrugged.

Roxy continued, "I think we should have a bet to see who falls in love first, who has a commitment ceremony first…all that gooey stuff."

Toni was tempted to kick Roxy in the shin with her cowboy boot. Instead, she yawned loudly and said, "Let me know how the handicapping goes. I can't bet since I'm in a position to fix the race. I'm gonna hit the hay."

"It's not even ten o'clock," Roxy complained.

Toni kissed her on the cheek. "I know, but you're such a fascinating conversationalist that you wear me out."

She got up and Heidi did the same. "I'm gonna take off, too." She kissed Roxy, and they both went around to the side of the bar to kiss Jackie goodnight.

When they got outside, Heidi said, "Feel like walking me home? You don't look tired."

Smiling, Toni asked, "What do I look?"

"Irritated. Sometimes Roxy doesn't know when to stuff a sock in it."

They started walking in the direction of Heidi's house. "I almost stuck my boot in it," Toni admitted. "And that would have hurt."

"Sometimes Roxy is like a little brother. You know you can't kick her butt or you'll get in trouble, but you really want to."

"My little brother isn't half as obnoxious as Roxy," Toni said, chuckling.

"She just does it because she knows she can."

"Yeah, but I don't have to like it."

Toni had her hands in her pockets, and Heidi threaded her hand around Toni's arm. "How is it going with Noel?"

"Good. I feel like I'm flying blind most of the time," she chuckled, "but I think it's going well."

"Count your blessings that she doesn't have any kids. That makes everything so much harder."

"Really? Why?"

"Lots of little things, and a few big things. Like…we probably would have moved in together if not for her son. But she has joint custody of him and her ex has already said she'd fight her about taking him out of state."

Toni's mouth dropped open and she stared at her. "You're at that point already?"

"Sure." She looked at Toni quizzically. "You're not?"

"No. Not at all."

"Wow. I didn't want to give Roxy the satisfaction, but we've already crossed the I-love-you barrier."

"Amazing." Toni's eyes had taken on that hooded quality they often had when something was troubling her.

"You're not there yet?" Heidi asked gently, squeezing Toni's bicep with her hand.

"No." She didn't say anything for a little while. Then, her voice full of uncertainty, she asked, "Should we have done that by now?"

"I can't say. Every couple is different." They walked on in silence for another few moments, then Heidi asked, "How serious are you?"

Immediately, Toni replied, "I'm very serious."

Something about the way she sounded made Heidi ask, "Do you think Noel is less serious than you are?"

Toni knew that Heidi wasn't the best person to confide in. She had an agenda, even though Toni wasn't always sure what it was. But at this point in her life she honestly didn't have anyone other than Noel to talk to about this. And there were so many questions flying around in her head that she felt like she might combust.

"I honestly don't know. How can you tell something like that?"

Heidi didn't reply immediately. Toni's stomach was in knots when she finally said, "Has she talked about moving here?"

"Yeah." She tried to keep the panic from her voice. "She doesn't want to move here. I think she liked it well enough this summer, but she's made it clear that Baltimore is her home. She hasn't changed her mind about running The Sandpiper either, so don't bother to ask about that."

"But she hasn't talked about selling it lately, so that's a good sign."

"I'm not sure that's true, but I'll take it."

"What did she say about the future?"

"Not much. When we first started…dating, she said I'd be the last person she'd choose if she was looking for a permanent relationship." Heidi let out an outraged squawk, so Toni hurried to add, "She had good reason to say that. I made it perfectly clear that I didn't want a girlfriend."

"What?" Heidi's confusion was evident from her expression. "Why would you tell her you didn't want a girlfriend if you were just starting to date?"

Caught in her lie about timing, Toni tried to think her way out of it. The best she could come up with was, "I told her I wanted to date her…but that I hadn't wanted a girlfriend for a very long time. I think she was teasing a little bit. You know, trying not to sound too serious."

"Nonetheless, that's pretty rude. She can be pretty abrupt. Standoffish too. I know we both thought that when we first met her."

Toni shot her a piercing look. "You didn't say that then. You said you liked her."

"I do. But I'm not going to like her if she's screwing around with you."

"I don't think she is. I think she's just not sure of me. Not that I blame her. I've got a rotten track record."

Heidi let go of Toni's arm, moving to encircle her waist. She hugged her. "You weren't a good partner, but you've been a great friend. I'm pretty sure you've learned a lot over the years. I think Noel would be lucky to get you."

Toni shrugged, looking a little self-conscious. "She has said one promising thing. She's told me several times that if we both want this to work out, it will."

Heidi nodded thoughtfully. "That is promising…if you both want it."

The emphasis Heidi put on that qualifier made Toni feel like throwing up. When she said it that way, it sounded like the kind of thing Noel would say to make sure she had an out.

"Don't worry about it. Any smart woman would be lucky to have you."

Toni recognized Heidi's reassuring tone of voice from the dozens of times she had proclaimed that Max wasn't as sick as they both knew she was. The mere fact that she was using it made Toni more anxious than if she'd said nothing. She knew she shouldn't ask, but she couldn't help herself. "Give me your best guess. From what I've said, do you think she's in love with me?"

The seconds ticked away, each one giving more time for Toni's jaw to clench painfully. Finally, Heidi said, "No, I don't think she is. But that doesn't mean she won't be. Maybe it's just hard for her to commit. Has she been in other relationships besides the one she just got out of?"

"Yeah. A bunch of them. If she's afraid to commit, I think she's just afraid of committing to me."

Heidi blew out a stream of air, making a soft whistling sound. "Ooo."

Growing more agitated by the moment, Toni said, "I've been

going over something in my mind. She didn't invite me to her family Thanksgiving gathering, even though she said she wanted to after I called her on it. That just didn't sound right to me, even though I tried to convince myself that it didn't mean anything."

"I could be wrong, and I hope I am, but if she were in love with you..." Heidi's voice trailed off, leaving Toni to fill in the blank.

Toni was feeling sick and wishing she'd never allowed herself to get into this conversation. "That's what I think too. I know she likes me a lot, but I don't think she loves me."

"How do you get along with her parents? It's always a good sign when a woman wants to show you off?"

Another kick to the gut. "I haven't met them."

"Really? Don't they live close to Noel?"

"Yeah." She fought back against the bile in her gut. "I think so. Somewhere in Maryland."

"How about her friends? I know you must spend time with her friends when you visit her."

"No. I've never met any of them." Her head swirled, trying to process all of these horrible facts.

"Ooo, that's not good." Heidi hugged her again, then patted her back under her jacket. "No, no, forget I said that. She just got out of a relationship. She's probably taking this really, really slowly. Don't give it another thought."

The thoughts were already embedded in Toni's brain as though etched in granite. "Or she's biding her time until she finds someone she thinks is more worthy of the risk."

"Well, that's possible, I guess. But not likely. I know you hate this kind of turmoil, but it comes with the territory. When you're trying to get to know someone it's always like this."

"Always? Really?"

"Sure. A new relationship is always filled with ups and downs."

Toni let the words wash over her. Ups and downs were one

thing, but this felt like a roller coaster. Things had been so much easier when she'd kept her friends close and her lovers distant.

⌒

By the time Toni got home she was in a lather. She didn't anger easily, and when she did, her anger usually flared and burned itself out quickly. But tonight she ruminated over what Heidi had said, finding herself getting angrier by the minute. Love was about risk, and she had taken more risks than she ever had. She'd been the one to ask Noel out, she'd been the one to pursue her, she'd been the one to ask her to spend the night that first time, she'd been the one who suggested they get together after Noel left town. Every single risk had been from her! What was Noel putting into this? Sure, they got along great sexually, but that wasn't what mattered now. What mattered now was going that next step. And Noel had shown no inclination to move her foot, much less take a step.

Toni didn't know how she would do it, but she resolved to pull back. There was no way she was going to be left hanging if Noel didn't want to proceed. She'd done pretty well on her own all of these years, and there was no reason she wouldn't do well if this didn't work out. She went into her bathroom and poured some antacids into her hand. Chewing quickly to get rid of the chalky taste, she swore to herself that she was going to pull back and not go another inch until Noel made it clear she was equally invested.

⌒

It was almost eleven o'clock when her cell phone rang. She was certain it was Noel. They hadn't talked to each other yet, and they never missed a day. Her muscles twitched, desperate to pick up the phone. But she refused, determined to maintain her self-respect.

⌒

Despite Noel's tender message, Toni didn't return her call. She also barely slept. But she felt a little more in control, even if it did seem like there was a quart of acid in her gut. When she got out of the shower the next morning, she heard her phone ringing, but again she didn't answer. She knew Noel would be in school soon, so she waited until she knew her phone would be off to return her call. Her message was perfunctory. "Hi, it's Toni. I was out last night and didn't get a chance to call you back. Running late today. Have a good one."

⌒

Toni argued with herself all day long. She had a feeling she was being unreasonable, but she also felt that Noel was taking advantage of her. It didn't feel like that when they were together, but when they were apart, she felt like she could see things in a different, clearer light. Still, even though some things seemed in sharper focus, she was woefully confused. She was certain Heidi was on her side, but it seemed as though she was trying to create doubt. Heidi knew more than anyone that Toni had a hard time figuring relationships out. Still, Heidi hadn't brought any of this up. She was just replying to Toni's questions.

By the time Toni got home, she felt like she'd worked three days instead of one. Her body ached and her head throbbed. She'd been castigating herself over what she now knew was her imprudent decision to pursue this relationship with such gusto. She knew from watching her friends that there was as much heartache as love in each of these journeys. She should have known better. Tired to the bone, she dropped her keys, shucked her coat, and lay down on the couch, her boots still on her feet.

⌐⌐

Some time later, Toni heard her phone ringing. She tried to wake up, but her mind and body didn't cooperate. Feeling like her limbs were covered in lead, she closed her eyes again, falling asleep immediately. She had no idea how much time had passed, but she was wakened once again by someone pounding on the front door. Her heart began to race as it often did when she was pulled from a deep sleep. She stumbled to the front door, getting her feet tangled in her discarded jacket. Biting back a curse, she opened the door to find a worried-looking Noel. "Are you all right?"

Toni nodded mutely. She stepped back and let Noel enter. "Are you sick? She put her hands on Toni's flushed cheeks. "I've been so worried about you!" She hugged her hard, then stepped back to look around the room lit only by the porch light. "Why don't you have any lights on? No TV?" She moved across the room and turned a table lamp on. "And your jacket's on the floor." She took another long look at Toni. "Were you sleeping with your clothes on?" She extended her hands and crossed back over to her. "Sweetheart, tell me what's wrong."

Toni fell into her embrace and let her body and soul soak up the concern she could feel flowing into her. "You've never called me sweetheart," she said, bursting into tears.

Noel patted her back, then rubbed it. "You're very, very sweet. And you have my heart." She pulled away and placed the back of her hand on Toni's forehead. "I think you have a fever, too. When did you start to feel bad?"

Strangely, a big grin settled onto Toni's face. "Last night. I thought I was just in a bad mood."

"You're never in a bad mood, but you are coming down with

something. I'm so glad I came down to see you. I'm gonna stay until you're better, so don't even try to argue with me. Come on now." She tugged Toni towards the bedroom. "Have you eaten?"

"No, my stomach's been upset."

"I'm going to get you into bed, then get you a little something." She undressed her quickly and put her to bed, tucking the covers up to her chin. "You rest while I go over to the diner. I'm sure you don't have anything here."

"Noel?" Toni said quietly.

"Yeah?"

"I thought you were busy this weekend."

"I was. But you come first." She started to walk away, then stopped. Turning to look at Toni, she said, "Did you doubt that?" Seeing the lack of certainty in Toni's dark eyes, she said, "You never should. You'll always come first."

Toni watched her leave and was suddenly overcome with a sense of serenity that she hadn't felt in quite a while. She snuggled down into the covers and happily waited for Noel to return.

⌒

By Sunday evening, Toni's fever had broken and her appetite was back. Noel didn't want to leave, but since Toni insisted she was going to work the next day, it made sense for her to go home. As she sometimes did, she called her sister to have some company for the long drive. They spent a while talking about Toni's health, then April brought up a topic they had discussed frequently.

"It sure would be easier for both of you if you would move down there."

"I thought your family was supposed to want you to stay close to home," Noel commented dryly.

"No, you got it wrong. Your family is supposed to help you not screw things up."

"Why are you so sure I'm going to screw this up? I think I'm doing fine. I took a risk this weekend and called her 'sweetheart.'"

April waited a beat, then said, "You're kidding."

"No," Noel said proudly, "I did."

"You've been seeing her for six months! It took six months and a virus to get you to say something most people would say on the third date?"

"I've never said something like that on a third date. You know I'm cautious."

"You slept with her pretty quickly," April said, chuckling evilly.

"I had no control over that. It didn't even occur to me to resist her." She moaned in frustration. "You have no idea, April. I've never been this attracted to anyone. She's like a big chocolate Easter bunny and I'm a hungry five-year-old."

"Then get on with it. Make some plans. Commit to her."

"I have. We're both committed to seeing only each other and trying to make it work."

April must have cupped her hand around the receiver, because her voice sounded like it was coming from a megaphone. "It's been six months. You need to make a move."

"I'm going to. I'm going to. I'm pretty certain I'm going to spend the summer there again. If things go well, maybe we'll be able to make some plans then."

"You want to wait another nine months? You can create a human being in nine months!"

"You know Toni is commitment phobic. I don't want to rush her."

"You can insist that Toni's the one who's afraid, but I think it's you. And if you don't get off your butt and make some progress you're going to lose her. And I would truly hate for that to happen."

"So would I! You know how much I care for her. But I won't be completely surprised if she's not able to make this work. I'm not at all sure that I'm going to be the first woman to convince Toni Hooper to settle down."

"Don't forget what they say about the lottery. You can't win if you don't play."

Part Thirteen

*T*hey spent the weekend before Christmas in Rehoboth. Noel had made more trips to Delaware than Toni had to Maryland, but she claimed to prefer it that way. They were relaxing in bed on Sunday afternoon, debating whether or not to go into the living room to watch the Ravens on TV. Noel was in favor, but she could tell by the way Toni's gaze was fixed on her that another round of lovemaking was in the offing.

"Oh! I keep forgetting to ask if you've firmed up your plans for Christmas."

"Yeah, we have. My mom, dad and I are going to my brother's on Tuesday. We'll stay until we're finished with the addition, and we're guessing it will take a week."

Noel started to kiss her way across Toni's chest, knowing it would distract her but unable to resist. "I was thinking more of our plans. You know I want you to come to my parents' for Christmas Eve and Christmas day and Boxing Day and…"

"Boxing Day?"

"Never mind. We don't celebrate that."

"It's not gonna be easy. I checked on MapQuest and my brother's house is sixty miles from your parents'."

"Ugh! That's sucks."

"I know. And since my dad and I are going to be there primarily to do the addition, I can't sneak out very often."

"You're well worth a sixty-mile drive. When do you guys celebrate?"

"Christmas Eve. How about you?"

"The same. What about Christmas day?"

"It's just going to be me and my parents at my brother's house, because he and his family are going to his wife's parents. But my dad's planning on working." She smiled and acted like she was hammering something onto the bed. "Once he gets going, he doesn't want to stop."

"I hate to leave my family on Christmas Eve. My poor grandmother is hanging onto her faculties by a thread."

"You need to be there. And I know your nieces and nephews really want you there."

"Same for yours. Maiden aunts are very popular on Christmas."

Toni laughed. "That's the truth. And I always get stuck putting everything together since neither my brother nor my brother-in-law have any mechanical ability."

"How do you think your mom would take it if I wanted to come over on Christmas Day?"

Toni's eyes closed while she scratched her head. Finally, she said, "You won't have fun, but I can handle her."

"No." Noel put her hand on Toni's shoulder and shook it. "I want a serious answer."

Toni met her gaze, not saying anything for over a minute. When she did speak her words were measured. "It'd be more fun if we met somewhere else. I'll be able to get away by five o'clock. I'll come up to your house."

"No, no. I don't want you to work all day and have to drive that far." She could tell that Toni's sexual desire had evaporated. "Is your mom really that difficult?"

With a sad smile, she nodded briefly. "The holidays are a real powder keg. It might be okay, but I sure wouldn't count on it."

Noel decided to try to banish the troubling thoughts she could see going through Toni's head. "You know what would be fun," she said, jumping out of bed. "I want to test your powers of concentration." Giving her a curious look, Toni took her hand and allowed herself to be led from the bed. They went into the living room where Noel urged her to lie on the sofa as she got on her knees in front of her. "I want to turn the game on and have you do play-by-play while I play with you."

"That is the goofiest idea you've ever had," Toni said, laughing.

Noel was fully aware of how goofy it was. But she was also pleased to see the sparkle back in Toni's eyes, her ulterior motive.

⌒

Noel was putting some finishing touches on the gifts she bought for her nieces and nephews when her cell phone rang on Christmas Eve morning. When she saw the name on the display she got up and made a dash for her old bedroom. "Hi," she said, quietly closing the door. "I miss you!"

"I miss you, too. My taskmaster father gave us the day off, but there are so many people running around here that it's like a mad house."

"It's still quiet here. I could probably get away for a few hours…"

"I'd love to see you, but there's no way I could get away without bringing a kid or two with me. I've got one on my lap right now."

Charmed, Noel said, "Who do you have?"

"My girlfriend wants to know your name." Noel heard a little voice giggle. "This one doesn't talk much, that's why I let her stay in here with me. Do you want to say hello to Noel, Emma?" There were some rustling noises and a little cajoling, then Toni got back on. "No dice. Count your blessings," she added, chuckling.

"Where are you guys?"

"In my brother's bedroom. Little did I know that one day I'd have to go to his bedroom to get a little privacy. The rules have changed."

"It stinks that your cell phone isn't working."

"He lives way out in the sticks. One of those new developments chomping up all of the fantastic farmland that made Virginia so beautiful. But now it's just a bunch of massive houses on small lots, where you try to act like a baron on an eighth of an acre. "

"I can't tell how you feel about it," Noel giggled. "Don't hold back."

"I just don't understand living like this. It takes him over an hour to get to work on a good day. My sister-in-law leaves the house at seven to get the kids to school and day care, and nobody gets home again until after six. Then they run around like crazy people trying to get the kids fed and help my nephew with his homework, then they start getting them put to bed. They don't have any quiet time," she said, clearly puzzled. "How can you live without any quiet time?"

"I don't know. All I know is that I couldn't spend over two hours a day getting to and from work. Thank God neither of us has to."

"I wish I had some quiet time with you," Toni said softly. "I miss being able to just talk."

"This won't last forever. We have to keep it in perspective."

"Where are you going to be on Monday?"

"I'll probably still be at my parents'. Why? Can you get away?"

"No, but we've gotten a lot done and my mom and dad are gonna go home. I'm gonna stay and finish plumbing the bathroom. Why don't you come over on Monday and hang out?"

"That's the best offer I've had all week. I'd give an awful lot to see you today, but I understand how things are."

"I hope you don't think I always buckle under to my mom's demands. I really don't. I just try to choose my battles. If we're… what I mean is…I stand up to her when I need to."

Noel knew her well enough to know exactly what she was trying to say. Toni would force her mother to come to terms with Noel's presence if she was certain Noel was going to be a lasting part of the landscape. But if she wasn't, why go to the trouble? It hurt to think that Toni wasn't sure they'd be together for the next holiday. But that's the risk she knew she was taking when she allowed herself to fall for a woman so averse to lasting relationships.

⌒

A little bit before ten that evening, Noel felt her cell phone buzzing in her pocket. Her mother saw her jump, and when she pulled out the device and looked at it, she made eye contact with her mom who nodded indulgently. She dashed into the bathroom and said, "Hello?"

"Hi." There was something about the way Toni said just that one word that let Noel know that neither niece nor nephew sat on her lap.

"Hello, yourself. You have your naughty girl voice on."

Chuckling, Toni said, "I have a naughty girl voice?"

"You sure do. And I love it. Are all of the little Hoopers in bed?"

"I expect so. But I'm more interested in a certain Carpenter. Why don't you put on your coat and step outside."

Noel clapped her hand over her mouth, stopping herself from squealing with excitement. "You're here?"

"Yep. I can't stay very long, but it just wouldn't be Christmas without you."

"Come inside! April and Ed and the boys are still here. You can finally meet everyone."

"Don't take this the wrong way, but I don't have very long and I'd rather focus on you. Is that horribly rude?"

"Probably," Noel said, chuckling, "but I don't care. I'll be right out."

Toni watched the door and laughed to herself when April emerged with Noel. April glowered and shook her finger at Toni, but when Toni got out of a dark grey SUV and blew April a kiss, she got one back. Noel couldn't wait for her own kiss. She dashed right up to Toni and threw her arms around her. It was cold and windy, but they both felt a surge of warmth flow through their bodies when they held each other. "Let's get in. The car's nice and warm."

Noel ran to the passenger side and jumped in, grinning wildly. "I can't even tell you how excited I am to see you."

Toni smiled back. "Then that disgusting drive was worth it. I'd blow a hole in my head if I had to do that very often."

"You don't want to sit here in the driveway do you?"

"What do you have in mind?" Her grin suggested she hoped it was something racy.

Noel reached into her pocket and dangled a set of keys. "April's house. It's ten minutes from here."

Toni put the car in reverse. "Direct me."

⌣

April's house might have been ten minutes away, but Toni made it in six. Noel had a hand on her thigh and was rubbing it lasciviously, making Toni ignore the speed limit. By the time they got in the front door, they were wrapped in a passionate embrace, kissing and being kissed.

They wrestled each other out of coats, sweaters and Toni's

shirt, but Noel stopped Toni as she was starting to unbutton her blouse. She took both of Toni's hands and put them on her breasts. Her voice was low and sexy when she said, "Would you like your Christmas present?"

Toni's eyes were glazed when she said, "You already gave me a present."

Smiling, Noel put Toni's fingers on the top button of her blouse. "This is a bonus. Go ahead and open it."

Hurriedly, Toni undid the buttons, stopping to marvel at the wonderful gift. Noel was wearing a black bra that presented her breasts as though a pair of hands were holding them up. The bra stopped just below her nipples, leaving the top half of each breast completely exposed. "You wore this to Christmas dinner with your grandmother?"

"No!" Noel started to laugh. "When you called, I grabbed April and ran upstairs to get my coat and ask her to cover for me. I was just going to go to your car and make out, but she suggested we go to her house. She insisted I put this bra on."

"You've got the strangest family."

"She was with me when I bought it. It was her idea."

"I can't imagine my sister ever suggesting anything to enhance my sex life."

Noel laughed. "I think April is as interested in mine and she is in her own. I hate to admit this, but my mom's not far behind April." She kissed Toni, running her hands along her scalp to hold her close. "I really want you to meet my family. But tonight...tonight I want you to focus on these."

Toni brushed her thumbs across Noel's nipples, her gaze so intent that it almost burned. "Does April know how much I love your breasts?"

Noel sucked in a breath when Toni pinched her. "Uh-huh. So does my mom."

Stunned, Toni leaned back and stared for a few seconds. "A lesser woman would let that screw with her mind." She was laughing when she leaned over and captured one of the beautifully presented nipples in her mouth. Her smile was luminous when she tilted her face and looked into Noel's eyes. "Luckily for you, I'm not a lesser woman."

That look...that smile...the cocky confidence that Toni sometimes showed when she was aroused shot Noel's desire into orbit. There was nothing...nothing that had ever turned her on as much as Toni's dominant side. It wasn't always in full force, and that just made it all the more alluring.

Toni could easily show her sweet, even shy, side and Noel loved that part of her as well. Sometimes she was so tender—achingly so—that Noel thought her heart would break from the feelings that welled up inside of her. But nothing turned her on like Toni's aggressive side. That was a whole new dimension to arousal, and she craved it like a drug when she hadn't seen it for a week or two.

Having those bright, shining eyes looking at her like she was about to become dinner was just the Christmas present she'd been hoping for, worth far more than any tangible gift Toni could have presented.

Every part of Noel tingled, but her breasts felt like thousands of tiny pins were dancing on them. Her pussy felt swollen and exquisitely sensitive, even though Toni hadn't touched it.

Suddenly, the air left her lungs as Toni pushed her, hard, against the front door. Noel grabbed the frame, trying to hang on as Toni devoured her. The black bra was still in place, but Noel couldn't even see it, given Toni's dark head which flitted from breast to breast, ravenously consuming Noel's flesh.

She put her hands on Toni's head, not to control her, but to tease her. Toni's head was remarkably sensitive, and scratching and rubbing her scalp was a surefire way to turn her on. Not that Toni needed a lot of help at the moment. She was in a frenzy, making soft, hungry moans and whimpers as she moved against Noel almost frantically.

A fist was insinuated between Noel's thighs, and she sank onto it, seeking blessed relief. Toni pressed it into her, and Noel responded, grinding her hips to feel the firm pulsing in every part of her pussy. Her heart was beating hard, feeling like it was thrumming in her breasts as Toni continued to suckle them.

Then everything shifted. Noel found herself in front of Toni, who was now against the door. One hand grasped and squeezed a breast while the other dove into her slacks, blindly fumbling for her sex. Noel thrust her hips up, trying to spread her legs while remaining standing. Toni's fingers slid into place, surrounding her clit, which felt like it had doubled in size.

As soon as Toni touched it, Noel gasped in relief, then tried to hold still, knowing that Toni knew just what to do. In their months together, Toni had learned her body like no other lover ever had. She seemed to read Noel's cues like a gifted musician reads the conductor. Tonight she didn't disappoint. She pressed her fingers around the hypersensitive flesh and squeezed—just enough—to make Noel bite her lip as she squirmed against her. "Yes, yes," she moaned, her feet tapping on the wood floor, unable to stay still.

Toni leaned into her and bit her neck, still pressing against her clit and pinching a pink nipple. Noel pushed back, her entire body weight pushing Toni against the door. Moving her hand just an inch, Toni slid into Noel, who nearly lost control of her legs. She fought to stay upright as that life-giving hand filled her while still rocking against her clit.

Noel's body curled into itself as she cried out. Toni was wrapped around her, holding her up with one arm, while the other remained buried between her legs. Every movement felt like a tiny orgasm as Toni slowly and gently continued to move, making Noel come until she could no longer fight gravity. They collapsed onto the floor in a heap, then started to laugh, continuing until Noel, with extreme reluctance, slowly extracted Toni's fingers from her body. "Who says Christmas is for kids?"

⌐

By ten forty-five they were back in the car. Toni drove with one hand while Noel seductively sucked on the fingers of the other. "Please don't do that," Toni moaned. "I've got a long drive ahead of me."

"I'm just trying to keep you alert," Noel said, giving her a naughty grin.

"If I were any more alert something would burst."

Noel kissed Toni's hand and put it on her breast, giving her an unrepentant grin.

"That's not a lot better, you know. Thank April and your mom and your grandmother for picking out such a nice present for me."

Noel took Toni's thumb and index finger and pressed them around her hard nipple. "Silly girl. My grandmother had nothing to do with this. She's a Carpenter. It's my mom's side of the family who are obsessed with sex."

"I love your mom's side of the family," Toni said dreamily.

They pulled up in front of the house and seconds later the porch light flipped on and off a few times. The door opened and April's sons stood in the doorway, waving madly. Toni shook her head. "The boys don't know about the bra, do they?"

"God, I hope not, but you never know with April."

Toni waved back and someone must've told them to close the door because they turned and looked like they were trying to convince an adult of something, then quickly closed it. "This has been quite an interesting little trip." She reached over and tried to make Noel's blouse look like she hadn't been rolling around the floor in it.

"How did you get away?"

"There were a lot of people over, and the little kids were in bed or asleep on the floor. My sister's car was blocking mine so I told her to give me her keys."

"You didn't say where you were going?"

"She knew. I've been mooning over you all week, and I made her use her fancy phone to get directions for me earlier today. She knew I was waiting for the opportunity to make a jailbreak."

"Will your mom be angry?"

"Yep. But I already got my knit hat and gloves with the matching Christmas sweater, so I'm good."

Noel giggled. "I can't see you in a Christmas sweater."

"The day you see me in a knit hat is the day I move to Greenland. But my mom doesn't notice little details like that."

"I'm glad you like the present I gave you better."

Toni looked over her shoulder to see the porch light flipping on and off again. "I guess you'd better go in."

"I guess so. This time it might really be my grandmother." She got out and dashed around to Toni's window. She leaned down and they kissed, their earlier frantic caresses giving way to ones soft and slow and tender.

"I'm so glad I got to see you," Toni said.

"Seeing you was better than having Santa and all of the reindeer prancing around on my roof." Noel kissed her one last time and started to stand up. Toni blinked a couple of times, then her mouth opened and closed. She said something that was too quiet for Noel to hear, so she started to lean into the window, catching a breathy, "I'm in love with you," before Toni popped the car into reverse and nearly left tire tread in her hurry to drive away.

⌒

Toni's heart was racing so quickly she was afraid she was having a coronary. Even though it was cold, she was covered in sweat. She shrugged out of her coat, glad that she had waited until the very end to say what had been aching in her chest for days.

She wasn't absolutely certain, but she thought Noel looked both stunned and pleased as the car hurtled down the driveway. She was almost certain that flicker of emotion that flashed just before Noel leapt backwards was pleasure. Or terror.

⌒

Noel made her way to the furthest reaches of Virginia on Monday morning. Toni's brother's house was just as she expected it to be—a very large, lot-filling behemoth. It had taken her a while to find his street, traversing street signs that heralded ridges, vales, and mews, none of which she'd noticed from a topographical standpoint.

She walked around to the back of the house, assuming that's where Toni would be. She let her ears lead her, spying her lover at the end of a nail gun. Careful not to surprise her when she was wielding a power tool, Noel opened the newly installed French doors and waved her hands. Toni's head shot up and she beamed. She carefully put the nail gun down and walked over to Noel, then hugged her brashly. She held on for a long time and burrowed her face against Noel's ear. "I've missed you."

"I've missed you, too." She summoned the courage she'd been trying to build and added, "I love you, too. It scares me to death, but I love you."

"What? Did you say something?" Toni reached up and removed a pair of custom fitted hearing protectors. "I'm deaf with these things in."

"Uhm…" Having Toni looking right into her eyes made her nerves kick in, and she chickened out and mumbled, "It's been killing me not to talk to you."

"I know. It's hard when I'm not in my own space. Plus, my dad's been working me to exhaustion."

"It looks great. Did you do all of this last week?"

"No, he had someone local pour the foundation. We just did the framing."

"I'm amazed you got so much done. That's a lot of work."

"It was. I think my brother was happy to go back to work." Toni laughed, her eyes twinkling. "My dad yelled at him all week. 'How can you get to be a thirty-five-year-old man and not know how to tell if something's plumb?'"

"Luckily, his sister knows all about plumb." Noel gave her an enthusiastic hug. "How can I help?"

"Well…" Toni scratched her head, and Noel could just see how diplomatic she was trying to be. "Do you have any experience?"

"Sure do." She tossed her head, letting her French braid fly over her shoulder. "Girly girls know their way around hammers and nails, too. We did a lot of our own work when we renovated our house. If nothing else, I'm great at following instructions."

Toni took off her glove and tenderly stroked Noel's face, looking into her eyes as though she were under a spell. "You always do just as you're told in bed."

"So do you." They stood there assessing one another, then Noel said, "We broke my sister's house in. Want to do your brother's?"

"Desperately." Toni grasped her and started to kiss her. In seconds their hands were wildly running over each other's bodies. Things started off hot and got hotter quickly. After a stunningly short time, Toni said, "Let's go to a motel."

"We've got a great big house right here. No one is home, right?"

"Right." Toni's eyes darted from Noel to the doorway of the main house. "But where would we go? I'm certainly not gonna do it in my brother's bedroom. I'd never get over that."

Noel pulled back and looked at her, trying to avoid giggling. "Why, Toni Hooper, I believe I've finally found a sexual hang-up in that fantastic body." She put her hands on her waist and tickled, making Toni laugh and twitch out of the way.

"Wouldn't you think it was a little funny if I could go right into my brother's bedroom and do all sorts of nasty things?"

Noel played with the buttons on her denim jacket. "There's nothing nasty about what we do."

"I mean nasty in a good way. Nasty as in hot."

"Well, in that case…I suppose I do like having a girlfriend with some boundaries."

Toni giggled, her eyes nearly closing. "I'm glad you don't have any because I loved going over to April's the other night."

"You little rat!" She took a swing and tried to hit Toni on the butt, but Toni was too fast for her and darted out of the way. Noel started to chase her, following Toni from the addition into the main house. They ran through the living room, dining room and kitchen and were headed upstairs when they heard a door open and slam and the sound of little feet running up the stairs after them.

"Toni?" A woman's voice called out.

"Uh-oh," Toni said, her eyes wide. "We've been caught."

⌒

At about nine o'clock Toni walked Noel out to her car. "My sister-in-law meant it when she said she'd love to have you stay overnight."

"I know she did, and it was very sweet of her to offer. I had a great time tonight, but I don't think either of us would be comfortable sleeping together on the sofa bed in the family room."

"It'd be fun," Toni said with false enthusiasm. "I'm sure a couple of kids would get in with us…it'd be a real party."

"My sentiments exactly. You go back to your nephew's little single bed, and I'll go back to Baltimore."

"But you'll come tomorrow?"

"You couldn't keep me away. I'm going to bring a change of clothes, and after we're done working, I'll take you and any of your favorite relatives out to dinner."

"We'll see about that. I might want to have you all to myself. After I exploit your tile-laying skills. You did a great job on the floor. Tomorrow you can start on the walls."

Noel got into her car and rolled the window down. She turned the car on to start the heater, taking some of the chill out. "I'll wait until traffic calms down to leave in the morning."

"Okay. Sounds good."

Toni leaned in and kissed her goodbye. Noel put her hand on the side of Toni's face, then slid it back and scratched behind her ear, a place she knew was particularly sensitive. She kissed her tenderly, put the car in gear, then whispered, "I'm in love with you, too," as she stomped on the gas pedal. She was just able to hear Toni's laughter ring out over the sound of squealing tires.

⌒

Noel would have kicked herself if she could have moved her leg enough to do it. She had firmly decided that she wasn't going to tell Toni she loved her until they'd had a frank discussion about fidelity. But when she'd seen those limpid brown eyes gazing at her that morning, she lost her mind. Having dodged that bullet once, why jump in front of it now? They needed to talk, not just fall into bed! Her imprudent words gnawed at her for a few minutes, then she decisively pulled over and searched her cell phone for Toni's brother's number. She dialed before she could talk herself out of it, and when Toni got on the phone, she said, "I'm going to find a motel and check in. Wanna join me?"

"Oh, Noel. You're such a romantic!"

It hit her like a slap in the face. Toni thought she wanted to be with her to celebrate their declaration of love. It was too late to be honest now, so she tried to be smooth. "I'll call you back in a few minutes when I find a place. I can't wait to see you."

⌐

A half hour later they were embracing in a fairly nice motel room. Toni had stopped and bought a bottle of champagne and some fading, but well-intentioned flowers, making Noel feel even worse about her true motive for wanting to talk. As nearly always happened when they were together, she lost track of her intentions for a good hour, during which Toni nearly made her forget her name. They lay in bed, Toni resting against the headboard, one arm draped across the wood. Noel's head in Toni's lap, her legs dangling over the side of the bed. Fingertip by fingertip, Toni fed Noel drops of wine, smiling down at her. "It could take us three days to finish the bottle at this rate."

"I'm on vacation. No rush."

"Have I ever told you I love your hair? It looks fantastic against my legs. Maybe I should have been a blonde."

"No, no, no. Your hair is perfect for you. It looks like milk chocolate."

Toni's smile grew, and she looked like she was about to say something, but didn't.

"What?" Noel asked.

Toni shook her head. "Nothing. Just thinking about

something."

"Come on." Noel rolled onto her side and captured some skin between her teeth. "Tell."

"Nothing big. I just remembered that Heidi says that, too." A frown started to form, and she said, "I don't like to talk about personal things she's said to me. That seems kinda…I don't know…rude or something."

"Rude?"

"Yeah. That's in the past and that's where it should stay. You don't need to hear about things that went on between Heidi and me."

Noel moved so she was on her back again. She was trying to wedge her concerns into the conversation, and it was hard to do with Toni looking right at her, innocence nearly pouring from her expression. "I don't think it's a bad idea to talk about our past relationships. Particularly the things we learned from them."

Toni's laugh was sharp and short. "I learned to stay away from being in a committed relationship. That's about it."

Still afraid to look at her, Noel said, "But that's changed. Maybe we should talk about what's different now."

Toni had been stroking her idly, but she stilled, her hand resting on Noel's arm. "Almost everything's different. I'm not the same person I was then."

She couldn't stop herself. She had to look into Toni's eyes. "How can that be? How does a person change?"

"It's been decades. I was a girl then. Shouldn't I have changed in all that time?"

"Decades? How's that possible?"

"Why wouldn't it be possible? She was my first girlfriend, and that was twenty years ago."

Noel sat up, shocked. "Your first girlfriend? She was your first?"

"Yeah. I'd had some awkward encounters with a couple of girls, but she was the first person I had a full sexual experience with."

"I'm stunned. Make that flabbergasted."

Toni put a hand on her and tried to push her back down but Noel resisted. "What's so surprising?"

Noel shook her head as though trying to dislodge unpleasant thoughts. "Either I've been jumping to some conclusions or I've been misled."

"About what?"

"About you." She pulled away, then stood and started to walk across the room. When she reached the window she leaned against the frame and stared out for a few minutes. "I wasn't going to tell you this," she said softly, "because I didn't want to hurt your relationship with her, but I'm not sure Heidi has your best interests at heart."

By the time her sentence was finished Toni was standing behind her, her arms around Noel's waist. "Tell me what she said."

Surprisingly, she didn't sound angry. Her voice had a note of resignation in it, but Noel didn't comment on that. Maybe she could circle back around and get to that, but the big issue was Heidi's fiendish subterfuge, not Toni's inability to find fault with her friends.

Noel continued, "I like Heidi. I really do. But I think she intentionally led me to believe that what she knows about you is pretty recent."

"Yeah. So...? She knows an awful lot about me."

Noel turned so that she could see Toni's eyes. They were full of equal amounts of curiosity and trepidation. "She tried to convince me that you couldn't be faithful. And, even though she didn't specifically say so, I think she wanted me to believe that she had recent evidence of that."

Toni let go and moved back to the bed. She sat down on the edge, bending over, her face in her hands. After a few long moments, she sat up and shook her head. "Here's the whole truth about us. I was nineteen and Heidi was twenty-five or six when we met. I was desperate to have sex and she was very willing."

"Who wouldn't be?"

Toni's smile was a little sad when she continued. "I liked her a lot, but I don't think I was ever in love with her." She looked up at Noel with a touching amount of vulnerability in her eyes. "Do you know what I mean? I loved her, but I don't think I was in love with her. There wasn't any spark there. I just needed to have human contact."

"I understand." Noel walked over, sat, and snugged an arm around her waist. She leaned her head against Toni's and waited quietly for her to continue at her own pace.

"I wasn't in any position to be in a relationship. I was just figuring out that I was a lesbian, but Heidi was sure that we were made for each other. I was at fault for not knowing my own mind better, and I let her think what she wanted to think because I didn't want to hurt her."

"You're a kind person."

"Kind people don't cheat." Her words were full of self-recrimination. "I was living in an apartment with two other women when I met Roxy one night at a bar. It didn't take long for her to move in and for us to start sleeping together. I was such a jerk."

"You were a very young woman, Toni. Cut yourself a little slack."

"I don't deserve any. There's no excuse for treating a person like that. One of the best things Max ever did for me was kick my ass about that."

"Max did that?"

"Yeah. She and I were just starting to be friends. She'd only had The Sandpiper a little while and it needed a lot of repair. I was just trying to figure out how to get work and she needed a lot of it. It worked out great," she said, chuckling. "I worked like a dog and she paid me like one. But she also gave me great recommendations to everybody she knew. She set me up."

"Tell me what she told you about Heidi."

"It wasn't so much about Heidi as it was Roxy. She said there were always women who could turn your head, but that people with class didn't allow that to happen. She made me admit that I took the easy way out by having sex with Roxy."

"What do you mean 'the easy way?'"

"I knew Heidi would break up with me if I cheated on her. I was really attracted to Roxy, so I did it. That saved me from having to gut it up and do it the right way."

"So you wanted out of the relationship anyway?"

"I did. Like I said, I cared for Heidi, but we never had much spark. I was very grateful to her for helping me figure out that I was a lesbian, but she didn't make my heart race. Once Roxy did, I knew that I couldn't stay with Heidi."

"How long were you together?"

"Mmm, I'd just finished my class work at trade school, so it was May or June. I think Roxy moved in around September."

"You were only together for a couple of months?"

"Yeah, I guess so." She narrowed her eyes, deep in thought. "It seemed like a very long time. I felt trapped pretty much right away."

"That's interesting. Surprising, too. I got the impression you were together for years and years. Do you think Heidi still…"

"Yeah. I've always felt she'd like to get back together, but since she broke up with her last girlfriend, it's been more obvious." She looked at Noel, her eyes expressing how helpless she felt. "In some ways she treats me like she has an interest in who I'm with, and I don't have the heart to tell her to knock it off."

"I do," Noel said, her eyes narrowing.

"No! Don't tell her I told you this!"

Noel wrapped her arms around Toni and squeezed her tightly. "I'm teasing. She'd have to do something flagrant for me to clock her." She held up a fist. "But I would."

"I appreciate that, but I care for Heidi. I need to handle my relationship with her in my own way." She let go of Noel and sat back against the headboard again. "I really wish she hadn't gone behind my back to talk to you."

"You know, I don't want to tell you how to behave, but if I were you, I'd be furious. You don't even seem…ticked off."

"I am." She locked her fingers around her knee and rocked a little, looking like she was thinking. "But I don't have the right to get too mad at her after what I did."

"Toni!" Noel put her hands on her hips and shook her. "It's been twenty years! Get over it."

"I can't," she said, looking irritated. "You have to own up to your mistakes, and I made a huge one."

"Twenty years ago!"

"There's no statute of limitations on bad behavior."

"Maybe not, but that doesn't give Heidi carte blanche to hold it over your head, either. She made it sound like you broke up a year or two ago. I can't believe that wasn't intentional."

"Nah." Toni shook her head quickly. "Heidi's not like that. She loves me. She'd never try to hurt me."

"I hope that's true. I really do." She put her arms around her and hugged tightly. "I love you, too."

Smiling, Toni said, "It feels so good to hear that. And even better to say it and mean it. I felt like I was forcing it when I told Heidi I loved her."

"And you don't feel that way with me?"

"Not for a second." She put her hands on Noel's waist and tugged on her until they were snuggled together. "I love you. No doubts. None at all."

Part Fourteen

*A*few days later, on New Year's Eve, Noel paced around her apartment, trying to avoid looking at herself in the mirror. A half hour earlier she had decided she was happy with the way she looked, but since then she had changed something every time she took another glance. Toni had refused to reveal what she was wearing to the party, and even though Noel had made it clear that this was a black-and-white themed party, she was a little worried that Toni would show up in her jeans and cowboy boots. She was sure that Toni would look fantastic in anything she wore, but Noel had to admit to herself that she wanted to blend in at this particular event.

She had been certain that she would skip this year, given that Janet and Heather would be sure to attend. But Toni could tell she wasn't being completely honest when she said she didn't want to go. After a tortured discussion, Toni pulled the truth out of her. She loved going to this party, partly because she got to catch up with people that she didn't see very often. But she also enjoyed getting dressed up and dancing. Once she had revealed that, Toni was insistent. They would go and dance until the band stopped.

Toni rang the bell at ten minutes before eight. Noel took a quick look at her watch, smiling when she saw that she was, as always, early. She opened the door and decided in a second that they should skip the party. Not because Toni wasn't dressed appropriately. She was. In fact, she looked so utterly fantastic that Noel couldn't imagine sharing her with anyone else.

Stepping inside, Toni grasped Noel's hands and turned her so the light would better illuminate her. "Let's stay home," she said, her dark eyes sparkling. "I'm not normally jealous, but I know everyone there will try to talk you into going home with them, and I don't feel like fighting."

"You're so sweet." She tilted her head and kissed Toni's soft pink lips. "And so beautiful."

"Thanks. My sister dressed me."

"She…helped you buy the clothes?"

"No, she lent me the clothes. We wear roughly the same size."

Noel took her hand and turned her so she could view her from all angles. "There's nothing rough about the way these clothes fit you." Toni wore a woman's shawl-collar tuxedo, the jacket hip length and nipped in at the waist. Her shirt was made of piqué, and had a bib front and stand-up collar. In lieu of the traditional tie, she had accented her outfit with a purple and black striped, opera-length silk scarf. She looked elegant, fashionable and luscious, and the small splash of color gave her just the right note of individuality.

Toni leaned in and took a kiss. "I could say the same about you. This dress is smooooooth."

Noel tilted her head and tried to act like she was embarrassed by the compliment. But she'd shopped for two days for the dress, determined to find something that she knew would appeal to Toni's sensibility. She knew she'd been successful when Toni's eyes dilated the moment she saw her. Noel usually didn't like the fact that she was so thin. But every once in a while it worked to her advantage.

She was able to wear a tight-bodiced, strapless black dress with a full skirt and still look svelte.

"Your hair looks so fantastic." Toni couldn't stop herself from threading her fingers through it. "I wish you'd wear it down like this all the time."

"Then it wouldn't look special when I did."

"You're right, as usual. Are you ready to go?"

"I guess I am. I'm not even going to try to convince you that I'm not nervous."

"You don't have a thing to worry about. I'm the one who should be nervous. I'm sure I'm going to have to clock somebody for drooling on you, and I'm just not the violent type."

⌒

They'd been at the party for almost an hour; dancing, talking, stealing kisses from one another and having a fantastic time when Toni said, "Janet just got here, right?"

Noel blinked in surprise. "How did you know?"

"Your body tensed up. I could feel it all across here." She drew her finger across Noel's back. "I know you."

Noel looked into her eyes and realized that was undoubtedly true. She also saw complete understanding which felt like a warm caress. She was so enraptured by the look in Toni's eyes that she gasped in surprise when someone touched her on the shoulder. "Janet!" She cleared her throat and took a breath, trying to sound natural. "How are you?"

"I'm good. You remember Heather."

"Indeed, I do." Her hands had been on Toni's hips and she slid her arm around her waist and stood next to her. "This is Toni Hooper. Toni, Janet and Heather." Toni shook their hands and nodded perfunctorily.

"Nice party," Janet said. "Have you been here long?"

"Seems like minutes," Toni said. "The music has been fantastic."

"Janet hates to dance, don't you honey," Heather said.

"Yeah, it's not something I'm good at."

"You can't get good unless you practice," Toni said. "If nothing else it's a great excuse to snuggle up to a beautiful woman." She winked rakishly and twirled Noel, then they started to dance, their laughter filling the corner of the room.

⌐⌐

Later, they sat at the edge of the party, watching idly and chatting. "I feel sorry for Janet," Toni said, sounding deeply thoughtful.

"Sorry for her? That's...odd."

"No, it's not. She doesn't know what's important in life. That sucks."

"How do you know that about her?"

"Mmm, Max used to tell me that what's important is finding a good woman and sticking with her. She always said that there was no substitute for character." She looked at Noel and said, "That's one of the best pieces of advice I've ever gotten."

"How do you know Janet doesn't have that?"

Toni blew a raspberry, making Noel laugh at her antics. "No way. I know I'm prejudiced, but there's just nothing wrong with you."

Noel's laugh grew louder. "Boy, you're under some kinda spell I hope never ends."

"I mean it. I truly do. You're kind and giving and thoughtful and smart and gorgeous. But most of all, you're honest. You have very good character. That's not something you just acquired. Janet gave that away. She voluntarily traded you and all of your wonderful qualities for something untested."

"Heather's pretty, you've got to hand her that."

"Yeah, she's nice looking, and she's very young. So what? There's always going to be something or someone attractive that catches your interest. You can spend your life chasing that or be thankful for what you have and keep working to make it better."

Noel caressed Toni's cheek, gazing into her eyes for a long time. "Now, that was deep."

"I'm not teasing. Every one of us is aging at the same rate. Heather isn't going to stay in her twenties. Yes, she's always going to be fifteen years younger than Janet, but she's still going to age. Beauty fades. Character doesn't."

"I see what you mean, but that's not the way our society views things."

"That's because society is screwed up. You don't give up something classic and proven just because something shiny and new catches your eye. To me, our relationship should be like a beautiful old home. You repair, you renovate and you restore. You never destroy it. Never."

Noel gazed at Toni for almost a minute before she spoke. She wanted to let the words linger in her mind, to turn them around a couple of times, and to relish them like a delicious bit of cookie. "I can see how much you believe that."

"I do. I don't wish Janet ill, but that relationship isn't gonna last. For one thing, they're both cheaters, and you can't trust a cheater. I did that once in my life, and I'd cut off an arm before I'd do it again."

Noel threw her arms around her and hugged tightly. Toni continued, "As long as we're together, I will never get close to another woman. If I'm even tempted, I'll tell you about it, and we'll figure out how to work things through."

Noel lifted her head and gazed at Toni for a minute. "That's the sexiest thing anyone has ever said to me."

Toni laughed when she put her arms around her. "Your back is covered with goosebumps."

She blinked, stunned. "I'm completely aroused. Completely."

"Did you ever think that we might just be remarkably hot for each other? Rather than in love, I mean."

Alarmed, Noel said, "Do you worry about that?"

"I did for a while, but not now. I've never been more attracted to a woman than I am to you, but I've also never been more interested in anyone. Talking to you makes my day and that's all I need to be happy."

Noel squeezed her tightly. "That's all?"

"I wish you lived closer, but distance isn't that big a problem. Lack of spark is. Been there, hated it."

"I've never had that experience." She pulled Toni close and kissed her. "And with you, I never will."

⌐

After they went back to Noel's apartment, Toni quickly shucked her clothes, brushed her teeth and got into bed while Noel was still carefully putting her jewelry away. Sensing Toni's eyes on her, and she looked over her shoulder and said, "What are you thinking about?"

"How can you tell I'm thinking?"

"I know you." She turned all the way around and gave her a love-filled smile. "I love that that's true."

"Me too. It's nice to be known. I was just thinking about how nice it is that you have all of the benefits of a really pretty woman and none of the detriments."

Noel slipped out of her dress and hung it in her closet. Wearing just a black strapless bra and black panties she knelt on the bed.

Resting back on her heels, she said, "That's a very nice compliment, but I'm not sure I know what you mean. I get the really pretty part, of course," she giggled, "but what are the detriments to being attractive?"

"Oh, they're not detriments for the attractive person. It's the people who surround the attractive person who have to suffer. For instance, most beautiful women have a very screwy relationship with food. I love that you can eat everything that isn't nailed down and not gain weight. That's so much nicer than going out with someone who acts like food is toxic."

"I know what you mean. Some of my friends have a very conflicted relationship with food. I really lucked out."

Toni ran her hand across Noel's concave belly. "You sure did. Max always looked like she was about six months pregnant. She couldn't lose it no matter what she tried"

Noel balled her hands into fists and shook them in front of herself. "Eww! Thank God I didn't inherit that trait."

Toni grasped Noel by the shoulders and pulled her close. "You got all of the best genes."

Now draped across Toni's body, Noel said, "I love the genes that made you so strong. I've always wanted a girlfriend who could pick me up, and now I finally got one."

"I was gonna ask about that. Janet was pretty femmy."

"All of my girlfriends have been, even though that's not really who I'm naturally attracted to. I'm attracted to women like you," she said, poking all over her body with her finger, "but you're the first woman I've ever met who had the personality and the character and the body that I love. You are the whole, beautiful package."

"I feel the same way about you. That's why I didn't even waste my time trying to make do with someone who didn't measure up."

"I find that hard to believe, but I'm very glad someone didn't get to you before I did." She tossed her hair over her shoulder then used Toni's hips to push herself up into a sitting position. "When we kissed at midnight I decided on a New Year's resolution."

Toni's eyes were shining brightly. "I did too," she said excitedly.

"Mine is that you're more important to me than my job or my home."

"That was my New Year's resolution!"

"I decided to…"

"I decided to…"

They stared at each other, then slowly added word by word, "To move to…Rehoboth…Baltimore."

"Baltimore?" Noel gasped.

"Rehoboth?"

"I need to be with you." Noel put her arms around Toni, who was struggling to sit up. "Nothing is more important than you are."

"I need to be with you. I'm sure I could make a living in Baltimore. You could sell The Sandpiper and we could renovate a really nice home here. You'd like that, wouldn't you?"

"Of course I would. But you wouldn't. You'd have to give up way too much to move here."

"You'd have to give up teaching to be with me."

"No, I wouldn't. I've been talking to Gloria, and she's done some looking around for me. I'm pretty sure I could get a job teaching in the county, if not in Rehoboth itself. To be honest, it might be nice to teach some kids who aren't so needy. Sometimes it really wears me down."

"But you said you can retire in just couple of years. You can't give that up. That'd be crazy!"

"Yeah, it is crazy. But I don't want to be away from you for that long."

"Then I'll move here for a couple of years."

"No! You'd have to give up fire fighting."

Toni looked like all the wind had been taken from her sails.

"Oh. I hadn't thought about that. I really love fire fighting."

"I argued with my family about this over the holidays. My dad flipped his lid when I said I was going to move without waiting to get my retirement."

"Your dad is right."

"Of course he is, financially. But there's more to life than money."

"I miss you, Noel, and I wish we lived together, but I think things have been going pretty well. I'm happier than I ever have been."

"I am too. But don't you want more?"

"I do. But I can wait a little while. You're well worth it."

"That's what my mother said. She thinks I should spend some time checking out the school districts in Delaware before I do anything rash."

"She probably thinks it's a good idea to make sure I can be in a relationship for more than ten minutes too." Toni's chin dipped down a little bit and her eyes were clouded.

Noel put her hand on Toni's face and tilted it up. "She didn't say anything like that. April has been singing your praises longer than I have. Besides, my parents aren't the types to give me relationship advice unless I ask for it. My mom just doesn't want me to give up my retirement benefits unless I absolutely have to."

"You don't have to. It's only two more years, right?"

"After this one. That seems like such a long time."

"It is. But you can spend that time deciding what to do with The Sandpiper…"

"Oh! I've already decided that. Andy spent a long time with me going over the best things to do. We think it makes the most sense to keep it open all year. He's got all sorts of ways to make sure you're protected financially in case it doesn't work out between us or if I die—"

"Wait! Wait! What's going on?"

"You're going to manage it, right?" She smiled, her heart soaring when she saw the excitement on Toni's face.

"You want to keep it?"

"Of course I want to keep it. Max knew exactly what she was doing when she left it to me." She cleared her throat, trying to keep talking through the emotion she felt welling up. "Somehow she knew."

Toni kissed her hard, her kiss packing the punch of a heart full of joy.

Noel tapped her on the shoulders, anxious to get back to sorting out their plans. "I'll do the paperwork and run the business side. You make nice with the guests, and make them feel at home. I think we can make enough money running it that neither of us would have to do other jobs if we didn't want to."

"I've never had a better offer in my life." Toni nearly glowed with happiness. "But we're not going to live there. You won't be happy. We'll live at my house." She was wriggling around the bed, bubbling with excitement. "I'll put a second story on with a guest room and a bath for when your family comes to visit."

"Oh, Toni. That's so sweet of you. But could we get that finished in two years? We still haven't touched that first bathroom, you know."

"You're so funny." She tickled Noel's sides, making her giggle and fight to get away. "You're the one who keeps me in bed all day. If you weren't so darned sexy, I could get something done."

"I wouldn't give up a minute we spend in bed. Not a minute."

"I wouldn't either. The best moments of my life have been lying in bed with you." She took a deep breath and stretched her arms out. "When I let myself think about it, it's hard for me to imagine how happy we're going to be."

Noel brushed a few warm tears from Toni's cheeks. "You're thinking about Max, aren't you?"

Toni's eyes shot open. "Do you know me that well?"

"No, I can't read your thoughts. But I'm thinking about her, too."

Sniffling, Toni asked, "What are you thinking about?"

"I was thinking about how happy she'd be to have you and me running her favorite place."

"You have no idea. That would have let her..." She trailed off, wiping away her tears. "She would have been at peace."

Noel sat next to Toni and leaned against her body. "I think about her a lot, you know."

"You do? You don't talk about her much."

"I'm still sorting things out in my head, but I think I've finally figured out why I didn't want to search for her."

"Because you were angry," Toni said, her voice soft and filled with understanding.

"Furious. To my very core." She put an arm around her, holding her close. "That's been hard to confront."

"It makes sense, Noel. It makes complete sense."

"But I'm not angry any more. Max made a huge sacrifice, and she did it to make sure I had the best upbringing I could have."

"That's why she wanted to meet you. She wanted to rest easy with her decision."

"I wish I'd been able to meet her. I could have thanked her for the second important gift she gave me."

"Second?"

"Yes. She took you under her wing, and helped make you into a fantastic woman. She was like a second mom to you, and that's a role she was great at."

"That's the truth. She propped me up when I really needed it."

"So she did her very best to be a good mother, even though it wasn't in the traditional way. I will always be immensely grateful to her for that." Noel didn't even try to stop her tears from flowing.

"She was a very generous woman."

"She would have been so proud of you."

"And you." She shifted around so they were face to face. "Let's agree on a joint New Year's resolution. Let's work on getting The Sandpiper in shape, figuring out how to manage it together and—"

Toni leaned over and silenced Noel with a kiss. "All we have to do is keep letting ourselves fall deeper in love. Everything else is just details."

Noel spent a few seconds staring into the warm depths of Toni's eyes. "I couldn't stop falling in love with you if I tried. And I'm never, ever going to try."

The End

By Susan X Meagher

Novels

Arbor Vitae
All That Matters
Cherry Grove
Girl Meets Girl
The Lies That Bind
The Legacy

Serial Novels

I Found My Heart In San Francisco
Awakenings
Beginnings
Coalescence
Disclosures
Entwined
Fidelity
Getaway
Honesty
Intentions

Anthologies

Undercover Tales
Outsiders

To purchase these books: *www.briskpress.com*
Author website: *www.susanxmeagher.com*
twitter.com/susanx
facebook.com/susanxmeagher